THE WORLD'S BEST ONE HUNDRED DETECTIVE STORIES

(IN TEN VOLUMES)

EUGENE THWING
EDITOR-IN-CHIEF

VOLUME EIGHT

FUNK & WAGNALLS COMPANY

NEW YORK AND LONDON

CONTENTS

THE WORLD'S BEST 100
DETECTIVE STORIES

ERNEST BRAMAH

THE LAST EXPLOIT OF HARRY THE ACTOR

THE one insignificant fact upon which turned the following incident in the joint experiences of Mr. Carlyle and Max Carrados was merely this: that having called upon his friend just at the moment when the private detective was on the point of leaving his office to go to the safe-deposit in Lucas Street, Piccadilly, the blind amateur accompanied him, and for ten minutes amused himself by sitting quite quietly among the palms in the centre of the circular hall while Mr. Carlyle was occupied with his deed-box in one of the little compartments provided for the purpose.

The Lucas Street depository was then (it has since been converted into a picture palace) generally accepted as being one of the strongest places in London. The front of the building was constructed to represent a gigantic safe door, and under the colloquial designation of "The Safe" the place had passed into a synonym for all that was secure and impregnable. Half of the marketable securities in the west of London were popularly reported to have seen the inside of its coffers at one time or another, together with the same generous proportion of family jewels. However exaggerated an estimate this might be, the substratum of truth was solid and auriferous enough to dazzle the imagination. When ordinary safes

(From "Max Carrados, Detective," by Ernest Bramah. Copyright, 1924, by Methuen & Co., Ltd., London.)

were being carried bodily away with impunity or ingeniously fused open by the scientifically equipped cracks-
man, nervous bond-holders turned with relief to the at-
tractions of an establishment whose modest claim was
summed up in its telegraphic address: "Impregnable."
To it went also the jewel-case between the lady's social
engagements, and when in due course "the family" jour-
neyed north—or south, east or west—whenever, in short,
the London house was closed, its capacious storerooms
received the plate-chest as an established custom. Not
a few traders also—jewellers, financiers, dealers in pictures, antiques and costly bijouterie, for instance, constantly used its facilities for any stock that they did not
require immediately to hand.

There was only one entrance to the place, an exaggerated keyhole, to carry out the similitude of the safe-door
alluded to. The ground floor was occupied by the ordinary
officers of the company; all the strong-rooms and safes
lay in the steel-cased basement. This was reached both
by a lift and by a flight of steps. In either case the visitor
found before him a grille of massive proportions. Behind
its bars stood a formidable commissionaire who never
left his post, his sole duty being to open and close the
grille to arriving and departing clients. Beyond this, a
short passage led into the round central hall where
Carrados was waiting. From this part, other passages
radiated off to the vaults and strong-rooms, each one
barred from the hall by a grille scarcely less ponderous
than the first one. The doors of the various private rooms
put at the disposal of the company's clients, and that of the
manager's office, filled the wall-space between the radiating
passages. Everything was very quiet, everything looked
very bright, and everything seemed hopelessly impregnable.

"But I wonder?" ran Carrados's dubious reflection, as
he reached this point.

"Sorry to have kept you so long, my dear Max," broke
in Mr. Carlyle's crisp voice. He had emerged from his
compartment and was crossing the hall, deed-box in hand.
"Another minute and I will be with you."

Carrados smiled and nodded and resumed his former expression, which was merely that of an uninterested gentleman waiting patiently for another. It is something of an attainment to watch closely without betraying undue curiosity, but others of the senses—hearing and smelling, for instance—can be keenly engaged while the observer possibly has the appearance of falling asleep.

"Now," announced Mr. Carlyle, returning briskly to his friend's chair, and drawing on his grey suède gloves. "You are in no particular hurry?"

"No," admitted the professional man, with the slowness of mild surprise. "Not at all. What do you propose?"

"It is very pleasant here," replied Carrados tranquilly. "Very cool and restful with this armoured steel between us and the dust and scurry of the hot July afternoon above. I propose remaining here for a few minutes longer."

"Certainly," agreed Mr. Carlyle, taking the nearest chair and eyeing Carrados as though he had a shrewd suspicion of something more than met the ear. "We may encounter a bishop, or a winning jockey, or even a musical comedy actress. Unfortunately it seems to be rather a slack time."

"Two men came down while you were in your cubicle," remarked Carrados casually. "The first took the lift. I imagine that he was a middle-aged, rather portly man. He carried a stick, wore a silk hat, and used spectacles for close sight. The other came by the stairway. I infer that he arrived at the top immediately after the lift had gone. He ran down the steps, so that the two were admitted at the same time, but the second man, though the more active of the pair, hung back for a moment in the passage and the portly one was the first to go to his safe."

Mr. Carlyle's knowing look expressed: "Go on, my friend; you are coming to something." But he merely contributed an encouraging "Yes?"

"When you emerged just now our second man quietly

opened the door of his pen a fraction. Doubtless he looked out. Then he closed it as quietly again. You were not his man, Louis."

"I am grateful," said Mr. Carlyle expressively. "What next, Max?"

"That is all; they are still closeted."

Both were silent for a moment. Mr. Carlyle's feeling was one of unconfessed perplexity. So far the incident was utterly trivial in his eyes; but he knew that the trifles which appeared significant to Max had a way of standing out like signposts when the time came to look back over an episode. Carrados's sightless faculties seemed indeed to keep him just a move ahead as the game progressed.

"Is there really anything in it, Max?" he asked at length.

"Who can say?" replied Carrados. "At least we may wait to see them go. Those tin deed-boxes now. There is one to each safe, I think?"

"Yes, so I imagine. The practice is to carry the box to your private lair and there unlock it and do your business. Then you lock it up again and take it back to your safe."

"Steady! our first man," whispered Carrados hurriedly. "Here, look at this with me." He opened a paper—a prospectus—which he pulled from his pocket, and they affected to study its contents together.

"You were about right, my friend," muttered Mr. Carlyle, pointing to a paragraph of assumed interest. "Hat, stick and spectacles. He is a clean-shaven, pink-faced old boy. I believe—yes, I know the man by sight. He is a bookmaker in a large way, I am told."

"Here comes the other," whispered Carrados.

The bookmaker passed across the hall, joined on his way by the manager whose duty it was to counterlock the safe, and disappeared along one of the passages. The second man sauntered up and down, waiting his turn. Mr. Carlyle reported his movements in an undertone and described him. He was a younger man than the other, of medium height, and passably well dressed in a quiet lounge suit, green Alpine hat and brown shoes. By the time the detective had reached his wavy chestnut hair, large and rather ragged moustache, and sandy, freckled complexion, the first man had completed his business and was leaving the place.

"It isn't an exchange lay, at all events," said Mr. Carlyle. "His inner case is only half the size of the other and couldn't possibly be substituted."

"Come up now," said Carrados, rising. "There is nothing more to be learned down here."

They requisitioned the lift, and on the steps outside the gigantic keyhole stood for a few minutes discussing an investment as a couple of trustees or a lawyer and a client who were parting there might do. Fifty yards away, a very large silk hat with a very curly brim marked the progress of the bookmaker towards Piccadilly.

The lift in the hall behind them swirled up again and the gate clashed. The second man walked leisurely out and sauntered away without a backward glance.

"He has gone in the opposite direction," exclaimed Mr. Carlyle, rather blankly. "It isn't the 'lame goat' nor the 'follow-me-on,' nor even the homely but efficacious sand-bag."

"What colour were his eyes?" asked Carrados.

"Upon my word, I never noticed," admitted the other.

"Parkinson would have noticed," was the severe comment.

"I am not Parkinson," retorted Mr. Carlyle, with asperity, "and strictly as one dear friend to another, Max, permit me to add, that while cherishing an unbounded admiration for your remarkable gifts, I have the strongest suspicion that the whole incident is a ridiculous mare's nest, bred in the fantastic imagination of an enthusiastic criminologist."

Mr. Carrados received this outburst with the utmost benignity. "Come and have a coffee, Louis," he suggested. "Mehmed's is only a street away."

Mehmed proved to be a cosmopolitan gentleman from

Mocha whose shop resembled a house from the outside and an Oriental divan when one was within. A turbaned Arab placed cigarettes and cups of coffee spiced with saffron before the customers, gave salaam and withdrew.

"You know, my dear chap," continued Mr. Carlyle, sipping his black coffee and wondering privately whether it was really very good or very bad, "speaking quite seriously, the one fishy detail—our ginger friend's watching for the other to leave—may be open to a dozen very innocent explanations."

"So innocent that to-morrow I intend taking a safe myself."

"You think that everything is all right?"

"On the contrary, I am convinced that something is very wrong."

"Then why——?"

"I shall keep nothing there, but it will give me the *entrée*. I should advise you, Louis, in the first place to empty your safe with all possible speed, and in the second to leave your business card on the manager."

Mr. Carlyle pushed his cup away, convinced now that the coffee was really very bad.

"But, my dear Max, the place—'The Safe'—is impregnable!"

"When I was in the States, three years ago, the head porter at one hotel took pains to impress on me that the building was absolutely fireproof. I at once had my things taken off to another hotel. Two weeks later the first place was burnt out. It *was* fireproof, I believe, but of course the furniture and the fittings were not and the walls gave way."

"Very ingenious," admitted Mr. Carlyle, "but why did you really go? You know you can't humbug me with your superhuman sixth sense, my friend."

Carrados smiled pleasantly, thereby encouraging the watchful attendant to draw near and replenish their tiny cups.

"Perhaps," replied the blind man, "because so many careless people were satisfied that it was fireproof."

"Ah-ha, there you are—the greater the confidence the greater the risk. But only if your self-confidence results in carelessness. Now do you know how this place is secured, Max?"

"I am told that they lock the door at night," replied Carrados, with bland malice.

"And hide the key under the mat to be ready for the first arrival in the morning," crowed Mr. Carlyle, in the same playful spirit. "Dear old chap! Well, let me tell you——"

"That force is out of the question. Quite so," admitted his friend.

"That simplifies the argument. Let us consider fraud. There again the precautions are so rigid that many people pronounce the forms a nuisance. I confess that I do not. I regard them as means of protecting my own property and I cheerfully sign my name and give my password, which the manager compares with his record-book before he releases the first lock of my safe. The signature is burned before my eyes in a sort of crucible there, the password is of my own choosing and is written only in a book that no one but the manager ever sees, and my key is the sole one in existence."

"No duplicate or master-key?"

"Neither. If a key is lost it takes a skilful mechanic half-a-day to cut his way in. Then you must remember that clients of a safe-deposit are not multitudinous. All are known more or less by sight to the officials there, and a stranger would receive close attention. Now, Max, by what combination of circumstances is a rogue to know my password, to be able to forge my signature, to possess himself of my key, and to resemble me personally? And, finally, how is he possibly to determine beforehand whether there is anything in my safe to repay so elaborate a plant?" Mr. Carlyle concluded in triumph and was so carried away by the strength of his position that he drank off the contents of his second cup before he realized what he was doing.

"At the hotel I just spoke of," replied Carrados, "there

was an attendant whose one duty in case of alarm was to secure three iron doors. On the night of the fire he had a bad attack of toothache and slipped away for just a quarter of an hour to have the thing out. There was a most up-to-date system of automatic fire alarm; it had been tested only the day before and the electrician, finding some part not absolutely to his satisfaction, had taken it away and not had time to replace it. The night watchman, it turned out, had received leave to present himself a couple of hours later on that particular night, and the hotel fireman, whose duties he took over, had missed being notified. Lastly, there was a big riverside blaze at the same time and all the engines were down at the other end of the city."

Mr. Carlyle committed himself to a dubious monosyllable. Carrados leaned forward a little.

"All these circumstances formed a coincidence of pure chance. Is it not conceivable, Louis, that an even more remarkable series might be brought about by design?"

"Our tawny friend?"

"Possibly. Only he was not really tawny." Mr. Carlyle's easy attitude suddenly stiffened into rigid attention. "He wore a false moustache."

"He wore a false moustache!" repeated the amazed gentleman. "And you cannot see! No, really, Max, this is beyond the limit!"

"If only you would not trust your dear, blundering old eyes so implicitly you would get nearer that limit yourself," retorted Carrados. "The man carried a five-yard aura of spirit gum, emphasized by a warm, perspiring skin. That inevitably suggested one thing. I looked for further evidence of making-up and found it—these preparations all smell. The hair you described was characteristically that of a wig—worn long to hide the joining and made wavy to minimize the length. All these things are trifles. As yet we have not gone beyond the initial stage of suspicion. I will tell you another trifle. When this man retired to a compartment with his deed-box, he never even opened it. Possibly it contains a brick and a newspaper. He is only watching."

"Watching the bookmaker."

"True, but it may go far wider than that. Everything points to a plot of careful elaboration. Still, if you are satisfied——"

"I am quite satisfied," replied Mr. Carlyle gallantly. "I regard 'The Safe' almost as a national institution, and as such I have an implicit faith in its precautions against every kind of force or fraud." So far Mr. Carlyle's attitude had been suggestive of a rock, but at this point he took out his watch, hummed a little to pass the time, consulted his watch again, and continued: "I am afraid that there were one or two papers which I overlooked. It would perhaps save me coming again to-morrow if I went back now——"

"Quite so," acquiesced Carrados, with perfect gravity. "I will wait for you."

For twenty minutes he sat there, drinking an occasional tiny cup of boiled coffee and to all appearance placidly enjoying the quaint atmosphere which Mr. Mehmed had contrived to transplant from the shores of the Persian Gulf.

At the end of that period Carlyle returned, politely effusive about the time he had kept his friend waiting but otherwise bland and unassailable. Anyone with eyes might have noticed that he carried a parcel of about the same size and dimensions as the deed-box that fitted his safe.

The next day Carrados presented himself at the safe-deposit as an intending renter. The manager showed him over the vaults and strong-rooms, explaining the various precautions taken to render the guile or force of man impotent: the strength of the chilled-steel walls, the casing of electricity-resisting concrete, the stupendous isolation of the whole inner fabric on metal pillars so that the watchman, while inside the building, could walk above, below, and all round the outer walls of what was really—although it bore no actual relationship to the advertising device of the front—a monstrous safe; and, finally, the arrangement which would enable the basement to be flooded with steam within three minutes of an alarm. These details were public property. "The Safe" was a show-place and its director held that no harm could come of displaying a strong hand.

Accompanied by the observant eyes of Parkinson, Carrados gave an adventurous but not a hopeful attention to these particulars. Submitting the problem of the tawny man to his own ingenuity, he was constantly putting before himself the question: How shall I set about robbing this place? and he had already dismissed force as impracticable. Nor, when it came to the consideration of fraud, did the simple but effective safeguards which Mr. Carlyle had specified seem to offer any loophole.

"As I am blind I may as well sign in the book," he suggested, when the manager passed to him a gummed slip for the purpose. The precaution against one acquiring particulars of another client might well be deemed superfluous in his case.

But the manager did not fall into the trap.

"It is our invariable rule in all cases, sir," he replied courteously. "What word will you take?" Parkinson, it may be said, had been left in the hall.

"Suppose I happen to forget it? How do we proceed?"

"In that case I am afraid that I might have to trouble you to establish your identity," the manager explained. "It rarely happens."

"Then we will say 'Conspiracy.' "

The word was written down and the book closed.

"Here is your key, sir. If you will allow me—your key-ring——"

A week went by and Carrados was no nearer the absolute solution of the problem he had set himself. He had, indeed, evolved several ways by which the contents of the safes might be reached, some simple and desperate, hanging on the razor-edge of chance to fall this way or that; others more elaborate, safer on the whole, but more liable to break down at some point of their ingenious intricacy. And setting aside complicity on the part of the manager—a condition that Carrados had satisfied himself did not exist—they all depended on a relaxation of the forms by which security was assured. Carrados continued to have several occasions to visit the safe during the week, and he "watched" with a quiet persistence that was deadly in its scope. But from beginning to end there was no indication of slackness in the business-like methods of the place; nor during any of his visits did the "tawny man" appear in that or any other disguise. Another week passed; Mr. Carlyle was becoming inexpressibly waggish, and Carrados himself, although he did not abate a jot of his conviction, was compelled to bend to the realities of the situation. The manager, with the obstinacy of a conscientious man who had become obsessed with the pervading note of security, excused himself from discussing abstract methods of fraud. Carrados was not in a position to formulate a detailed charge; he withdrew from active investigation, content to await his time.

It came, to be precise, on a certain Friday morning, seventeen days after his first visit to "The Safe." Returning late on the Thursday night, he was informed that a man giving the name of Draycott had called to see him. Apparently the matter had been of some importance to the visitor for he had returned three hours later on the chance of finding Mr. Carrados in. Disappointed in this, he had left a note. Carrados cut open the envelope and ran a finger along the following words:—

"DEAR SIR,—I have to-day consulted Mr. Louis Carlyle, who thinks that you would like to see me. I will call again in the morning, say at nine o'clock. If this is too soon or otherwise inconvenient I entreat you to leave a message fixing as early an hour as possible. Yours faithfully,   HERBERT DRAYCOTT.

"*P.S.*—I should add that I am the renter of a safe at the Lucas Street depository.   H.D."

A description of Mr. Draycott made it clear that he was not the West-End bookmaker. The caller, the servant explained, was a thin, wiry, keen-faced man. Carrados felt agreeably interested in this development, which seemed to justify his suspicion of a plot.

At five minutes to nine the next morning Mr. Draycott again presented himself.

"Very good of you to see me so soon, sir," he apolo-gized, on Carrados at once receiving him. "I don't know much of English ways—I'm an Australian—and I was afraid it might be too early."

"You could have made it a couple of hours earlier as far as I am concerned," replied Carrados. "Or you either for that matter, I imagine," he added, "for I don't think that you slept much last night."

"I didn't sleep at all last night," corrected Mr. Dray-cott. "But it's strange that you should have seen that. I understand from Mr. Carlyle that you—excuse me if I am mistaken, sir—but I understood that you were blind."

Carrados laughed his admission lightly.

"Oh yes," he said. "But never mind that. What is the trouble?"

"I'm afraid it means more than just trouble for me, Mr. Carrados." The man had steady, half-closed eyes, with the suggestion of depth which one notices in the eyes of those whose business it is to look out over great expanses of land or water; they were turned towards Carrados's face with quiet resignation in their frankness now. "I'm afraid it spells disaster. I am a working en-gineer from the Mount Magdalena district of Coolgardie. I don't want to take up your time with outside details, so I will only say that about two years ago I had an opportunity of acquiring a share in a very promising claim —gold, you understand, both reef and alluvial. As the work went on I put more and more into the undertaking —you couldn't call it a venture by that time. The results were good, better than we had dared to expect, but from one cause and another the expenses were terrible. We saw that it was a bigger thing than we had bargained for and we admitted that we must get outside help."

So far Mr. Draycott's narrative had proceeded smoothly

enough under the influence of the quiet despair that had come over the man. But at this point a sudden recollection of his position swept him into a frenzy of bitterness.

"Oh, what the blazes is the good of going over all this again!" he broke out. "What can you or anyone else do anyhow? I've been robbed, rooked, cleared out of everything I possess," and tormented by recollections and by the impotence of his rage the unfortunate engineer beat the oak table with the back of his hand until his knuckles bled.

Carrados waited until the fury had passed.

"Continue, if you please, Mr. Draycott," he said. "Just what you thought it best to tell me is just what I want to know."

"I'm sorry, sir," apologized the man, colouring under his tanned skin. "I ought to be able to control myself better. But this business has shaken me. Three times last night I looked down the barrel of my revolver, and three times I threw it away. . . . Well, we arranged that I should come to London to interest some financiers in the property. We might have done it locally or in Perth, to be sure, but then, don't you see, they would have wanted to get control. Six weeks ago I landed here. I brought with me specimens of the quartz and good samples of extracted gold, dust and nuggets, the clearing up of several weeks' working, about two hundred and forty ounces in all. That includes the Magdalena Lodestar, our lucky nugget, a lump weighing just under seven pounds of pure gold.

"I had seen an advertisement of this Lucas Street safe-deposit and it seemed just the thing I wanted. Besides the gold, I had all the papers to do with the claims—plans, reports, receipts, licences and so on. Then when I cashed my letter of credit I had about one hundred and fifty pounds in notes. Of course I could have left everything at a bank, but it was more convenient to have it, as it were, in my own safe, to get at any time, and to have a private room that I could take any gentlemen to. I hadn't a suspicion that anything could be wrong. Nego-

tiations hung on in several quarters—it's a bad time to
do business here, I find. Then, yesterday, I wanted something. I went to Lucas Street, as I had done half-a-dozen
times before, opened my safe, and had the inner case
carried to a room. . . . Mr. Carrados, it was empty!"

"Quite empty?"

"No." He laughed bitterly. "At the bottom was a sheet
of wrapper paper. I recognized it as a piece I had left
there in case I wanted to make up a parcel. But for that
I should have been convinced that I had somehow opened
the wrong safe. That was my first idea."

"It cannot be done."

"So I understand, sir. And, then, there was the paper
with my name written on it in the empty tin. I was
dazed; it seemed impossible. I think I stood there without
moving for minutes—it was more like hours. Then I closed
the tin box again, took it back, locked up the safe and
came out."

"Without notifying anything wrong?"

"Yes, Mr. Carrados." The steady blue eyes regarded
him with pained thoughtfulness. "You see, I reckoned it
out in that time that it must be someone about the place
who had done it."

"You were wrong," said Carrados.

"So Mr. Carlyle seemed to think. I only knew that
the key had never been out of my possession and I had
told no one of the password. Well, it did come over me
rather like cold water down the neck, that there was I
alone in the strongest dungeon in London and not a
living soul knew where I was."

"Possibly a sort of up-to-date Sweeney Todd's?"

"I'd heard of such things in London," admitted Draycott. "Anyway, I got out. It was a mistake; I see it now.
Who is to believe me as it is—it sounds a sort of unlikely
tale. And how do they come to pick on me? to know
what I had? I don't drink, or open my mouth, or hell
round. It beats me."

"They didn't pick on you—you picked on them," replied Carrados. "Never mind how; you'll be believed all

right. But as for getting anything back——" The un-finished sentence confirmed Mr. Draycott in his gloomiest anticipations.

"I have the numbers of the notes," he suggested, with an attempt at hopefulness. "They can be stopped, I take it?"

"Stopped? Yes," admitted Carrados. "And what does that amount to? The banks and the police stations will be notified and every little public-house between here and Land's End will change one for the scribbling of 'John Jones' across the back. No, Mr. Draycott, it's awkward, I dare say, but you must make up your mind to wait until you can get fresh supplies from home. Where are you staying?"

Draycott hesitated.

"I have been at the Abbotsford, in Bloomsbury, up to now," he said, with some embarrassment. "The fact is, Mr. Carrados, I think I ought to have told you how I was placed before consulting you, because I—I see no prospect of being able to pay my way. Knowing that I had plenty in the safe, I had run it rather close. I went chiefly yesterday to get some notes. I have a week's hotel bill in my pocket, and"—he glanced down at his trousers —"I've ordered one or two other things unfortunately."

"That will be a matter of time, doubtless," suggested the other encouragingly.

Instead of replying Draycott suddenly dropped his arms on to the table and buried his face between them. A minute passed in silence.

"It's no good, Mr. Carrados," he said, when he was able to speak; "I can't meet it. Say what you like, I simply can't tell those chaps that I've lost everything we had and ask them to send me more. They couldn't do it if I did. Understand, sir. The mine is a valuable one; we have the greatest faith in it, but it has gone beyond our depth. The three of us have put everything we own into it. While I am here they are doing labourers' work for a wage, just to keep going . . . waiting, oh, my God! waiting for good news from me!"

Carrados walked round the table to his desk and wrote. Then, without a word, he held out a paper to his visitor.

"What's this?" demanded Draycott, in bewilderment. "It's—it's a cheque for a hundred pounds."

"It will carry you on," explained Carrados imperturbably. "A man like you isn't going to throw up the sponge for this set-back. Cable to your partners that you require copies of all the papers at once. They'll manage it, never fear. The gold . . . must go. Write fully by the next mail. Tell them everything and add that in spite of all you feel that you are nearer success than ever."

Mr. Draycott folded the cheque with thoughtful deliberation and put it carefully away in his pocket-book.

"I don't know whether you've guessed as much, sir," he said in a queer voice, "but I think that you've saved a man's life to-day. It's not the money, it's the encouragement . . . and faith. If you could see you'd know better than I can say how I feel about it."

Carrados laughed quietly. It always amused him to have people explain how much more he would learn if he had eyes.

"Then we'll go on to Lucas Street and give the manager the shock of his life," was all he said. "Come, Mr. Draycott, I have already rung up the car."

But, as it happened, another instrument had been destined to apply that stimulating experience to the manager. As they stepped out of the car opposite "The Safe" a taxicab drew up and Mr. Carlyle's alert and cheery voice hailed them.

"A moment, Max," he called, turning to settle with his driver, a transaction that he invested with an air of dignified urbanity which almost made up for any small pecuniary disappointment that may have accompanied it. "This is indeed fortunate. Let us compare notes for a moment. I have just received an almost imploring message from the manager to come at once. I assumed that it was the affair of our colonial friend here, but he went on to mention Professor Holmfast Bulge. Can it really be possible that he also has made a similar discovery?"

"What did the manager say?" asked Carrados.

"He was practically incoherent, but I really think it must be so. What have you done?"

"Nothing," replied Carrados. He turned his back on "The Safe" and appeared to be regarding the other side of the street. "There is a tobacconist's shop directly opposite?"

"There is."

"What do they sell on the first floor?"

"Possibly they sell 'Rubbo.' I hazard the suggestion from the legend 'Rub in Rubbo for Everything' which embellishes each window."

"The windows are frosted?"

"They are, to half-way up, mysterious man."

Carrados walked back to his motor-car.

"While we are away, Parkinson, go across and buy a tin, bottle, box or packet of 'Rubbo.' "

"What is 'Rubbo,' Max?" chirped Mr. Carlyle with insatiable curiosity.

"So far we do not know. When Parkinson gets some, Louis, you shall be the one to try it."

They descended into the basement and were passed in by the grille-keeper, whose manner betrayed a discreet consciousness of something in the air. It was unnecessary to speculate why. In the distance, muffled by the armoured passages, an authoritative voice boomed like a sonorous bell heard under water.

"What, however, are the facts?" it was demanding, with the causticity of baffled helplessness. "I am assured that there is no other key in existence; yet my safe has been unlocked. I am given to understand that without the password it would be impossible for an unauthorized person to tamper with my property. My password, deliberately chosen, is 'anthropophaginian,' sir. Is it one that is familiarly on the lips of the criminal classes? But my safe is empty! What is the explanation? Who are the guilty persons? What is being done? Where are the police?"

"If you consider that the proper course to adopt is to

stand on the doorstep and beckon in the first constable
who happens to pass, permit me to say, sir, that I differ
from you," retorted the distracted manager. "You may
rely on everything possible being done to clear up the
mystery. As I told you, I have already telephoned for
a capable private detective and for one of my directors."

"But that is not enough," insisted the professor angrily.
"Will one mere private detective restore my £6000
Japanese 4½ per cent. bearer bonds? Is the return of my
irreplaceable notes on 'Polyphyletic Bridal Customs among
the mid-Pleistocene Cave Men' to depend on a solitary
director? I demand that the police shall be called in—as
many as are available. Let Scotland Yard be set in mo-
tion. A searching inquiry must be made. I have only been
a user of your precious establishment for six months, and
this is the result."

"There you hold the key of the mystery, Professor
Bulge," interposed Carrados quietly.

"Who is this, sir?" demanded the exasperated professor
at large.

"Permit me," explained Mr. Carlyle, with bland assurance. "I am Louis Carlyle, of Bampton Street. This
gentleman is Mr. Max Carrados, the eminent amateur
specialist in crime."

"I shall be thankful for any assistance towards eluci-
dating this appalling business," condescended the professor sonorously. "Let me put you in possession of the
facts——"

"Perhaps if we went into your room," suggested Carrados to the manager, "we should be less liable to inter-
ruption."

"Quite so; quite so," boomed the professor, accepting
the proposal on everyone else's behalf. "The facts, sir, are
these: I am the unfortunate possessor of a safe here, in
which, a few months ago, I deposited—among less important matter—sixty bearer bonds of the Japanese Im-
perial Loan—the bulk of my small fortune—and the
manuscript of an important projected work on 'Polyphyletic Bridal Customs among the mid-Pleistocene Cave

Men.' To-day I came to detach the coupons which fall due on the fifteenth, to pay them into my bank a week in advance, in accordance with my custom. What do I find? I find the safe locked and apparently intact, as when I last saw it a month ago. But it is far from being intact, sir. It has been opened, ransacked, cleared out. Not a single bond, not a scrap of paper remains."

It was obvious that the manager's temperature had been rising during the latter part of this speech and now he boiled over.

"Pardon my flatly contradicting you, Professor Bulge. You have again referred to your visit here a month ago as your last. You will bear witness of that, gentlemen. When I inform you that the professor had access to his safe as recently as on Monday last you will recognize the importance that the statement may assume."

The professor glared across the room like an infuriated animal, a comparison heightened by his notoriously hircine appearance.

"How dare you contradict me, sir!" he cried, slapping the table sharply with his open hand. "I was not here on Monday."

The manager shrugged his shoulders coldly.

"You forget that the attendants also saw you," he remarked. "Cannot we trust our own eyes?"

"A common assumption, yet not always a strictly reliable one," insinuated Carrados softly.

"I cannot be mistaken."

"Then can you tell me, without looking, what colour Professor Bulge's eyes are?"

There was a curious and expectant silence for a minute. The professor turned his back on the manager and the manager passed from thoughtfulness to embarrassment.

"I really do not know, Mr. Carrados," he declared loftily at last. "I do not refer to mere trifles like that."

"Then you can be mistaken," replied Carrados mildly yet with decision.

"But the ample hair, the venerable flowing beard, the prominent nose and heavy eyebrows——"

"These are just the striking points that are most easily
counterfeited. They 'take the eye.' If you would ensure
yourself against deception, learn rather to observe the eye
itself, and particularly the spots on it, the shape of the
finger-nails, the set of the ears. These things cannot be
simulated."

"You seriously suggest that the man was not Professor
Bulge—that he was an impostor?"

"The conclusion is inevitable. Where were you on Monday, Professor?"

"I was on a short lecturing tour in the Midlands. On
Saturday I was in Nottingham. On Monday in Birming-
ham. I did not return to London until yesterday."

Carrados turned to the manager again and indicated
Draycott, who so far had remained in the back-
ground.

"And this gentleman? Did he by any chance come here
on Monday?"

"He did not, Mr. Carrados. But I gave him access to
his safe on Tuesday afternoon and again yesterday."

Draycott shook his head sadly.

"Yesterday I found it empty," he said. "And all Tuesday afternoon I was at Brighton, trying to see a gentleman on business."

The manager sat down very suddenly.

"Good God, another!" he exclaimed faintly.

"I am afraid the list is only beginning," said Carrados.
"We must go through your renters' book."

The manager roused himself to protest.

"That cannot be done. No one but myself or my deputy
ever sees the book. It would be—unprecedented."

"The circumstances are unprecedented," replied Carrados.

"If any difficulties are placed in the way of these gentlemen's investigations, I shall make it my duty to bring
the facts before the Home Secretary," announced the professor, speaking up to the ceiling with the voice of a
brazen trumpet.

Carrados raised a deprecating hand.

"May I make a suggestion?" he remarked. "Now, I am blind. If, therefore——?"

"Very well," acquiesced the manager. "But I must request the others to withdraw."

For five minutes Carrados followed the list of safe-renters as the manager read them to him. Sometimes he stopped the catalogue to reflect a moment; now and then he brushed a finger-tip over a written signature and compared it with another. Occasionally a password interested him. But when the list came to an end he continued to look into space without any sign of enlightenment.

"So much is perfectly clear and yet so much is incredible," he mused. "You insist that you alone have been in charge for the last six months?"

"I have not been away a day this year."

"Meals?"

"I have my lunch sent in."

"And this room could not be entered without your knowledge while you were about the place?"

"It is impossible. The door is fitted with a powerful spring and a feather-touch self-acting lock. It cannot be left unlocked unless you deliberately prop it open."

"And, with your knowledge, no one has had an opportunity of having access to this book?"

"No," was the reply.

Carrados stood up and began to put on his gloves.

"Then I must decline to pursue my investigation any further," he said icily.

"Why?" stammered the manager.

"Because I have positive reason for believing that you are deceiving me."

"Pray sit down, Mr. Carrados. It is quite true that when you put the last question to me a circumstance rushed into my mind which—so far as the strict letter was concerned—might seem to demand 'Yes' instead of 'No.' But not in the spirit of your inquiry. It would be absurd to attach any importance to the incident I refer to."

"That would be for me to judge."

"You shall do so, Mr. Carrados. I live at Windermere Mansions with my sister. A few months ago she got to know a married couple who had recently come to the opposite flat. The husband was a middle-aged, scholarly man who spent most of his time in the British Museum. His wife's tastes were different; she was much younger, brighter, gayer; a mere girl in fact, one of the most charming and unaffected I have ever met. My sister Amelia does not readily——"

"Stop!" exclaimed Carrados. "A studious middle-aged man and a charming young wife! Be as brief as possible. If there is any chance it may turn on a matter of minutes at the ports. She came here, of course?"

"Accompanied by her husband," replied the manager stiffly. "Mrs. Scott had travelled and she had a hobby of taking photographs wherever she went. When my position accidentally came out one evening she was carried away by the novel idea of adding views of a safe-deposit to her collection—as enthusiastic as a child. There was no reason why she should not; the place has often been taken for advertising purposes."

"She came, and brought her camera—under your very nose!"

"I do not know what you mean by 'under my very nose.' She came with her husband one evening just about our closing time. She brought her camera, of course—quite a small affair."

"And contrived to be in here alone?"

"I take exception to the word 'contrived.' It—it happened. I sent out for some tea, and in the course——"

"How long was she alone in here?"

"Two or three minutes at the most. When I returned she was seated at my desk. That was what I referred to. The little rogue had put on my glasses and had got hold of a big book. We were great chums, and she delighted to mock me. I confess that I was startled—merely instinctively—to see that she had taken up this book, but the next moment I saw that she had it upside down."

"Clever! She couldn't get it away in time. And the camera, with half-a-dozen of its specially sensitized films already snapped over the last few pages, by her side!"

"That child!"

"Yes. She is twenty-seven and has kicked hats off tall men's heads in every capital from Petersburg to Buenos Ayres! Get through to Scotland Yard and ask if Inspector Beedel can come up."

The manager breathed heavily through his nose.

"To call in the police and publish everything would ruin this establishment—confidence would be gone. I cannot do it without further authority."

"Then the professor certainly will."

"Before you came I rang up the only director who is at present in town and gave him the facts as they then stood. Possibly he has arrived by this. If you will accompany me to the boardroom we will see."

They went up to the floor above, Mr. Carlyle joining them on the way.

"Excuse me a moment," said the manager.

Parkinson, who had been having an improving conversation with the hall porter on the subject of land values, approached.

"I am sorry, sir," he reported, "but I was unable to procure any 'Rubbo.' The place appears to be shut up."

"That is a pity; Mr. Carlyle had set his heart on it."

"Will you come this way, please?" said the manager, reappearing.

In the boardroom they found a white-haired old gentleman who had obeyed the manager's behest from a sense of duty, and then remained in a distant corner of the empty room in the hope that he might be overlooked. He was amiably helpless and appeared to be deeply aware of it.

"This is a very sad business, gentlemen," he said, in a whispering, confiding voice. "I am informed that you recommend calling in the Scotland Yard authorities. That would be a disastrous course for an institution that depends on the implicit confidence of the public."

"It is the only course," replied Carrados.

"The name of Mr. Carrados is well known to us in connection with a delicate case. Could you not carry this one through?"

"It is impossible. A wide inquiry must be made. Every port will have to be watched. The police alone can do that." He threw a little significance into the next sentence. "I alone can put the police in the right way of doing it."

"And you will do that, Mr. Carrados?"

Carrados smiled engagingly. He knew exactly what constituted the great attraction of his services.

"My position is this," he explained. "So far my work has been entirely amateur. In that capacity I have averted one or two crimes, remedied an occasional injustice, and now and then been of service to my professional friend, Louis Carlyle. But there is no reason at all why I should serve a commercial firm in an ordinary affair of business for nothing. For any information I should require a fee, a quite nominal fee of, say, one hundred pounds."

The director looked as though his faith in human nature had received a rude blow.

"A hundred pounds would be a very large initial fee for a small firm like this, Mr. Carrados," he remarked in a pained voice.

"And that, of course, would be independent of Mr. Carlyle's professional charges," added Carrados.

"Is that sum contingent on any specific performance?" inquired the manager.

"I do not mind making it conditional on my procuring for you, for the police to act on, a photograph and a description of the thief."

The two officials conferred apart for a moment. Then the manager returned.

"We will agree, Mr. Carrados, on the understanding that these things are to be in our hands within two days. Failing that——"

"No, no!" cried Mr. Carlyle indignantly, but Carrados good-humouredly put him aside.

"I will accept the condition in the same sporting spirit that inspires it. Within forty-eight hours or no pay. The cheque, of course, to be given immediately the goods are delivered?"

"You may rely on that."

Carrados took out his pocket-book, produced an envelope bearing an American stamp, and from it extracted an unmounted print.

"Here is the photograph," he announced. "The man is called Ulysses K. Groom, but he is better known as 'Harry the Actor.' You will find the description written on the back."

Five minutes later, when they were alone, Mr. Carlyle expressed his opinion of the transaction.

"You are an unmitigated humbug, Max," he said, "though an amiable one, I admit. But purely for your own private amusement you spring these things on people."

"On the contrary," replied Carrados, "people spring these things on me."

"Now this photograph. Why have I heard nothing of it before?"

Carrados took out his watch and touched the fingers.

"It is now three minutes to eleven. I received the photograph at twenty past eight."

"Even then, an hour ago you assured me that you had done nothing."

"Nor had I—so far as result went. Until the keystone of the edifice was wrung from the manager in his room, I was as far away from demonstrable certainty as ever."

"So am I—as yet," hinted Mr. Carlyle.

"I am coming to that, Louis. I turn over the whole thing to you. The man has got two clear days' start and the chances are nine to one against catching him. We know everything, and the case has no further interest for me. But it is your business. Here is your material.

"On that one occasion when the 'tawny' man crossed our path, I took from the first a rather more serious view of his scope and intention than you did. That same day I sent a cipher cable to Pierson of the New York service.

I asked for news of any man of such and such a description—merely negative—who was known to have left the States; an educated man, expert in the use of disguises, audacious in his operations, and a specialist in 'dry' work among banks and strong-rooms."

"Why the States, Max?"

"That was a sighting shot on my part. I argued that he must be an English-speaking man. The smart and inventive turn of the modern Yank has made him a specialist in ingenious devices, straight or crooked. Unpickable locks and invincible lock-pickers, burglar-proof safes and safe-specializing burglars, come equally from the States. So I tried a very simple test. As we talked that day and the man walked past us, I dropped the words 'New York' —or, rather, 'Noo Y'rk'—in his hearing."

"I know you did. He neither turned nor stopped."

"He was that much on his guard; but into his step there came—though your poor old eyes could not see it, Louis—the 'psychological pause,' an absolute arrest of perhaps a fifth of a second; just as it would have done with you if the word 'London' had fallen on your ear in a distant land. However, the whys and the wherefores don't matter. Here is the essential story.

"Eighteen months ago 'Harry the Actor' successfully looted the office safe of M'Kenkie, J. F. Higgs & Co., of Cleveland, Ohio. He had just married a smart but very facile third-rate vaudeville actress—English by origin— and wanted money for the honeymoon. He got about five hundred pounds, and with that they came to Europe and stayed in London for some months. That period is marked by the Congreave Square post office burglary, you may remember. While studying such of the British institutions as most appealed to him, the 'Actor's' attention became fixed on this safe-deposit. Possibly the implied challenge contained in its telegraphic address grew on him until it became a point of professional honour with him to despoil it; at all events he was presumedly attracted by an undertaking that promised not only glory but very solid profit. The first part of the plot was, to the most skilful criminal 'impersonator' in the States, mere skittles. Spreading over those months he appeared at 'The Safe' in twelve different characters and rented twelve safes of different sizes. At the same time he made a thorough study of the methods of the place. As soon as possible he got the keys back again into legitimate use, having made duplicates for his own private ends, of course. Five he seems to have returned during his first stay; one was received later, with profuse apologies, by registered post; one was returned through a leading Berlin bank. Six months ago he made a flying visit here, purely to work off two more. One he kept from first to last, and the remaining couple he got in at the beginning of his second long residence here, three or four months ago.

"This brings us to the serious part of the cool enterprise. He had funds from the Atlantic and South-Central Mail-car coup when he arrived here last April. He appears to have set up three establishments; a home, in the guise of an elderly scholar with a young wife, which, of course, was next door to our friend the manager; an observation point, over which he plastered the inscription 'Rub in Rubbo for Everything' as a reason for being; and, somewhere else, a dressing-room with essential conditions of two doors into different streets.

"About six weeks ago he entered the last stage. Mrs. Harry, with quite ridiculous ease, got photographs of the necessary page or two of the record-book. I don't doubt that for weeks before then everyone who entered the place had been observed, but the photographs linked them up with the actual men into whose hands the 'Actor's' old keys had passed—gave their names and addresses, the numbers of their safes, their passwords and signatures. The rest was easy."

"Yes, by Jupiter; mere play for a man like that," agreed Mr. Carlyle, with professional admiration. "He could contrive a dozen different occasions for studying the voice and manner and appearance of his victims. How much has he cleared?"

"We can only speculate as yet. I have put my hand

on seven doubtful callers on Monday and Tuesday last.
Two others he had ignored for some reason; the remaining two safes had not been allotted. There is one point
that raises an interesting speculation."

"What is that, Max?"

"The 'Actor' has one associate, a man known as 'Billy
the Fondant,' but beyond that—with the exception of his
wife, of course—he does not usually trust anyone. It is
plain, however, that at least seven men must latterly
have been kept under close observation. It has occurred
to me——"

"Yes, Max?"

"I have wondered whether Harry has enlisted the innocent services of one or other of our clever private inquiry
offices."

"Scarcely," smiled the professional. "It would hardly
pass muster."

"Oh, I don't know. Mrs. Harry, in the character of a
jealous wife or a suspicious sweetheart, might reasonably——"

Mr. Carlyle's smile suddenly faded.

"By Jupiter!" he exclaimed. "I remember——"

"Yes, Louis?" prompted Carrados, with laughter in his
voice.

"I remember that I must telephone to a client before
Beedel comes," concluded Mr. Carlyle, rising in some
haste.

At the door he almost ran into the subdued director,
who was wringing his hands in helpless protest at a new
stroke of calamity.

"Mr. Carrados," wailed the poor old gentleman in a
tremulous bleat, "Mr. Carrados, there is another now—
Sir Benjamin Gump. He insists on seeing me. You will
not—you will not desert us?"

"I should have to stay a week," replied Carrados
briskly, "and I'm just off now. There will be a procession.
Mr. Carlyle will support you, I am sure."

He nodded "Good-morning" straight into the eyes of
each and found his way out with the astonishing cer-

tainty of movement that made so many forget his in-
firmity. Possibly he was not desirous of encountering
Draycott's embarrassed gratitude again, for in less than
a minute they heard the swirl of his departing car.

"Never mind, my dear sir," Mr. Carlyle assured his
client, with impenetrable complacency. "Never mind. *I*
will remain instead. Perhaps I had better make myself
known to Sir Benjamin at once."

The director turned on him the pleading, trustful look
of a cornered dormouse.

"He is in the basement," he whispered. "I shall be
in the boardroom—if necessary."

Mr. Carlyle had no difficulty in discovering the centre
of interest in the basement. Sir Benjamin was expansive
and reserved, bewildered and decisive, long-winded and
short-tempered, each in turn and more or less all at
once. He had already demanded the attention of the
manager, Professor Bulge, Draycott and two underlings
to his case and they were now involved in a babel of
inutile reiteration. The inquiry agent was at once drawn
into a circle of interrogation that he did his best to
satisfy impressively while himself learning the new
facts.

The latest development was sufficiently astonishing.
Less than an hour before Sir Benjamin had received a
parcel by district messenger. It contained a jewel-case
which ought at that moment to have been securely reposing in one of the deposit safes. Hastily snatching it
open, the recipient's incredible forebodings were realized.
It was empty—empty of jewels, that is to say, for, as
if to add a sting to the blow, a neatly inscribed card
had been placed inside, and on it the agitated baronet read
the appropriate but at the moment rather gratuitous
maxim: "Lay not up for yourselves treasures upon
earth——"

The card was passed round and all eyes demanded the
expert's pronouncement.

" '—where moth and rust doth corrupt and where
thieves break through and steal.' H'm," read Mr. Carlyle

with weight. "This is a most important clue, Sir Benjamin——"

"Hey, what? What's that?" exclaimed a voice from the other side of the hall. "Why, damme if I don't believe you've got another! Look at that, gentlemen; look at that. What's on, I say? Here now, come; give me my safe. I want to know where I am."

It was the bookmaker who strode tempestuously in among them, flourishing before their faces a replica of the card that was in Mr. Carlyle's hand.

"Well, upon my soul this is most extraordinary," exclaimed that gentleman, comparing the two. "You have just received this, Mr.—Mr. Berge, isn't it?"

"That's right, Berge—'Iceberg' on the course. Thank the Lord Harry, I can take my losses coolly enough, but this—this is a facer. Put into my hand half-an-hour ago inside an envelope that ought to be here and as safe as in the Bank of England. What's the game, I say? Here, Johnny, hurry and let me into my safe."

Discipline and method had for the moment gone by the board. There was no suggestion of the boasted safeguards of the establishment. The manager added his voice to that of the client, and when the attendant did not at once appear he called again.

"John, come and give Mr. Berge access to his safe at once."

"All right, sir," pleaded the harassed key-attendant, hurrying up with the burden of his own distraction. "There's a silly fathead got in what thinks this is a left-luggage office, so far as I can make out—a foreigner."

"Never mind that now," replied the manager severely. "Mr. Berge's safe: No. 01724."

The attendant and Mr. Berge went off together down one of the brilliant colonnaded vistas. One or two of the others who had caught the words glanced across and became aware of a strange figure that was drifting indecisively towards them. He was obviously an elderly German tourist of pronounced type—long-haired, spectacled, outrageously garbed and involved in the mental abstraction of his philosophical race. One hand was occupied with the manipulation of a pipe, as markedly Teutonic as its owner; the other grasped a carpet-bag that would have ensured an opening laugh to any low comedian.

Quite impervious to the preoccupation of the group, the German made his way up to them and picked out the manager.

"This was a safety deposit, *nicht wahr?*"

"Quite so," acquiesced the manager loftily, "but just now——"

"Your fellow was dense of gomprehension." The eyes behind the clumsy glasses wrinkled to a ponderous humour. "He forgot his own business. Now this goot bag——"

Brought into fuller prominence, the carpet-bag revealed further details of its overburdened proportions. At one end a flannel shirt cuff protruded in limp dejection; at the other an ancient collar, with the grotesque attachment known as a "dickey," asserted its presence. No wonder the manager frowned his annoyance. "The Safe" was in low enough repute among its patrons at that moment without any burlesque interlude to its tragic hour.

"Yes, yes," he whispered, attempting to lead the would-be depositor away, "but you are under a mistake. This is not——"

"It was a safety deposit? Goot. Mine bag—I would deposit him in safety till the time of mine train. *Ja?*"

"*Nein, nein!*" almost hissed the agonized official. "Go away, sir, go away! It isn't a cloakroom. John, let this gentleman out."

The attendant and Mr. Berge were returning from their quest. The inner box had been opened and there was no need to ask the result. The bookmaker was shaking his head like a baffled bull.

"Gone, no effects," he shouted across the hall. "Lifted from 'The Safe,' by crumb!"

To those who knew nothing of the method and operation of the fraud it seemed as if the financial security
of the Capital was tottering. An amazed silence fell, and
in it they heard the great grille door of the basement
clang on the inopportune foreigner's departure. But, as
if it was impossible to stand still on that morning of
dire happenings, he was immediately succeeded by a
dapper, keen-faced man in severe clerical attire who had
been let in as the intruder passed out.

"Canon Petersham!" exclaimed the professor, going
forward to greet him.

"My dear Professor Bulge!" reciprocated the canon.
"You here! A most disquieting thing has happened to
me. I must have my safe at once." He divided his attention between the manager and the professor as he
monopolized them both. "A most disquieting and—and
outrageous circumstance. My safe, please—yes, yes, Rev.
Henry Noakes Petersham. I have just received by hand
a box, a small box of no value but one that I *thought*,
yes, I am convinced that it was the one, a box that was
used to contain certain valuables of family interest which
should at this moment be in my safe here. No. 7436?
Very likely, very likely. Yes, here is my key. But not
content with the disconcerting effect of that, professor,
the box contained—and I protest that it's a most un-
seemly thing to quote *any* text from the Bible in this
way to a clergyman of my position—well, here it is.
'Lay not up for yourselves treasures upon earth——' Why,
I have a dozen sermons of my own in my desk now on
that very verse. I'm particularly partial to the very need-
ful lesson that it teaches. And to apply it to *me!* It's
monstrous!"

"No. 7436, John," ordered the manager, with weary
resignation.

The attendant again led the way towards another ar-
mour-plated aisle. Smartly turning a corner, he stumbled
over something, bit a profane exclamation in two, and
looked back.

"It's that bloomin' foreigner's old bag again," he explained across the place in aggrieved apology. "He left it here after all."

"Take it upstairs and throw it out when you've finished," said the manager shortly.

"Here, wait a minute," pondered John, in absent-minded familiarity. "Wait a minute. This is a funny go. There's a label on that wasn't here before. *'Why not look inside?'*"

"'Why not look inside?'" repeated someone.

"That's what it says."

There was another puzzled silence. All were arrested by some intangible suggestion of a deeper mystery than they had yet touched. One by one they began to cross the hall with the conscious air of men who were not curious but thought that they might as well see.

"Why, curse my crumpet," suddenly exploded Mr. Berge, "if that ain't the same writing as these texts!"

"By gad, but I believe you are right," assented Mr. Carlyle. "Well, why not look inside?"

The attendant, from his stooping posture, took the verdict of the ring of faces and in a trice tugged open the two buckles. The central fastening was not locked, and yielded to a touch. The flannel shirt, the weird collar and a few other garments in the nature of a "top-dressing" were flung out and John's hand plunged deeper. . . .

Harry the Actor had lived up to his dramatic instinct. Nothing was wrapped up; nay, the rich booty had been deliberately opened out and displayed, as it were, so that the overturning of the bag, when John the key-bearer in an access of riotous extravagance lifted it up and strewed its contents broadcast on the floor, was like the looting of a smuggler's den, or the realization of a speculator's dream, or the bursting of an Aladdin's cave, or something incredibly lavish and bizarre. Banknotes fluttered down and lay about in all directions, relays of sovereigns rolled away like so much dross, bonds and scrip for thousands and tens of thousands clogged the downpouring stream of jewellery and unset gems. A yellow stone the size of a four-pound weight and twice as heavy dropped plump upon the canon's toes and sent him hopping and grimacing to the wall. A ruby-hilted kris cut across the manager's wrist as he strove to arrest the splendid rout. Still the miraculous cornucopia deluged the ground, with its pattering, ringing, bumping, crinkling, rolling, fluttering produce until, like the final tableau of some spectacular ballet, it ended with a golden rain that masked the details of the heap beneath a glittering veil of yellow sand.

"My dust!" gasped Draycott.

"My fivers, by golly!" ejaculated the bookmaker, initiating a plunge among the spoil.

"My Japanese bonds, coupons and all, and—yes, even the manuscript of my work on 'Polyphyletic Bridal Customs among the mid-Pleistocene Cave Men.' Hah!" Something approaching a cachinnation of delight closed the professor's contribution to the pandemonium, and eyewitnesses afterwards declared that for a moment the dignified scientist stood on one foot in the opening movement of a can-can.

"My wife's diamonds, thank heaven!" cried Sir Benjamin, with the air of a schoolboy who was very well out of a swishing.

"But what does it mean?" demanded the bewildered canon. "Here are my family heirlooms—a few decent pearls, my grandfather's collection of camei and other trifles—but who——?"

"Perhaps this offers some explanation," suggested Mr. Carlyle, unpinning an envelope that had been secured to the lining of the bag. "It is addressed 'To Seven Rich Sinners.' Shall I read it for you?"

For some reason the response was not unanimous, but it was sufficient. Mr. Carlyle cut open the envelope.

"MY DEAR FRIENDS,—Aren't you glad? Aren't you happy at this moment? Ah yes; but not with the true joy of regeneration that alone can bring lightness to the afflicted soul. Pause while there is yet time. Cast off the burden of your sinful lusts, for what shall it profit a man if he shall gain the whole world and lose his own soul? (Mark, chap. viii., *v.* 36.)

"Oh, my friends, you have had an all-fired narrow squeak. Up till the Friday in last week I held your wealth in the hollow of my ungodly hand and rejoiced in my nefarious cunning, but on that day as I with my guilty female accomplice stood listening with worldly amusement to the testimony of a converted brother at a meeting of the Salvation Army on Clapham Common, the gospel light suddenly shone into our rebellious souls and then and there we found salvation. Hallelujah!

"What we have done to complete the unrighteous scheme upon which we had laboured for months has only been for your own good, dear friends that you are, though as yet divided from us by your carnal lusts. Let this be a lesson to you. Sell all you have and give it to the poor —through the organization of the Salvation Army by preference—and thereby lay up for yourselves treasures where neither moth nor rust doth corrupt and where thieves do not break through and steal. (Matthew, chap. vi., *v.* 20.)

"Yours in good works,
"PRIVATE HENRY, THE SALVATIONIST.

"*P.S.* (in haste).—I may as well inform you that no crib is really uncrackable, though the Cyrus J. Coy Co.'s Safe Deposit on West 24th Street, N. Y., comes nearest the kernel. And even that I could work to the bare rock if I took hold of the job with both hands—that is to say I could have done in my sinful days. As for you, I should recommend you to change your T.A. to 'Peanut.'

"U. K. G."

"There sounds a streak of the old Adam in that post-script, Mr. Carlyle," whispered Inspector Beedel, who had just arrived in time to hear the letter read.

ERNEST BRAMAH

THE COMEDY AT FOUNTAIN COTTAGE

CARRADOS had rung up Mr. Carlyle soon after the inquiry agent had reached his office in Bampton Street on a certain morning in April. Mr. Carlyle's face at once assumed its most amiable expression as he recognized his friend's voice.

"Yes, Max," he replied, in answer to the call, "I am here and at the top of form, thanks. Glad to know that you are back from Trescoe. Is there—anything?"

"I have a couple of men coming in this evening whom you might like to meet," explained Carrados. "Manoel the Zambesia explorer is one and the other an East-End slum doctor who has seen a few things. Do you care to come round to dinner?"

"Delighted," warbled Mr. Carlyle, without a moment's consideration. "Charmed. Your usual hour, Max?" Then the smiling complacence of his face suddenly changed and the wire conveyed an exclamation of annoyance. "I am really very sorry, Max, but I have just remembered that I have an engagement. I fear that I must deny myself after all."

"Is it important?"

"No," admitted Mr. Carlyle. "Strictly speaking, it is not in the least important; this is why I feel compelled to keep it. It is only to dine with my niece. They have just got into an absurd doll's house of a villa at Groat's Heath and I had promised to go there this evening."

"Are they particular to a day?"

There was a moment's hesitation before Mr. Carlyle replied.

"I am afraid so, now it is fixed," he said. "To you, Max, it will be ridiculous or incomprehensible that a third to dinner—and he only a middle-aged uncle—should make a straw of difference. But I know that in their bijou way it will be a little domestic event to Elsie—an added anxiety in giving the butcher an order, an extra course for dinner, perhaps; a careful drilling of the one diminutive maid-servant, and she is such a charming little woman—eh? Who, Max? No! No! I did not say the maid-servant; if I did it is the fault of this telephone. Elsie is such a delightful little creature that, upon my soul, it would be too bad to fail her now."

"Of course it would, you old humbug," agreed Carrados, with sympathetic laughter in his voice. "Well, come to-morrow instead. I shall be alone."

"Oh, besides, there is a special reason for going, which for the moment I forgot," explained Mr. Carlyle, after accepting the invitation. "Elsie wishes for my advice with regard to her next-door neighbour. He is an elderly man of retiring disposition and he makes a practice of throwing kidneys over into her garden."

"Kittens! Throwing kittens?"

"No, no, Max. Kidneys. Stewed k-i-d-n-e-y-s. It is a little difficult to explain plausibly over a badly vibrating telephone, I admit, but that is what Elsie's letter assured me, and she adds that she is in despair."

"At all events it makes the lady quite independent of the butcher, Louis!"

"I have no further particulars, Max. It may be a solitary diurnal offering, or the sky may at times appear to rain kidneys. If it is a mania the symptoms may even have become more pronounced and the man is possibly showering beef-steaks across by this time. I will make full inquiry and let you know."

"Do," assented Carrados, in the same light-hearted spirit. "Mrs. Nickleby's neighbourly admirer expressed his feelings by throwing cucumbers, you remember, but this man puts him completely in the shade."

It had not got beyond the proportions of a jest to

either of them when they rang off—one of those whimsical occurrences in real life that sound so fantastic in outline. Carrados did not give the matter another thought until the next evening when his friend's arrival revived the subject.

"And the gentleman next door?" he inquired among his greetings. "Did the customary offering arrive while you were there?"

"No," admitted Mr. Carlyle, beaming pleasantly upon all the familiar appointments of the room, "it did not, Max. In fact, so diffident has the mysterious philanthropist become, that no one at Fountain Cottage has been able to catch sight of him lately, although I am told that Scamp—Elsie's terrier—betrays a very self-conscious guilt and suspiciously muddy paws every morning."

"Fountain Cottage?"

"That is the name of the toy villa."

"Yes, but Fountain something, Groat's Heath—Fountain Court: wasn't that where Metrobe——?"

"Yes, yes, to be sure, Max. Metrobe the traveller, the writer and scientist——"

"Scientist!"

"Well, he took up spiritualism or something, didn't he? At any rate, he lived at Fountain Court, an old red-brick house in a large neglected garden there, until his death a couple of years ago. Then, as Groat's Heath had suddenly become a popular suburb with a tube railway, a land company acquired the estate, the house was razed to the ground and in a twinkling a colony of Noah's ark villas took its place. There is Metrobe Road here, and Court Crescent there, and Mansion Drive and what not, and Elsie's little place perpetuates another landmark."

"I have Metrobe's last book there," said Carrados, nodding towards a point on his shelves. "In fact he sent me a copy. 'The Flame beyond the Dome' it is called—the queerest farrago of balderdash and metaphysics imaginable. But what about the neighbour, Louis? Did you settle what we might almost term 'his hash'?"

"Oh, he is mad, of course. I advised her to make as little

fuss about it as possible, seeing that the man lives next door and might become objectionable, but I framed a note for her to send which will probably have a good effect."

"Is he mad, Louis?"

"Well, I don't say that he is strictly a lunatic, but there is obviously a screw loose somewhere. He may carry indiscriminate benevolence towards Yorkshire terriers to irrational lengths. Or he may be a food specialist with a grievance. In effect he is mad on at least that one point. How else are we to account for the circumstances?"

"I was wondering," replied Carrados thoughtfully.

"You suggest that he really may have a sane object?"

"I suggest it—for the sake of argument. If he has a sane object, what is it?"

"That I leave to you, Max," retorted Mr. Carlyle conclusively. "If he has a sane object, pray what is it?"

"For the sake of the argument I will tell you that in half-a-dozen words, Louis," replied Carrados, with good-humoured tolerance. "If he is not mad in the sense which you have defined, the answer stares us in the face. His object is precisely that which he is achieving."

Mr. Carlyle looked inquiringly into the placid, unemotional face of his blind friend, as if to read there whether incredible as it might seem, Max should be taking the thing seriously after all.

"And what is that?" he asked cautiously.

"In the first place he has produced the impression that he is eccentric or irresponsible. That is sometimes useful in itself. Then what else has he done?"

"What else, Max?" replied Mr. Carlyle, with some indignation. "Well, whatever he wishes to achieve by it I can tell you one thing else that he has done. He has so demoralized Scamp with his confounded kidneys that Elsie's neatly arranged flower-beds—and she took Fountain Cottage principally on account of an unusually large garden—are hopelessly devastated. If she keeps the dog up, the garden is invaded night and day by an army of peregrinating feline marauders that scent the booty from afar. He has gained the everlasting annoyance of an other-

wise charming neighbour, Max. Can you tell me what he
has achieved by that?"

"The everlasting esteem of Scamp probably. Is he a
good watch-dog, Louis?"

"Good heavens, Max!" exclaimed Mr. Carlyle, coming to
his feet as though he had the intention of setting out for
Groat's Heath then and there, "is it possible that he is
planning a burglary?"

"Do they keep much of value about the house?"

"No," admitted Mr. Carlyle, sitting down again with
considerable relief. "No, they don't. Bellmark is not particularly well endowed with worldly goods—in fact, between ourselves, Max, Elsie could have done very much
better from a strictly social point of view, but he is a
thoroughly good fellow and idolizes her. They have no
silver worth speaking of, and for the rest—well, just the
ordinary petty cash of a frugal young couple."

"Then he probably is not planning a burglary. I confess
that the idea did not appeal to me. If it is only that, why
should he go to the trouble of preparing this particularly
succulent dish to throw over his neighbour's ground when
cold liver would do quite as well?"

"If it is not only that, why should he go to the trouble,
Max?"

"Because by that bait he produces the greatest disturbance of your niece's garden."

"And, if sane, why should he wish to do that?"

"Because in those conditions he can the more easily
obliterate his own traces if he trespasses there at
nights."

"Well, upon my word, that's drawing a bow at a venture,
Max. If it isn't burglary, what motive could the man have
for any such nocturnal perambulation?"

An expression of suave mischief came into Carrados's
usually imperturbable face.

"Many imaginable motives surely, Louis. You are a man
of the world. Why not to meet a charming little
woman——"

"No by gad!" exclaimed the scandalized uncle warmly;

"I decline to consider the remotest possibility of that explanation. Elsie——"

"Certainly not," interposed Carrados, smothering his quiet laughter. "The maid-servant, of course."

Mr. Carlyle reined in his indignation and recovered himself with his usual adroitness.

"But, you know, that is an atrocious libel, Max," he added. "I never said such a thing. However, is it probable?"

"No," admitted Carrados. "I don't think that in the circumstances it is at all probable."

"Then where are we, Max?"

"A little further than we were at the beginning. Very little. . . . Are you willing to give me a roving commission to investigate?"

"Of course, Max, of course," assented Mr. Carlyle heartily. "I—well, as far as I was concerned, I regarded the matter as settled."

Carrados turned to his desk and the ghost of a smile might possibly have lurked about his face. He produced some stationery and indicated it to his visitor.

"You don't mind giving me a line of introduction to your niece?"

"Pleasure," murmured Carlyle, taking up a pen. "What shall I say?"

Carrados took the inquiry in its most literal sense and for reply he dictated the following letter:—

" 'MY DEAR ELSIE . . .'

"If that is the way you usually address her," he parenthesized.

"Quite so," acquiesced Mr. Carlyle, writing.

" 'The bearer of this is Mr. Carrados, of whom I have spoken to you.'

"You have spoken of me to her, I trust, Louis?" he put in.

"I believe that I have casually referred to you," admitted the writer.

"I felt sure you would have done. It makes the rest easier.

" 'He is not in the least mad although he frequently does things which to the uninitiated appear more or less eccentric at the moment. I think that you would be quite safe in complying with any suggestion he may make.

" 'Your affectionate uncle,

" 'LOUIS CARLYLE.' "

He accepted the envelope and put it away in a pocket-book that always seemed extraordinarily thin for the amount of papers it contained.

"I may call there to-morrow," he added.

Neither again referred to the subject during the evening, but when Parkinson came to the library a couple of hours after midnight to know whether he would be required again, he found his master rather deeply immersed in a book and a gap on the shelf where *The Flame beyond the Dome* had formerly stood.

It is not impossible that Mr. Carlyle supplemented his brief note of introduction with a more detailed communication that reached his niece by the ordinary postal service at an earlier hour than the other. At all events, when Mr. Carrados presented himself at the toy villa on the following afternoon he found Elsie Bellmark suspiciously disposed to accept him and his rather gratuitous intervention among her suburban troubles as a matter of course.

When the car drew up at the bright green wooden gate of Fountain Cottage another visitor, apparently a good-class working man, was standing on the path of the trim front garden, lingering over a reluctant departure. Carrados took sufficient time in alighting to allow the man to pass through the gate before he himself entered. The last exchange of sentences reached his ear.

"I'm sure, marm, you won't find anyone to do the work at less."

"I can quite believe that," replied a very fair young lady who stood nearer the house, "but, you see, we do all the gardening ourselves, thank you."

Carrados made himself known and was taken into the daintily pretty drawing-room that opened on to the lawn behind the house.

"I do not need to ask if you are Mrs. Bellmark," he had declared.

"I have Uncle Louis's voice?" she divined readily.

"The niece of his voice, so to speak," he admitted. "Voices mean a great deal to me, Mrs. Bellmark."

"In recognizing and identifying people?" she suggested.

"Oh, very much more than that. In recognizing and identifying their moods—their thoughts even. There are subtle lines of trouble and the deep rings of anxious care quite as patent to the ear as to the sharpest eye sometimes."

Elsie Bellmark shot a glance of curiously interested speculation to the face that, in spite of its frank, open bearing, revealed so marvellously little itself.

"If I had any dreadful secret, I think that I should be a little afraid to talk to you, Mr. Carrados," she said, with a half-nervous laugh.

"Then please do not have any dreadful secret," he replied, with quite youthful gallantry. "I more than suspect that Louis has given you a very transpontine idea of my tastes. I do not spend all my time tracking murderers to their lair, Mrs. Bellmark, and I have never yet engaged in a hand-to-hand encounter with a band of cut-throats."

"He told us," she declared, the recital lifting her voice into a tone that Carrados vowed to himself was wonderfully thrilling, "about this: He said that you were once in a sort of lonely underground cellar near the river with two desperate men whom you could send to penal servitude. The police, who were to have been there at a certain time, had not arrived, and you were alone. The men had heard that you were blind, but they could hardly believe it. They were discussing in whispers which could not be overheard what would be the best thing to do, and they had just agreed that if you really were blind they would risk the attempt to murder you. Then, Louis said, at that very moment you took a pair of scissors from your pocket, and coolly asking them why they did not have a lamp down there, you actually snuffed the candle that stood on the table before you. Is that true?"

Carrados's mind leapt vividly back to the most desperate moment of his existence, but his smile was gently deprecating as he replied:

"I seem to recognize the touch of truth in the inclination to do *anything* rather than fight," he confessed. "But, although he never suspects it, Louis really sees life through rose-coloured opera glasses. Take the case of your quite commonplace neighbour——"

"That is really what you came about?" she interposed shrewdly.

"Frankly, it is," he replied. "I am more attracted by a turn of the odd and grotesque than by the most elaborate tragedy. The fantastic conceit of throwing stewed kidneys over into a neighbour's garden irresistibly appealed to me. Louis, as I was saying, regards the man in the romantic light of a humanitarian monomaniac or a demented food reformer. I take a more subdued view and I think that his action, when rightly understood, will prove to be something quite obviously natural."

"Of course it is very ridiculous, but all the same it has been desperately annoying," she confessed. "Still, it scarcely matters now. I am only sorry that it should have been the cause of wasting your valuable time, Mr. Carrados."

"My valuable time," he replied, "only seems valuable to me when I am, as you would say, wasting it. But is the incident closed? Louis told me that he had drafted you a letter of remonstrance. May I ask if it has been effective?"

Instead of replying at once she got up and walked to the long French window and looked out over the garden where the fruit trees that had been spared from the older cultivation were rejoicing the eye with the promise of their pink and white profusion.

"I did not send it," she said slowly, turning to her visitor again. "There is something that I did not tell Uncle Louis, because it would only have distressed him without doing any good. We may be leaving here very soon."

"Just when you had begun to get it well in hand?" he said, in some surprise.

"It is a pity, is it not? but one cannot foresee these things. There is no reason why you should not know the cause, since you have interested yourself so far, Mr. Carrados. In fact," she added, smiling away the seriousness of the manner into which she had fallen, "I am not at all sure that you do not know already."

He shook his head and disclaimed any such prescience.

"At all events you recognized that I was not exactly light-hearted," she insisted. "Oh, you did not say that *I* had dark rings under my eyes, I know, but the cap fitted excellently. . . . It has to do with my husband's business. He is with a firm of architects. It was a little venturesome taking this house—we had been in apartments for two years—but Roy was doing so well with his people and I was so enthusiastic for a garden that we did—scarcely two months ago. Everything seemed quite assured. Then came this thunderbolt. The partners—it is only a small firm, Mr. Carrados—required a little more capital in the business. Someone whom they know is willing to put in two thousand pounds, but he stipulates for a post with them as well. He, like my husband, is a draughtsman. There is no need for the services of both and so——"

"Is it settled?"

"In effect, it is. They are as nice as can be about it but that does not alter the facts. They declare that they would rather have Roy than the new man and they have definitely offered to retain him if he can bring in even one thousand pounds. I suppose they have some sort of compunction about turning him adrift, for they have asked him to think it over and let them know on Monday. Of course, that is the end of it. It may be—I don't know—I don't

like to think, how long before Roy gets another position
equally good. We must endeavour to get this house off our
hands and creep back to our three rooms. It is . . . luck."

Carrados had been listening to her wonderfully musical
voice as another man might have been drawn irresistibly
to watch the piquant charm of her delicate face.

"Yes," he assented, almost to himself, "it is that strange,
inexplicable grouping of men and things that, under one
name or another, we all confess . . . just luck."

"Of course you will not mention this to Uncle Louis
yet, Mr. Carrados?"

"If you do not wish it, certainly not."

"I am sure that it would distress him. He is so soft-
hearted, so kind, in everything. Do you know, I found
out that he had had an invitation to dine somewhere and
meet some quite important people on Tuesday. Yet he
came here instead, although most other men would have
cried off, just because he knew that we small people would
have been disappointed."

"Well, you can't expect me to see any self-denial in
that," exclaimed Carrados. "Why, I was one of them
myself."

Elsie Bellmark laughed outright at the expressive disgust
of his tone.

"I had no idea of that," she said. "Then there is another
reason. Uncle is not very well off, yet if he knew how
Roy was situated he would make an effort to arrange
matters. He would, I am sure, even borrow himself in
order to lend us the money. That is a thing Roy and I are
quite agreed on. We will go back; we will go under, if it is
to be; but we will not borrow money, not even from
Uncle Louis."

Once, subsequently, Carrados suddenly asked Mr.
Carlyle whether he had ever heard a woman's voice roll
like a celestial kettle-drum. The professional gentleman
was vastly amused by the comparison, but he admitted that
he had not.

"So that, you see," concluded Mrs. Bellmark, "there is
really nothing to be done."

"Oh, quite so; I am sure that you are right," assented her visitor readily. "But in the meanwhile I do not see why the annoyance of your next-door neighbour should be permitted to go on."

"Of course: I have not told you that, and I could not explain it to uncle," she said. "I am anxious not to do anything to put him out because I have a hope—rather a faint one, certainly—that the man may be willing to take over this house."

It would be incorrect to say that Carrados pricked up his ears—if that curious phenomenon has any physical manifestation—for the sympathetic expression of his face did not vary a fraction. But into his mind there came a gleam such as might inspire a patient digger who sees the first speck of gold that justifies his faith in an unlikely claim.

"Oh," he said, quite conversationally, "is there a chance of that?"

"He undoubtedly did want it. It is very curious in a way. A few weeks ago, before we were really settled, he came one afternoon, saying he had heard that this house was to be let. Of course I told him that he was too late, that we had already taken it for three years."

"You were the first tenants?"

"Yes. The house was scarcely ready when we signed the agreement. Then this Mr. Johns, or Jones—I am not sure which he said—went on in a rather extraordinary way to persuade me to sublet to him. He said that the house was dear and I could get plenty, more convenient, at less rent, and it was unhealthy, and the drains were bad, and that we should be pestered by tramps and it was just the sort of house that burglars picked on, only he had taken a sort of fancy to it and he would give me a fifty-pound premium for the term."

"Did he explain the motive for this rather eccentric partiality?"

"I don't imagine that he did. He repeated several times that he was a queer old fellow with his whims and fancies and that they often cost him dear."

"I think we all know that sort of old fellow," said Carrados. "It must have been rather entertaining for you, Mrs. Bellmark."

"Yes, I suppose it was," she admitted. "The next thing we knew of him was that he had taken the other house as soon as it was finished."

"Then he would scarcely require this?"

"I am afraid not." It was obvious that the situation was not disposed of. "But he seems to have so little furniture there and to live so solitarily," she explained, "that we have even wondered whether he might not be there merely as a sort of caretaker."

"And you have never heard where he came from or who he is?"

"Only what the milkman told my servant—our chief source of local information, Mr. Carrados. He declares that the man used to be the butler at a large house that stood here formerly, Fountain Court, and that his name is neither Johns nor Jones. But very likely it is all a mistake."

"If not, he is certainly attached to the soil," was her visitor's rejoinder. "And, apropos of that, will you show me over your garden before I go, Mrs. Bellmark?"

"With pleasure," she assented, rising also. "I will ring now and then I can offer you tea when we have been round. That is, if you——?"

"Thank you, I do," he replied. "And would you allow my man to go through into the garden—in case I require him?"

"Oh, certainly. You must tell me just what you want without thinking it necessary to ask permission, Mr. Carrados," she said, with a pretty air of protection. "Shall Amy take a message?"

He acquiesced and turned to the servant who had appeared in response to the bell.

"Will you go to the car and tell my man—Parkinson—that I require him here? Say that he can bring his book; he will understand."

"Yes, sir."

They stepped out through the French window and sauntered across the lawn. Before they had reached the other side Parkinson reported himself.

"You had better stay here," said his master, indicating the sward generally. "Mrs. Bellmark will allow you to bring out a chair from the drawing-room."

"Thank you, sir; there is a rustic seat already provided," replied Parkinson.

He sat down with his back to the houses and opened the book that he had brought. Let in among its pages was an ingeniously contrived mirror.

When their promenade again brought them near the rustic seat Carrados dropped a few steps behind.

"He is watching you from one of the upper rooms, sir," fell from Parkinson's lips as he sat there without raising his eyes from the page before him.

The blind man caught up to his hostess again.

"You intended this lawn for croquet?" he asked.

"No; not specially. It is too small, isn't it?"

"Not necessarily. I think it is in about the proportion of four by five all right. Given that, size does not really matter for an unsophisticated game."

To settle the point he began to pace the plot of ground, across and then lengthways. Next, apparently dissatisfied with this rough measurement, he applied himself to marking it off more exactly by means of his walking-stick. Elsie Bellmark was by no means dull but the action sprang so naturally from the conversation that it did not occur to her to look for any deeper motive.

"He has got a pair of field-glasses and is now at the window," communicated Parkinson.

"I am going out of sight," was the equally quiet response. "If he becomes more anxious tell me afterwards."

"It is quite all right," he reported, returning to Mrs. Bellmark with the satisfaction of bringing agreeable news. "It should make a splendid little ground, but you may have to level up a few dips after the earth has set."

A chance reference to the kitchen garden by the visitor took them to a more distant corner of the enclosure where the rear of Fountain Cottage cut off the view from the next house windows.

"We decided on this part for vegetables because it does not really belong to the garden proper," she explained. "When they build farther on this side we shall have to give it up very soon. And it would be a pity if it was all in flowers."

With the admirable spirit of the ordinary English-woman, she spoke of the future as if there was no cloud to obscure its prosperous course. She had frankly declared their position to her uncle's best friend because in the circumstances it had seemed to be the simplest and most straightforward thing to do; beyond that, there was no need to whine about it.

"It is a large garden," remarked Carrados. "And you really do all the work of it yourselves?"

"Yes; I think that is half the fun of a garden. Roy is out here early and late and he does all the hard work. But how did you know? Did uncle tell you?"

"No; you told me yourself."

"I? Really?"

"Indirectly. You were scorning the proffered services of a horticultural mercenary at the moment of my arrival."

"Oh, I remember," she laughed. "It was Irons, of course. He is a great nuisance, he is so stupidly persistent. For some weeks now he has been coming time after time, trying to persuade me to engage him. Once when we were all out he had actually got into the garden and was on the point of beginning work when I returned. He said he saw the milkmen and the grocers leaving samples at the door so he thought that he would too!"

"A practical jester evidently. Is Mr. Irons a local character?"

"He said that he knew the ground and the conditions round about here better than anyone else in Groat's Heath," she replied. "Modesty is not among Mr. Irons's handicaps. He said that he—— How curious!"

"What is, Mrs. Bellmark?"

"I never connected the two men before, but he said

that he had been gardener at Fountain Court for seven years."

"Another family retainer who is evidently attached to the soil."

"At all events they have not prospered equally, for while Mr. Johns seems able to take a nice house, poor Irons is willing to work for half-a-crown a day, and I am told that all the other men charge four shillings."

They had paced the boundaries of the kitchen garden, and as there was nothing more to be shown Elsie Bellmark led the way back to the drawing-room. Parkinson was still engrossed in his book, the only change being that his back was now turned towards the high paling of clinker-built oak that separated the two gardens.

"I will speak to my man," said Carrados, turning aside.

"He hurried down and is looking through the fence, sir," reported the watcher.

"That will do then. You can return to the car."

"I wonder if you would allow me to send you a small hawthorn-tree?" inquired Carrados among his felicitations over the teacups five minutes later. "I think it ought to be in every garden."

"Thank you—but is it worth while?" replied Mrs. Bellmark, with a touch of restraint. As far as mere words went she had been willing to ignore the menace of the future, but in the circumstances the offer seemed singularly inept and she began to suspect that outside his peculiar gifts the wonderful Mr. Carrados might be a little bit obtuse after all.

"Yes; I think it is," he replied, with quiet assurance.

"In spite of——?"

"I am not forgetting that unless your husband is prepared on Monday next to invest one thousand pounds you contemplate leaving here."

"Then I do not understand it, Mr. Carrados."

"And I am unable to explain as yet. But I brought you a note from Louis Carlyle, Mrs. Bellmark. You only glanced at it. Will you do me the favour of reading me the last paragraph?"

She picked up the letter from the table where it lay and complied with cheerful good-humour.

"There is some suggestion that you want me to accede to," she guessed cunningly when she had read the last few words.

"There are some three suggestions which I hope you will accede to," he replied. "In the first place I want you to write to Mr. Johns next door—let him get the letter to-night—inquiring whether he is still disposed to take this house."

"I had thought of doing that shortly."

"Then that is all right. Besides, he will ultimately decline."

"Oh," she exclaimed—it would be difficult to say whether with relief or disappointment—"do you think so? Then why——"

"To keep him quiet in the meantime. Next I should like you to send a little note to Mr. Irons—your maid could deliver it also to-night, I dare say?"

"Irons! Irons the gardener?"

"Yes," apologetically. "Only a line or two, you know. Just saying that, after all, if he cares to come on Monday you can find him a few days' work."

"But in any circumstances I don't want him."

"No; I can quite believe that you could do better. Still, it doesn't matter, as he won't come, Mrs. Bellmark; not for a half-a-crown a day, believe me. But the thought will tend to make Mr. Irons less restive, also. Lastly, will you persuade your husband not to decline his firm's offer until Monday?"

"Very well, Mr. Carrados," she said, after a moment's consideration. "You are Uncle Louis's friend and therefore our friend. I will do what you ask."

"Thank you," said Carrados. "I shall endeavour not to disappoint you."

"I shall not be disappointed because I have not dared to hope. And I have nothing to expect because I am still completely in the dark."

"I have been there for nearly twenty years, Mrs. Bellmark."

"Oh, I am sorry!" she cried impulsively.

"So am I—occasionally," he replied. "Good-bye, Mrs. Bellmark. You will hear from me shortly, I hope. About the hawthorn, you know."

It was, indeed, in something less than forty-eight hours that she heard from him again. When Bellmark returned to his toy villa early on Saturday afternoon Elsie met him almost at the gate with a telegram in her hand.

"I really think, Roy, that everyone we have to do with here goes mad," she exclaimed, in tragi-humorous despair. "First it was Mr. Johns or Jones—if he is Johns or Jones— and then Irons who wanted to work here for half of what he could get at heaps of places about, and now just look at this wire that came from Mr. Carrados half-an-hour ago."

This was the message that he read:

Please procure sardine tin-opener, mariner's compass and bottle of champagne. Shall arrive 6.45 bringing Cratægus Coccinea.—CARRADOS.

"Can anything be more absurd?" she demanded.

"Sounds as though it was in code," speculated her husband. "Who's the foreign gentleman he's bringing?"

"Oh that's a kind of special hawthorn—I looked it up. But a bottle of champagne, and a compass, and a sardine tin-opener! What possible connection is there between them?"

"A very resourceful man might uncork a bottle of champagne with a sardine tin-opener," he suggested.

"And find his way home afterwards by means of a mariner's compass?" she retorted. "No, Roy dear, you are not a sleuth-hound. We had better have our lunch."

They lunched, but if the subject of Carrados had been tabooed the meal would have been a silent one.

"I have a compass on an old watch-chain somewhere," volunteered Bellmark.

"And I have a tin-opener in the form of a bull's head," contributed Elsie.

"But we have no champagne, I suppose?"

"How could we have, Roy? We never have had any. Shall you mind going down to the shops for a bottle?"

"You really think that we ought?"

"Of course we must, Roy. We don't know what mightn't happen if we didn't. Uncle Louis said that they once failed to stop a jewel robbery because the jeweller neglected to wipe his shoes on the shop door-mat, as Mr. Carrados had told him to do. Suppose Johns is a desperate anarchist and he succeeded in blowing up Buckingham Palace because we——"

"All right. A small bottle, eh?"

"No. A large one. Quite a large one. Don't you see how exciting it is becoming?"

"If you are excited already you don't need much champagne," argued her husband.

Nevertheless he strolled down to the leading wine-shop after lunch and returned with his purchase modestly draped in the light summer overcoat that he carried on his arm. Elsie Bellmark, who had quite abandoned her previous unconcern, in the conviction that "something was going to happen," spent the longest afternoon that she could remember, and even Bellmark, in spite of his continual adjurations to her to "look at the matter logically," smoked five cigarettes in place of his usual Saturday afternoon pipe and neglected to do any gardening.

At exactly six-forty-five a motor car was heard approaching. Elsie made a desperate rally to become the self-possessed hostess again. Bellmark was favourably impressed by such marked punctuality. Then a Regent Street delivery van bowled past their window and Elsie almost wept.

The suspense was not long, however. Less than five minutes later another vehicle raised the dust of the quiet suburban road, and this time a private car stopped at their gate.

"Can you see any policeman inside?" whispered Elsie.

Parkinson got down and opening the door took out a

small tree which he carried up to the porch and there deposited. Carrados followed.

"At all events there isn't much wrong," said Bellmark. "He's smiling all the time."

"No, it isn't really a smile," explained Elsie; "it's his normal expression."

She went out into the hall just as the front door was opened.

"It is the 'Scarlet-fruited thorn' of North America," Bellmark heard the visitor remarking. "Both the flowers and the berries are wonderfully good. Do you think that you would permit me to choose the spot for it, Mrs. Bellmark?"

Bellmark joined them in the hall and was introduced.

"We mustn't waste any time," he suggested. "There is very little light left."

"True," agreed Carrados. "And Coccinea requires deep digging."

They walked through the house, and turning to the right passed into the region of the vegetable garden. Carrados and Elsie led the way, the blind man carrying the tree, while Bellmark went to his outhouse for the required tools.

"We will direct our operations from here," said Carrados, when they were half-way along the walk. "You told me of a thin iron pipe that you had traced to somewhere in the middle of the garden. We must locate the end of it exactly."

"My rosery!" sighed Elsie, with premonition of disaster, when she had determined the spot as exactly as she could. "Oh, Mr. Carrados!"

"I am sorry, but it might be worse," said Carrados inflexibly. "We only require to find the elbow-joint. Mr. Bellmark will investigate with as little disturbance as possible."

For five minutes Bellmark made trials with a pointed iron. Then he cleared away the soil of a small circle and at about a foot deep exposed a broken inch pipe.

"The fountain," announced Carrados, when he had examined it. "You have the compass, Mr. Bellmark?"

"Rather a small one," admitted Bellmark.

"Never mind, you are a mathematician. I want you to strike a line due east."

The reel and cord came into play and an adjustment was finally made from the broken pipe to a position across the vegetable garden.

"Now a point nine yards, nine feet and nine inches along it."

"My onion bed!" cried Elsie tragically.

"Yes; it is really serious this time," agreed Carrados. "I want a hole a yard across, digging here. May we proceed?"

Elsie remembered the words of her uncle's letter—or what she imagined to be his letter—and possibly the preamble of selecting the spot had impressed her.

"Yes, I suppose so. Unless," she added hopefully, "the turnip bed will do instead? They are not sown yet."

"I am afraid that nowhere else in the garden will do," replied Carrados.

Bellmark delineated the space and began to dig. After clearing to about a foot deep he paused.

"About deep enough, Mr. Carrados?" he inquired.

"Oh, dear no," replied the blind man.

"I am two feet down," presently reported the digger.

"Deeper!" was the uncompromising response.

Another six inches were added and Bellmark stopped to rest.

"A little more and it won't matter which way up we plant Coccinea," he remarked.

"That is the depth we are aiming for," replied Carrados.

Elsie and her husband exchanged glances. Then Bellmark drove his spade through another layer of earth.

"Three feet," he announced, when he had cleared it.

Carrados advanced to the very edge of the opening.

"I think that if you would loosen another six inches with the fork we might consider the ground prepared," he decided.

Bellmark changed his tools and began to break up the soil. Presently the steel prongs grated on some obstruction.

"Gently," directed the blind watcher. "I think you will find a half-pound cocoa tin at the end of your fork."

"Well, how on earth you spotted that——!" was wrung from Bellmark admiringly, as he cleared away the encrusting earth. "But I believe you are about right." He threw up the object to his wife, who was risking a catastrophe in her eagerness to miss no detail. "Anything in it besides soil, Elsie?"

"She cannot open it yet," remarked Carrados. "It is soldered down."

"Oh, I say," protested Bellmark.

"It is perfectly correct, Roy. The lid is soldered on."

They looked at each other in varying degrees of wonder and speculation. Only Carrados seemed quite untouched.

"Now we may as well replace the earth," he remarked.

"Fill it all up again?" asked Bellmark.

"Yes; we have provided a thoroughly disintegrated subsoil. That is the great thing. A depth of six inches is sufficient merely for the roots."

There was only one remark passed during the operation.

"I think I should plant the tree just over where the tin was," Carrados suggested. "You might like to mark the exact spot." And there the hawthorn was placed.

Bellmark, usually the most careful and methodical of men, left the tools where they were, in spite of a threatening shower. Strangely silent, Elsie led the way back to the house and taking the men into the drawing-room switched on the light.

"I think you have a tin-opener, Mrs. Bellmark?"

Elsie, who had been waiting for him to speak, almost jumped at the simple inquiry. Then she went into the next room and returned with the bull-headed utensil.

"Here it is," she said, in a voice that would have amused her at any other time.

"Mr. Bellmark will perhaps disclose our find."

Bellmark put the soily tin down on Elsie's best tablecover without eliciting a word of reproach, grasped it firmly with his left hand, and worked the opener round the top.

"Only paper!" he exclaimed, and without touching the contents he passed the tin into Carrados's hands.

The blind man dexterously twirled out a little roll that crinkled pleasantly to the ear, and began counting the leaves with a steady finger.

"They're bank-notes!" whispered Elsie in an awe-struck voice. She caught sight of a further detail. "Bank-notes for a hundred pounds each. And there are dozens of them!"

"Fifty, there should be," dropped Carrados between his figures. "Twenty-five, twenty-six——"

"Good God," murmured Bellmark; "that's five thousand pounds!"

"Fifty," concluded Carrados, straightening the edges of the sheaf. "It is always satisfactory to find that one's calculations are exact." He detached the upper ten notes and held them out. "Mrs. Bellmark, will you accept one thousand pounds as a full legal discharge of any claim that you may have on this property?"

"Me—I?" she stammered. "But I have no right to any in any circumstances. It has nothing to do with us."

"You have an unassailable moral right to a fair proportion, because without you the real owners would never have seen a penny of it. As regards your legal right"—he took out the thin pocket-book and extracting a business-looking paper, spread it open on the table before them—"here is a document that concedes it. 'In consideration of the valuable services rendered by Elsie Bellmark, etc., etc., in causing to be discovered and voluntarily surrendering the sum of five thousand pounds deposited and not relinquished by Alexis Metrobe, late of, etc., etc., deceased, Messrs. Binstead & Polegate, solicitors, of 77a Bedford Row, acting on behalf of the administrator and next-of-kin of the said, etc., etc., do hereby'—well, that's what they do. Signed, witnessed and stamped at Somerset House."

"I suppose I shall wake presently," said Elsie dreamily.

"It was for this moment that I ventured to suggest the third requirement necessary to bring our enterprise to a successful end," said Carrados.

"Oh, how thoughtful of you!" cried Elsie. "Roy, the champagne."

Five minutes later Carrados was explaining to a small but enthralled audience.

"The late Alexis Metrobe was a man of peculiar character. After seeing a good deal of the world and being many things, he finally embraced spiritualism, and in common with some of its most pronounced adherents he thenceforward abandoned what we should call 'the common-sense view.'

"A few years ago, by the collation of the Book of Revelations, a set of Zadkiel's Almanacs, and the complete works of Mrs. Mary Baker Eddy, Metrobe discovered that the end of the world would take place on the tenth of October, 1910. It therefore became a matter of urgent importance in his mind to ensure pecuniary provision for himself for the time after the catastrophe had taken place."

"I don't understand," interrupted Elsie. "Did he expect to survive it?"

"You cannot understand, Mrs. Bellmark, because it is fundamentally incomprehensible. We can only accept the fact by the light of cases which occasionally obtain prominence. Metrobe did not expect to survive, but he was firmly convinced that the currency of this world would be equally useful in the spirit-land into which he expected to pass. This view was encouraged by a lady medium at whose feet he sat. She kindly offered to transmit to his banking account in the Hereafter, without making any charge whatever, any sum that he cared to put into her hands for the purpose. Metrobe accepted the idea but not the offer. His plan was to deposit a considerable amount in a spot of which he alone had knowledge, so that he could come and help himself to it as required."

"But if the world had come to an end——?"

"Only the material world, you must understand, Mrs. Bellmark. The spirit world, its exact impalpable counterpart, would continue as before and Metrobe's hoard would be spiritually intact and available. That is the prologue.

"About a month ago there appeared a certain advertisement in a good many papers. I noticed it at the time and three days ago I had only to refer to my files to put my hand on it at once. It reads:

" 'Alexis Metrobe. Any servant or personal attendant of the late Alexis Metrobe of Fountain Court, Groat's Heath, possessing special knowledge of his habits and movements, may hear of something advantageous on applying to Binstead & Polegate, 77a Bedford Row, W.C.'

"The solicitors had, in fact, discovered that five thousand pounds' worth of securities had been realized early in 1910. They readily ascertained that Metrobe had drawn that amount in gold out of his bank immediately after, and there the trace ended. He died six months later. There was no hoard of gold and not a shred of paper to show where it had gone, yet Metrobe lived very simply within his income. The house had meanwhile been demolished but there was no hint or whisper of any lucky find.

"Two inquirers presented themselves at 77a Bedford Row. They were informed of the circumstances and offered a reward, varying according to the results, for information that would lead to the recovery of the money. They are both described as thoughtful, slow-spoken men. Each heard the story, shook his head, and departed. The first caller proved to be John Foster, the ex-butler. On the following day Mr. Irons, formerly gardener at the Court, was the applicant.

"I must now divert your attention into a side track. In the summer of 1910 Metrobe published a curious work entitled *The Flame beyond the Dome*. In the main it is an eschatological treatise, but at the end he tacked on an epilogue, which he called 'The Fable of the Chameleon.' It is even more curious than the rest and with reason, for under the guise of a speculative essay he gives a cryptic account of the circumstances of the five thousand pounds and, what is more important, details the exact particulars of its disposal. His reason for so doing is characteristic of the man. He was conscious by experience that he possessed an utterly treacherous memory, and having had occasion to move the treasure from one spot to another he feared that when the time came his bemuddled shade would be unable to locate it. For future reference, therefore, he embodied the details in his book, and to make sure that plenty of copies should be in existence he circulated it by the only means in his power—in other words, he gave a volume to everyone he knew and to a good many people whom he didn't.

"So far I have dealt with actualities. The final details are partly speculative but they are essentially correct. Metrobe conveyed his gold to Fountain Court, obtained a stout oak coffer for it, and selected a spot *west* of the fountain. He chose a favourable occasion for burying it, but by some mischance Irons came on the scene. Metrobe explained the incident by declaring that he was burying a favourite parrot. Irons thought nothing particular about it then, although he related the fact to the butler, and to others, in evidence of the general belief that 'the old cock was quite barmy.' But Metrobe himself was much disturbed by the accident. A few days later he dug up the box. In pursuance of his new plan he carried his gold to the Bank of England and changed it into these notes. Then transferring the venue to one due *east* of the fountain, he buried them in this tin, satisfied that the small space it occupied would baffle the search of anyone not in possession of the exact location."

"But, I say!" exclaimed Mr. Bellmark. "Gold might remain gold, but what imaginable use could be made of bank-notes after the end of the world?"

"That is a point of view, no doubt. But Metrobe, in spite of his foreign name, was a thorough Englishman. This world might come to an end, but he was satisfied that somehow the Bank of England would ride through it all right. I only suggest that. There is much that we can only guess."

"That is all there is to know, Mr. Carrados?"

"Yes. Everything comes to an end, Mrs. Bellmark. I

sent my car away to call for me at eight. Eight has struck. That is Harris announcing his arrival."

He stood up, but embarrassment and indecision marked the looks and movements of the other two.

"How can we possibly take all this money, though?" murmured Elsie, in painful uncertainty. "It is entirely your undertaking, Mr. Carrados. It is the merest fiction bringing me into it at all."

"Perhaps in the circumstances," suggested Bellmark. nervously—"you remember the circumstances, Elsie?— Mr. Carrados would be willing to regard it as a loan——"

"No, no!" cried Elsie impulsively. "There must be no half measures. We know that a thousand pounds would be nothing to Mr. Carrados, and he knows that a thousand pounds are everything to us." Her voice reminded the blind man of the candle-snuffing recital. "We will take this great gift, Mr. Carrados, quite freely, and we will not spoil the generous satisfaction that you must have in doing a wonderful and a splendid service by trying to hedge our obligation."

"But what can we ever do to thank Mr. Carrados?" faltered Bellmark mundanely.

"Nothing," said Elsie simply. "That is it."

"But I think that Mrs. Bellmark has quite solved that," interposed Carrados.

ERNEST BRAMAH

THE CURIOUS CIRCUMSTANCES OF THE TWO LEFT SHOES

At the time when the Enderleighs lost their silver the Monkey Burglar was at the height of his fame. The Monkey Burglar, should you by this date have forgotten, was the one who invariably gained access by leaping from a tree on to an upper story window-sill. So strong was habit that there were said to be cases of the Monkey Burglar going through this performance at houses where the front door stood open, or where a builder's ladder, left in position overnight, was reared against the very point he gained by the more sensational flight. During the thick of the burglary season that year each number of *Punch* regularly contained one or more jokes about the Monkey; no pantomime was complete without a few references to him; and the burgled invariably tried to claim distinction as authentic victims. In this, the Press, to do it justice, worthily seconded their endeavours.

The Enderleighs lived near Silver Park at that time, in one of the old-fashioned cottages that have long, delightful gardens running down to the river edge. They were a young couple, setting themselves a very moderate standard until the day when Enderleigh's wonderful qualities should be suitably recognised by a partnership. In the meanwhile he was something exceptionally responsible but not so exceptionally rewarded in connection with a firm of estate agents and surveyors. Max Carrados had heard of him favourably from one or two friends and was not unwilling to put business in the young man's way. An opportunity came when the blind criminologist had, as trustee, to deal

(From "Max Carrados's Mysteries," by Ernest Bramah. Copyright by Hodder and Stoughton, Limited, London, England.)

with an estate down in Warwickshire. He ascertained that Enderleigh was not debarred from doing work on his own account, and gave him a commission to inspect the property and make a general report. Business being slack, there was no difficulty in arranging a few days' leave of absence from the office, and the proposal was gratefully accepted.

On his return—he had conscientiously managed to cover the ground within two days—Enderleigh looked in at The Turrets before proceeding home and found Mr. Carrados at leisure.

"I thought that I would leave the report with you now," he explained, "in case you cared to glance over it and ask me about any details while it's all fresh in my mind. I wrote up my notes in the train on the way back."

"Good man," smiled Carrados, accepting the docket. "I should have liked you to stay while we discussed the matter, but I am afraid that someone else has a prior lien on your time."

"In what way?"

"A few hours ago Mrs. Enderleigh rang me up on the 'phone, and there is what I might describe as a standing order for you to communicate with her from here at the earliest moment."

"Good heavens!" exclaimed Enderleigh in some trepidation. "What's up, I wonder? Nothing wrong that you know of?"

"Nothing at all," replied Carrados with reassuring unconcern. "Your wife was in exceptional spirits, I gathered, but somewhat cryptical. However, there is the means of setting your mind at rest," and he indicated the instrument. "I'll leave you to it."

"Please don't go." Enderleigh seemed to be toying with the moment as if rather unwilling to set his mind at rest. "I was startled for a second, but if my wife herself spoke to you there can't be anything much the matter. The fact is," he confided with a certain shy complacency, "she has been getting rather fanciful of late—not an unusual phase of the situation, I understand."

Mr. Carrados murmured his discreet congratulations,

and his visitor summed up enough indifference to make the call.

"Holy Moses!" the blind man heard him mutter, and there followed a rapid fusillade of "How?" and "When?" and "What?" and "You don't mean it!" all indicating consternation and surprise, as long as the colloquy lasted.

"Here's a pretty go," announced Mr. Enderleigh, hanging up the receiver. "We've been burgled!"

"The deuce!" exclaimed Carrados sympathetically. "I hope your wife isn't much upset?"

"No, I don't think so. In fact, she seems rather set up, because some of our neighbours were robbed in a very commonplace way lately, and she's determined that this must have been the authentic Monkey."

"Much taken?"

"Apparently the silver chest and nothing else. Myra rather fancied that I would call here on my way from something I had said—that's why she rang you up—and she wants me to go straight on. I hope you don't mind?"

"Of course not. I had hoped that you would keep me company for an hour or two, but that's out of the question now. . . . I'll tell you what, though: I will make a bargain with you. Stay another fifteen minutes, in which we can have a snack of some kind in place of dinner. In the meanwhile I will have a car got out that will land you at your place quicker than any other way you could go; and in return you shall invite me to inspect the depredation."

"That's certainly a bargain from my side of the transaction," replied Enderleigh. "If it isn't putting you out, I'll accept like a shot."

"Not a bit," declared his host with more than polite formality. He moved across to the house telephone and quickly distributed the necessary orders. "I love anything that comes suddenly along. It may be the beginning of—what adventure?"

"Well, as to that, of course there are two sides," said the domesticated Enderleigh. "This is quite sudden enough for me, but I certainly don't love it."

Carrados was as good as his literal word, and fifteen minutes after he had spoken the lean form of his speedy Redshank car glided down the drive into the high road and then stretched out for Silver Park.

"Now that it's come to this, I may as well tell you about our silver," explained Mr. Enderleigh to his companion, on a confidential impulse. "We happen to have rather a lot—more than people in our modest way generally sport, I mean. Myra's father was a fruit-grower and won a lot of cups and plates in his time. I used to be something of a runner and I amassed a few more, and when we got married our friends showered cruets and cake baskets down on us galore. The consequence is that there was a solid half-hundredweight of the metal reposing in a specially made case in the dining-room at Homecroft. Of course it ought to have been kept at the bank, and at first it was, but Myra liked to see an assortment out on the sideboard, so that it got to be a nuisance sending it backwards and forwards. Then I said that if we had it in the house it ought to be kept up in the bedroom for safety, and Myra found that she couldn't even lift the chest and decided that it would be too inconvenient to have it there. What with one thing and another, the confounded silver got to become a bit of a sore point between us—it brought on the first unpleasantness we had. Then, as bad luck would have it, just when I was leaving the other morning to go on this job we must needs get arguing about it again. I suggested that as there would be only two women alone in the house—herself and the servant—it would be safer if I carried the box up and hid it under the bed. Myra—God knows why—retorted that if the silver was the danger-point it wasn't very kind to want to put it just under where she would be. One silly word led to another until I finally went off saying that I wished the damned stuff was at the bottom of the river."

"You seem to have got the next thing to what you asked for then," remarked Carrados. "The silver apparently won't trouble you again"; but Enderleigh demurred at this cheerful summary and shook his head.

"Oh, yes," he replied, "but when you wish a thing like that you don't really mean that you want it to happen."

"You are insured, I suppose?"

"Only partly, I'm afraid, because the value of the silver now exceeds the percentage allowed. And of course a lot of the things have associations, although there is nothing of antique value. I'm really wondering how Myra will take it when the excitement wears off."

But so far the excitement was on, and she welcomed them radiantly, albeit a shade mystified that Mr. Carrados should have chosen that moment to pay his call. It does not say much for the criminal expert's sense of publicity that neither his host nor hostess had the faintest idea of his uncanny reputation. To them he was simply the rich blind man who seemed as though he might be useful to Guy.

"But isn't it a shame, Mr. Carrados?" she cooed, when the first round of wonder and exclamation had been gone through. "Sergeant Lapworth declares that it can't possibly be the Monkey Burglar. And I was so relying on that to squelch the Higgses with."

Carrados divined an exchange of private glances, expostulatory from the husband, playfully defiant on her part.

"I have met Sergeant Lapworth once or twice and he seemed to know his work," said the visitor. "Did he say why it couldn't be?"

"Well, the only way they could have got in was by the side door. No fastenings have been forced or windows opened. And the Monkey wouldn't ever dream of using a side door."

"But how on earth could they do that?" demanded Enderleigh. "I mean without using force. Chloe fastens the door at night, doesn't she?"

"I'll show you if you don't mind accompanying me to the nether regions," said the light-hearted girl. "Chloe only locks the door, it seems—the bolts are too stiff to work—and Sergeant Lapworth says that these people—he's almost sure he knows the gang—have all manner of ingenious tools. There's a sort of pincers that you catch hold of a key with from the other side and turn it quite easily. You can see that the lock has been oiled to make it go."

"You found the door unlocked this morning?"

"No—I don't know. I never thought of that. But I suppose they could just as easily lock it again to cover their tracks, and as it happened it was not until this afternoon that I missed the silver chest. Then there are footprints on the bed from the gate to the side door. He found those as well. It's most wildly exciting discovering clues; I've been looking for some all the afternoon, but so far without success."

"Come on then," suggested Enderleigh. "You have a lamp or candle, I suppose?"

"Yes. Do you care to see our private morgue, Mr. Carrados—oh, I am sorry: I forgot!"

"That's very nice of you—to forget," smiled the blind man. "It shows that I'm not so helpless after all. Certainly I should like to come; I'm as keen on clues as you are."

The side door was the chief point of interest. It opened on to the garden from the scullery. The scullery—a dank and forbidding chamber that almost justified its epithet—in turn led into the kitchen, and the kitchen into the hall. But there were other ways of getting about, for it was an old house with many passages and on various levels. Most of the rooms appeared to have at least two doors. "I think that the man who built it must have been fond of French farces," remarked Mr. Enderleigh, pointing out this feature.

But even at the side door there was very little to see, the Enderleigh burglary being chiefly remarkable for its negative features. There was the oiled lock, and the key bore certain recent scratches, and that was all.

"If the bolts had been shot this would never have happened," said the master of the house. "Perhaps in future——"

"But the bolts can't be stirred, dear," protested Myra. "I've tried myself until my poor thumbs are nearly dislocated. And every one says that if burglars want to get in they will, even if they have to come down the chimney."

"I think the bolts might move if they were simply oiled," suggested Carrados. "The level is all right, you see."

"Chloe," called out Mr. Enderleigh—the kitchen door stood open—"is there any oil about?"

A young girl in cap and apron—a girl of quite unusual prettiness—appeared at the door.

"Oil, sir?" she repeated faintly, and she continued to look from one to another of them as though something was amiss.

"Yes, oil—ordinary oil—the sort you oil with, you know. There must be some about somewhere."

"Oh, yes—for the sewing machine," she replied, and disappeared to return with it in a moment.

"Now a feather."

The girl's eyes shot to a bucket holding kitchen refuse that stood beneath the sink; then rose to the level again as she continued to stand there.

"Feathers: in the middle dresser drawer, Chloe," prompted her mistress tartly. "Bless me," she confided to the others, "the girl's going dotty, I believe. Over-excitement isn't good for our poor sex."

"Now we want a chair or something for the top bolt," said Enderleigh.

"I think I can do it without, if you will allow me," put in Carrados. "I fancy that I am just a few inches to the good in that respect."

"But really, Mr. Carrados," protested the lady, "won't you get it on your clothes—or something?"

"That is only a matter of carelessness, not vision," replied Carrados. He gave the feather a dexterous turn in the neck of the bottle to remove the excess of oil before he withdrew it. "Children have the keenest sight, Mrs. Enderleigh, and yet look how they drop the jam about!"

"It's quite marvellous," she murmured, watching him apply the oil and then work the action until the bolt slid easily.

"Not so much as you might think," he assured her. "Frequently you are indebted to other senses when you think you are using your eyes, and they get all the credit. Several men have told me that they always close their eyes when they are doing certain delicate adjustments."

"I once knew a lady who always shut her eyes before she fired a gun off," contributed Enderleigh. "Yet she was fond of shooting, and often hit things."

"Dogs or keepers?" inquired Myra politely.

Certainly the burglary did not seem to have damped anyone's spirits. Presently they went out to look at the incriminating footprints—"viewing the body," Myra called it—by candlelight until they were tired of striking matches and the friendly darkness put Carrados at liberty to go down on hands and knees and touch the well-marked impressions with his eerily perceptive fingers in his own peculiar way.

"What's this—snowing?" Enderleigh had exclaimed as he opened the door to lead the way into the garden. A sprinkling of white showed on the bare earth before them.

"Goose!" retorted Myra fondly, "it's lime, of course. Old Benjamin—he's a sort of local unhandyman, Mr. Carrados, whom Guy employs one day a week to sit in the garden and smoke shag—put it on only yesterday. He said the soil was too 'thodden' for bulbs: it's always too something for Ben."

"It came in useful, all the same," said her husband. "You see, the lime being crushed down in the footprints shows that they were made after it was put there. That's important."

"Lapworth the Sleuth had already diagnosed that, O Fountain of Wisdom," mocked his wife. She leaned forward and struck him lightly on the arm. "You're it! Race you to the river, Guy!"

"Ssh!" warned Enderleigh with a nod towards their guest.

"Go, children—run," urged Carrados benignly. "I will follow at a pace more suited to my years."

"Hold up!" cried Myra, limping into a walk before they

were fairly off. "I forgot; my feet are as soft as mush to-day. Besides, I oughtn't to now."

"No, of course you oughtn't to," said Guy severely. "And we oughtn't to leave Mr. Carrados like that. God knows what sort of a lunatic asylum he'll think he's dropped on."

"Never mind: I got you away. Just one, Guy. And don't worry about him. He said his ears, but he meant his eyes, of course: his ears are sharp enough. That old man wouldn't take any harm if you put him down in the middle of a sawmill."

"Old!" exclaimed Mr. Enderleigh indignantly. "Great Scott! What next?"

They walked back to meet the advancing Carrados, and then they all strolled soberly down to the extremity of the garden and stood contemplating the slow, muddy river before they turned back again.

"You take Mr. Carrados into the dining-room, Guy," said Myra, hastening on ahead as they neared the house. "I'm going up to change my shoes—these are soaked."

"Yes, my lady, you are pretty high up already, I'm afraid," apostrophised her husband as they followed. "That's the way of it, Mr. Carrados. I shall think myself lucky if she isn't down below zero before the night is out."

"I've taken hot water up to the spare room, sir," said Chloe, as they passed her in the hall.

They washed their hands leisurely and went down to the dining-room. The maid had lit the lamp and was replenishing the fire. Still Mrs. Enderleigh did not appear. A few minutes passed rather flatly. Enderleigh made a half-hearted show of asking his guest if he was fond of this and that, but Carrados divined his vague uneasiness and soon they both frankly waited.

"Guy," said a queer little voice just outside the door—it had been left somewhat ajar—"do you mind coming here a minute?"

Enderleigh threw a quick, inquiring look across, and the blind man—informed by what sense, who shall say?—

nodded mute assent. Then the door closed and Carrados slowly turned his face to the four points of the room.

It was perhaps five minutes later that Enderleigh returned. He came thoughtfully across the room and stood close to his guest's chair.

"It's just as I was afraid," he said, pitching his voice cautiously. "Myra is now at a very minus stage indeed. And a curious thing—curious and trivial, and yet, I must admit, extraordinary—has happened to upset her. It's mixed up with one or two other matters, and I suppose that this burglary also—although that has nothing to do with it —has helped to put the emotional screw on. If you care to hear I will tell you with pleasure, especially as you have seen how bright she was a few minutes ago, but I don't want to bore you."

"Go on," said Carrados. "Curious and trivial things that are extraordinary have never bored me yet."

"Well, you shall judge. I indicated, over at your place, that we are expecting our little household to be increased in the course of a few months. Not unnaturally, Myra has to pass through a variety of new emotions on the subject, and she also has an unfortunate misgiving. It happened that her father was born club-footed and *his* father was disfigured in the same way. Of course, we tell her that its all nonsense, but there is undeniably an element of heredity in that sort of thing, and she knows it well enough. Just now she is doubly prone to take notice of any kind of suggestion or premonition that may come along, especially on that one unlucky possibility. You heard her say that she was going up to change her shoes? Well, this is what has happened: she went upstairs, kicked off her wet shoes, and proceeded to pull on another pair. They are shoes that she has worn quite comfortably at intervals for the past few weeks, but now one—the right foot—would not go on. Thinking nothing of it, she picked up a shoe-lift and tried again. Still it refused to accommodate, and then she went to the light and looked more closely. . . . It wasn't likely to fit, Carrados, for the extraordinary thing is that those shoes, which she has worn quite easily and naturally a dozen times in the last few weeks, are both for the left foot!"

There was a rattle of cups and glasses as the attractive maid nearly dropped the tray she was bringing in. Enderleigh looked sharply round, but the girl kept her face averted and quickly went out again.

"There's another who's certainly got the jumps," said her master. "But about those shoes. Of course it's ridiculous, but you see the inference? In each forerunning case it was the right foot that was wrong, and so poor Myra is miraculously endowed with two left shoes at this moment as a sort of admonition that an ordinary right will not be needed. . . . But you don't see anything in it, I expect?"

"On the contrary," replied Carrados slowly, "I see so much in it—so many thousand possibilities, all wrong but one—that I should like to go up into a very large, perfectly bare attic, lit by several twenty thousand candle power arc lamps, and there meditate."

"And the nearest thing I can offer you," said Enderleigh, "is the coal cellar. It's roomy as such places go and certainly practically empty now. For the rest——" He found the pleasantry difficult to sustain.

"So," continued the blind man seriously, "we must still proceed on directly material lines. I should very much like to handle the pair of shoes that has caused the trouble. Do you think Mrs. Enderleigh would allow me?"

"Why not?" assented the lady's husband. "I'll go and get them."

He went, and returned almost immediately—but empty-handed.

"She's coming down now. Much better," he whispered in the voice of a conspirator. "Bringing them." And almost at his heels a sobered Myra reappeared.

"I'm a hopeless little rabbit, Mr. Carrados," she apologised. "Please don't say anything nice about it, because I am."

"Rabbit!" ejaculated her natural protector loyally; "rabbit! Why, Mr. Carrados, that—that sylph has the

heart of a—a—well, I'm not strong on the faunas, but of
whatever is the antithesis of rabbit."

"That would be a ferret, wouldn't it?" asked Myra in
her funny way. "What a sad flatterer you are, Guy!"

"Go on," said Guy happily. "So long as you can
laugh——"

She waved a reassuring hand to him across the room as
she addressed their guest again.

"Of course, I know that he has told you all about it,
Mr. Carrados," she said. "Because when I taxed him he
began by saying, 'I only just——' Here is the mystery."

It was a pair of pretty bronze shoes, neat yet not fragile,
that she put into the blind man's hands. He held them one
by one, and as his long, delicately-formed fingers brushed
across their surface the two watchers received a curious
impression of seeing something read.

"I shouldn't mind—I shouldn't mind the shoes a par-
ticle," declared Myra—she felt compelled to speak to
break the almost hypnotic quest of those understanding
hands—"though, of course, they're no earthly use. But for
weeks I've been wearing them all right, and now I know
perfectly well that I couldn't. There's something wrong
with me somewhere, don't you see?"

"But, dearest," pleaded Guy soothingly, "there's some
perfectly simple explanation if only we could see it. Why,
only just now you said that your feet were tender. That's
probably it. You've got them sore, and so you can't put
on the shoe. If they were all right you'd jump into them
and not notice that anything was the matter, just as you
have been doing up to now."

"Don't talk tommy, Guy!" she exclaimed half wrath-
fully. "As if I could possibly put on two left shoes without knowing it, even if I could get them on. And yet," she
wailed, "I *have* been putting them on—that's the horrible
thing about it."

Carrados had apparently finished his scrutiny, for he was
listening to this exchange in his usual benign complacency,
and as he listened he absently rubbed his nose gently with
the polished toe of a shoe.

"Set your mind at rest, Mrs. Enderleigh," he remarked quietly, as he offered her the other one. "There is nothing wrong. You have never worn that shoe."

"I have never worn it?"

"Neither you nor anybody else. The shoe has not been worn."

"But look at the wear," she persisted, displaying the scarified sole. "Look at this worn lace."

"The lace, yes," he admitted, with unshaken confidence. "But not the shoe."

"But how can you possibly know that?"

"In exactly the same way that I could oil the bolt—by using other powers than that of sight."

"Do you mean——" began Enderleigh, but Carrados interrupted him with uplifted hand.

"If I may suggest, please don't say anything more about the shoes just yet. At this moment Sergeant Lapworth has come to the door and your servant is admitting him. Let us hear what he has to say."

Myra and Guy exchanged looks of bewilderment— almost of alarm—and then the girl's face cleared.

"Yes," she exclaimed, "I had forgotten to tell you. He did say that he would look in again after you got back, Guy."

"If you please, m'm," said Chloe at the door, "there's the detective here again, and he would like to see the master if it's convenient."

"Quite right," replied Myra. "Show him in here."

Sergeant Lapworth was a plain-clothes man of the local staff. If he had a fault it was that of giving the impression of knowing more than he would tell, a suggestion that resulted in people sometimes finding him less omniscient in the end than they had expected. The Enderleighs were rather surprised at the sudden respect that came over him when he recognised their blind visitor.

"One or two small matters I thought I'd like to see you about, sir," he said, addressing Mr. Enderleigh. "Those footprints by the side gate. I understand that no one came along that way between the time your gardener put the

lime there yesterday and my seeing them this afternoon?"

"That is quite right," agreed Myra. "We allow the milkman to come in at the front gate and go to the side door,
to save him carrying his can right round the other way.
No one else came; I asked Chloe particularly."

"You see the point, sir?" continued the sergeant, directing his voice at Mr. Carrados this time. "Whoever left
those footprints is the man we want to put our hands on.
We should like him to account for his movements last
night at all events. Old Ben certainly never made those
prints, sir. Now, I wonder," the sergeant's voice became
softly speculative as he leisurely felt in one or two pockets
and finally produced a neat paper template of a boot, "I
wonder if this suggests anything to either of you?"

Myra shook her head and passed the paper on to Enderleigh.

"It's a man's boot, I suppose," she said. "It is broader
than a woman's and the heel is twice as large. It's much
smaller than any of yours, Guy."

"Lord, yes," he agreed. "I'm miles beyond that."

"Perhaps," continued Sergeant Lapworth, becoming almost dreamy in his quiet detachment, "perhaps this might
help you more if you should ever have seen the original."
It was a small fancy button that he mysteriously produced
this time from the Aladdin's cave among his garments.
Myra's spirits went up.

"What a splendid clue, Mr. Lapworth!" she exclaimed.
"Where did you find it?"

"I don't want anything said about it just yet," he stipu-
lated. "As a matter of fact I picked it up in your scullery
this afternoon."

"It is a boot button, I suppose?" questioned Enderleigh.
"It strikes me as rather dressy."

"It is the top of a pearl boot button undoubtedly, I
should say," pronounced the sergeant. "One of those metal-
shanked things that they wire into the boot nowadays.
First question is, Does it belong to anyone of the house?
I dare say you have plenty of pairs of fancy boots and

shoes in use or put by, but it isn't a button that you would readily forget."

Myra breathlessly agreed that if she had had boot buttons like that she would never have forgotten it, and added that if Guy had appeared with them she could never have forgiven it—a *sotto-voce* effort that elicited nothing more than an anxious look from her husband.

"And how about the young person in the kitchen?" suggested Lapworth.

"I know Chloe's boots, and it certainly doesn't come from there," replied Chloe's mistress. "However, you had better ask her, to make sure. Shall I ring now?"

"Don't trouble," he replied, as he returned the precious relic to its hiding-place. "I can have a word with her as I go out. Now as regards the silver. Your good lady said that you would be able to make me out a list, sir."

"Of course," assented Enderleigh; "that's got to be done, hasn't it? And then there'll be the insurance people. And then a young man introducing himself as 'The Press.' I'll tell you what, sergeant, this being burgled isn't such a soft thing after all."

"I don't know, sir. It strikes me that you have come off uncommonly easy, seeing as how things were. No mess, no breakages, no odds and ends from every room that you can't remember until it's too late to claim. Just one big lot taken clean."

"It would be about as much as he could take, anyway," said the owner. "I shouldn't like to heft that case far."

"Yes, it would be a tidy load. I don't know that I ever remember the case being taken before. Reckon they had a car somewhere near."

"Anyway, nothing was overlooked," said Myra. "There were some tankards out on the sideboard here, and three dozen spoons of various sizes in the drawer, and they went too. I put them——"

"You put them what?" prompted her husband, for Myra had stopped as though she had said her say.

"I haven't the faintest notion, dear," she replied frankly.

"To tell the truth I think I was half asleep. Put what what?"

"Well, I think I'll be getting on along, sir," said Lapworth, reading in this a pretty obvious hint. "As soon as we hear from you——"

There was a hesitating knock at the door and Chloe entered with a card.

"Please, m'm," said the girl—Mrs. Enderleigh happened to be seated nearest to her—"there's a gentleman would like to see the master for a minute."

"'Wich'—'Mr. William Wich,'" read Myra. "Isn't there a Lady Wich a few houses away?"

"Trefusis—Lady Wich, madam," volunteered Lapworth. "There is a Mr. William, the son."

"I'd better go out and see what it is," said Enderleigh. "Probably only a minute—excuse me, won't you?"

For so short a gap it did not seem worth while discovering a topic of conversation, and so no one broke the minute's silence. If they had spoken their thoughts the exchange would have been something after this fashion:

"I wonder if Lady Wich ever intends to call—city knight's widow, I suppose. Now will Mr. Carrados go when the fat sergeant leaves, or does he expect that we have proper supper?"

"Bit of a card this Mr. Willie Wich from what I hear. Old party keeps him in pretty tight by all accounts. Larky; girls."

"She must stand five feet five—possibly six. At that, with the tread she has, she will take a $4\frac{1}{2}$ to 5. Yes, under any vigorous exercise she might reasonably split a pliant $3\frac{1}{2}$. There were certainly two definable personal exudations about the other shoe, and associable with them syringa—that's the girl—and cheiranthus—this one."

The door opened and Enderleigh entered, then standing aside he waited for someone else.

"Rather curious," he announced. "Mr. Wich has come to give us some information about our friend last night; so as we are all here—— My wife, Mr. Wich; Mr. Carrados; Sergeant Lapworth."

"It's really from my mother, you know," said the dapper youth who followed the host in. "She's a frightful invalid—heart and all that—so she sent me to tell you. We only just heard of what had happened: beastly shame——"

"We didn't know that you'd be interested," ventured Myra graciously.

"Eh? Oh, I mean rotten luck being burgled like that. Well, it seems that last night the mater was having a bad turn and she had to get up and sit at the open window to have air. That's how it takes her. It seems that from her bedroom window one can see most of your garden—we live a couple of houses along: Trefusis, you know—and as she sat there she distinctly saw someone go down your garden towards the river and disappear among the trees. She says she wasn't taking much notice of it at the time, because there was no reason why there should be anything wrong in that, and it being dark she didn't see a lot, and she was feeling pretty washed out as well. But she did notice that it seemed to be a man carrying something large and heavy, and when she heard of this she thought you'd better know."

"It's most awfully good of Lady Wich to send," gushed Myra; "and of you to come. We are just celebrating the event with frugal hospitality. Will you drink the toast 'Our Absent Friend,' Mr. Wich?"

"Eh? Oh, I don't mind, thank you."

"The river," mused Lapworth. "That's certainly an idea now: we couldn't find any likely motor wheel-tracks down the side road here. A boat waiting, you see. What time about would this be, sir?"

"Oh, about half-past twelve, she said."

"Ah!" The sergeant continued to regard Mr. Wich with an air of distant speculation while at the same time his hand went mechanically to his mysterious pocket. "I suppose you didn't by any chance happen to be in the neighbourhood yourself at about that hour, sir?"

The perfect respect of the tone could not wholly disguise a certain significance in the question, and Willie

Wich looked up to meet the sergeant's eyes on level terms. Enderleigh also found something arresting in the sudden tension that seemed to have involved two of his guests, while Carrados continued to have gaze into unseen space with the faint half smile of placid contemplation. Myra alone appeared to have no interest in the passage, and her face was turned away, but her lips were tight pressed to hold back a cry of generous warning and her heart was thudding like an engine beat, for in a flash her eyes had followed Lapworth's and in a flash had seen on her spruce guest's extended foot a boot with identical pearl buttons, of which the upper one was missing.

The gap between the question and the answer was almost as long as it takes to tell of it, for with their eyes meeting Wich paused to consider his reply as though a thought urged caution.

"What do you quite mean by that?" he asked guardedly. "You know, of course, that I live in the neighbourhood. Do you mean, was I at home?"

"Not exactly, sir," replied the sergeant. "You might have been passing this very house on your way home and thought you saw or heard something suspicious here and come nearer to investigate. Or you might have had a dog stray into this garden and come in to call it back, or a dozen things. What I should like to know is, Did you come into this house or garden last night for any purpose?"

"I did not," said Wich, his face relaxing into something like an amused grin. "What is more, sergeant, I have never before been in this house or garden in the course of my long and industrious life."

"That's quite definite, sir," Lapworth admitted. "In the circumstances would you mind stating where you were between the hours of eleven last night and two o'clock this morning?"

To those who knew him pretty well young Mr. Wich was something of a puzzle, and they complained that you never knew how he would take it and whether the fellow was quite the fool he sometimes seemed.

" 'In the circumstances,' sergeant, seems to imply the

existence of certain conditions of which I have no knowledge," he now replied. "Should I ever find myself in the dock of the Old Bailey, charged with the murder of a constable, or before the Surrey Petty Sessions accused of appropriating Mr. Enderleigh's ancestral plate, either of those eventualities would constitute an aggregation of circumstances that would enforce my acquiescence. At present I fail to see any reason why I should render an account of my trivial life and movements."

Sergeant Lapworth took out an irreproachably white pocket handkerchief and wiped his face profusely.

"Very good, sir," he remarked with dark significance. "Should you have any objection to my comparing this form"—here the sergeant dramatically produced his first exhibit—"with the boots you are now wearing?"

"Not the least," replied the buoyant young man, raising his right foot to facilitate the operation; "though I must protest against the attention thus gratuitously directed to my very unprepossessing footwear. Anything to assist the legitimate ends of justice. But not," he added severely, "of mere vulgar curiosity."

Without deigning to reply, Sergeant Lapworth went down on one knee and from that position fitted the paper impression against the proffered boot. It was at once plain to every one that the two outlines coincided perfectly. But an even more significant piece of evidence was to emerge, for as the sergeant performed this office he slyly inserted a nail in the angle of the instep and an appreciable sprinkling of white-peppered soil fell down into his hand.

"I must call your attention, sir, to the fact that this earth from your boot appears to correspond with the soil of the garden here."

"I say!" exclaimed Mr. Wich aghast, "I am sorry, Mrs. Enderleigh—bringing stuff like that into your pretty room!" Then with a bright look of toleration, "But I expect you know what servants are!"

"Lastly," said Sergeant Lapworth with admirable composure in spite of a rather flushed complexion, "I shall be glad if you will look at this button which corresponds exactly with those on your boot, where one is missing."

"Thank you," replied young Mr. Wich, passing it back again; "it's very good of you to have kept it for me, but it's really no use. It isn't a button you sew on, but one of those metal-shanked affairs and the shank is broken."

"Then I understand, sir, that you decline to assist us with any information?"

"Oh, no, you don't, sergeant—not if you understand the common or vernacular tongue, that is," retorted his antagonist. "So far, what I have declined is to give an account of my movements on the strength of an old button hypothetically lost at some time from my boot and a little piece of paper traced to measure. It may be the law that I have to if anyone shows me those: I must look that up. But you may remember that the only reason for my being here was to bring you information."

"Oh, yes," exclaimed Myra, completely won over by the suspect's ready nonchalance, "we are all sure that Mr. Wich is quite all right, Sergeant Lapworth. Aren't we, Guy?"

"Mrs. Enderleigh," put in Wich, gazing at her with melancholy admiration, "before I go I must unburden my mind, and I'm afraid you may think very poorly of me in consequence. I did *not* purloin your silver and I have not the faintest idea who did. Good-bye."

"Must you really go?" she asked. "Please be sure and thank Lady Wich from me, won't you? And any Thursday."

"If you would be so kind as to help a blind man to his car, Mr. Wich," interposed Carrados, and Enderleigh found his own proffered services quietly brushed aside.

"You don't say you are!" exclaimed Wich. "I never tumbled to it. And that's your little jigger waiting then? I'm looking forward to something on four wheels myself, but so far I have to be content with two."

"It's hardly worth while offering you a lift," said Carrados, when they were in the road, "but if you don't mind I should like to walk with you as far as your gate."

"Right-o," said Mr. Wich, wondering who this queer customer who had made up to him might be. "Lovely night, isn't it? What about your car?"

"It will follow presently; my driver understands. I have been trying to think where we have met before. Are you by any chance the Wich who made forty-nine for The Rest against Lord's Schools five years ago?"

"Oh, I say!" exclaimed his companion, becoming quite boyishly shy at the reference to this exploit. "You don't mean to say that you remember that? Were you at Lord's?"

"Yes. I am fond of the minor fixtures; I can hear more play in them than often comes out in first-class matches. We did not speak, but you passed, and I thought I recognised your step again. A Winchester fellow was commenting on the game for me. You were given run out."

"You must simply be a walking Wisden, sir," said Wich, brimming with admiration. And then with a curious intonation in his voice he added, "But why 'given'?"

"I remember some reference to it. . . . Were you out?"

"As a matter of fact I was not," he admitted.

"I don't think you made any fuss about it—quarrelled with the umpire or groused about the pavilion?"

"Well, should I be likely? . . . It was cricket."

"Yes. . . . And now about this business?"

They had reached the gate of Trefusis, but the young man made no movement towards it, and presently they fell to walking slowly on again.

"That isn't so easy. Not by a long, long way. I was taken by surprise, I must admit; I hadn't a notion that there'd be any trace. Of course it would have been simple enough to tell the sergeant how it came about, if that was all."

"You mean the lady in the case; or shall we say the girl in the shoes?"

"Partly; and then there is my mother. She would certainly have a heart attack if she found that William had been taking her neighbour's handmaiden out to midnight carnivals and other forms of penance."

"Is that quite—cricket?"

"Not absolutely M.C.C., perhaps, but it isn't to be inferred that I had the inklingest of who she was at first. And Chloe really is an awfully pretty girl, you know. What has she let out?"

"Nothing at all, so far as I am aware."

"Then how on earth do you come to know of her—and the shoes?"

"Very much, I suppose, in the same way that Sergeant Lapworth has come to know of you and the boot—because the traces are so obvious."

"I must say I think Chloe was a bit of a mutt to walk on the bed and then leave a button somewhere about. She might have learned better than that from the pictures surely."

"Chloe naturally had not foreseen that the escapade would coincide with a burglary. But I would not be too ready to blame her, my young friend," advised Carrados dryly. "The most disastrous blunder of all was made by someone else."

"That's a straight one," said Mr. Wich. "What did I do?"

"Suppose you tell me about it?" suggested Mr. Carrados. "Under the seal of confidence."

"I don't mind. I was going to see a lawyer first thing to-morrow to find out what I'd better do to circumvent the forces of law and order. Perhaps you could advise me?"

"Perhaps I could," admitted Carrados. "At all events I will."

"There really isn't very much to tell," said young Mr. Wich pensively. "I happened to be on the river alone a few months ago when I noticed a dazzling creature watching my feeble efforts from the bank. To have a nearer look I landed and asked her if she was not, excuse me, Miss Prendergast? She said no, but, how curious, she

had been almost sure that I was a certain Mr. Johnson.
This constituting a deputy introduction on established
lines I prevailed upon the bright vision to go for a
short cruise and even to accept some slight refreshment
of a light and portable nature.

"Under the auspices of the gods the idyll proceeded
with exemplary propriety to run its normal course. So
far as I was concerned the chief attraction was the extreme likelihood of detection and the certainty that every
one concerned would impute the very worst motives to
my conduct when they did find out.

"On our usual 'evening' last week I was indulging the
delightful being's passion for a harmless beverage known
as Tango Teaser when she espied a handbill announcing
a cheap fancy dance at one of the public halls a few
miles away and artlessly exclaimed:

" 'I should love to go to one of those.'

"Of course there was only one humanly possible reply
to a heart-cry like that, and I gallantly made it.

" 'And I should love to take you. Why not?'

"To this she said that it was absolutely impossible and
we fell to making the arrangements. She was to creep out
quietly by a side door after the others had gone to bed,
lock the door after her and bring the key, and meet
me at our usual trysting place—a spot a few hundred
yards from our respective abodes. I would be there with
my iron steed, and on the pillion thereof would whirl her
into fairyland.

"Everything went off as per schedule. The only con-
tretemps was that Chloe—have I mentioned that the
heroine was Chloe, by the way?—ripped one of her
shoes across and thus passed automatically into the retired list. I confess that I was surprised at the consternation the mishap occasioned the sweet chit, and then she
told me. Ashamed at the deficiency of her own pedal
outfit she had surreptitiously 'borrowed' a pair belonging
to her mistress. Detection would now inevitably follow,
disgrace, possibly dismissal. Sighs, tears—heavens!—re-
proaches. Again I did the insane chivalrous thing and

swore to replace the shoe within twelve hours or perish.

"The rest is obvious. Chloe knew where they had been bought—a shop in Oxford Street—and I was to hie me off at dawn and duplicate them. As there would be the business of giving the shoes the necessary 'wear' it would be simpler to keep only one, and this I was to put into a clump of ivy on the garden side wall. But when it came to parting a difficulty arose: it was essential for me to have the split shoe as a pattern; I could not allow the fair penitent to walk stocking-footed along the stony road; and it wasn't wise to risk being seen together any nearer our houses. The simple way out was for me to lend her one of mine, and this I recovered from the ivy bush when I put the other one in. And there, Mr. Carrados, you have the whole egg in a nutshell."

"Everything went off all right then?" inquired Carrados maliciously.

"Like a clock. I obtained the exact thing in the exact size, scrubbed it down to the exact appearance of the other and put in the old lace. The superfluous shoe was flung over into an orchard somewhere Isleworth way. There was nothing much in all that. But now you see why it was impossible to satisfy Sergeant Lapworth's inopportune curiosity."

"You may perhaps find it difficult to satisfy one or two other people as well. Did Chloe say anything when she let you in just now?"

"Why, yes; it struck me as ungracious at the time. The angel looked at me very weirdly and just said 'Idiot!' I thought she must be overwrought."

"I think it very likely. I told you that there had been other blunders besides Chloe's. What she wished to indicate by a single appropriate word, my budding Lothario, was that you had thrown away the wrong shoe, with the consequence that Mrs. Enderleigh is now on the verge of hysterics at an apparent miracle."

"No!" exclaimed Wich incredulously, "I could not. And yet, surely . . . Oh, good Lord, I did! I kept them to make a pair—the new one and the other, instead of . . . Well, I am a prize fathead! What will happen now?"

"What? Why the extreme probability that you have had your trouble for nothing and that Chloe will be sacked after all."

"Oh, I don't think that—not after seeing Mrs. Enderleigh. You and Chloe both misjudge her strangely. She seems the jolliest sort of girl to me. I bet she'll understand."

"I'll bet she will," assented Carrados grimly. "And when she understands that her pretty servant has been wearing her things, sneaking out at nights (to say nothing about giving burglars the chance of sneaking in) to foot it at dance-halls with the young spark from next-door-but-one, you may not find her quite so sympathetic as she was half an hour ago. If she doesn't take the opportunity of calling upon Lady Wich about it I'm badly out."

"It's a mug's business," said Mr. Wich with a qualmish note in his voice. "What had I better do?"

"What you had better do is to leave it in my hands and agree to my condition."

"What condition?"

"That you never go gallivanting with Chloe again. You both 'don't mean anything,' but suppose you did happen to get the girl discharged with a very dubious character? Should you see any alternative to behaving either as a fool or a knave to put it right?"

"Whew!" exclaimed Mr. Wich, easing the collar against his neck, "that's heart-to-heart stuff. Well, if you can bring it off I'm good for my part. Chloe certainly is a dazzling thing, but, strictly between ourselves, her mind is little more than an assortment of obsolete film captions."

. . . .

When Mr. Enderleigh returned from business the next day Myra greeted him with a subdued note. It was plain that the excitement had quite worn off.

"If Mr. Carrados is really going to be useful to you,

Guy, of course I shall do my best to amuse him. But I wonder all the same if he is going to make a practice of dropping in every evening."

"How so?" demanded Guy.

"He rang me up this afternoon and hoped that we should both be in later as he would like to call. I had to say we should be charmed."

"Just as well you did, my lady," remarked Guy. "Do you know that quite important people have a most extraordinary opinion of the man, and I am told that Scotland Yard will do anything to oblige him. That's what I've come across to-day."

"My gracious!" said Myra, deeply impressed; "it's just as well I fawned. Talking about police, I met Sergeant Lapworth in the road this morning and he seemed very odd. He said they had received instructions to go slow in taking any steps."

"That ought to suit them down to the ground," suggested Guy pessimistically. "We don't look like seeing any of our plate again, old girl."

"I don't know, Guy. It struck me that Sergeant Lapworth knew more than he would tell. He said that they expected developments."

"It used to be 'were investigating a clue,'" said the unimpressed gentleman.

Mrs. Enderleigh had named nine o'clock as a convenient hour and with the busy man's punctuality nine o'clock found Mr. Carrados walking up the Homecroft garden path. Looking out, the lady of the house felt a pleasant access of importance, arising from the notable proportions of the car waiting at her gate.

"How nice of you to come again!" she exclaimed playfully. "After the alarms and excursions of yesterday I hardly dared to hope it."

"Oh, yes," he replied prosaically, "your husband and I have some small business details to discuss."

"Of course," she assented quickly. "I am going to leave you at it."

"But first," he continued, "I have a bargain to offer you."

"Offer me? How exciting! Whatever can it be?"

"You really want to get your silver back again?"

"Why, naturally. Guy tells me that we shall only receive about half the value the way our policy goes—isn't it, Guy?"

"I'm afraid it is," admitted her husband.

"And that's only money. To both of us many of the things are priceless."

"While you have no particular affection for that odd pair of shoes?"

"Shoes? Oh, *those!* How ridiculous, Mr. Carrados! You are not coming like an up-to-date genie to offer silver plates for old shoes, are you?"

"You have guessed. But there's always a catch about these attractive bargains, you remember. If you agree to let the shoes go, everything connected with them goes also. You have no curiosity, make no inquiries, entertain no suspicions: it is to be as though they and all that appertains to them had never been."

"I wonder if I understand?" mused Myra with a sharp little look in his direction.

"I think you do," replied Carrados. "You are—forgive the homely phrase—no fool, Mrs. Enderleigh. If you do not quite understand yet it's only because you have not had time to think about it. You soon would."

"All right; I'll take it," said Myra, with a very sporting air.

"But do you mean that you actually know now where the silver is?" demanded Enderleigh.

"I know where the silver is," Carrados admitted.

"Where?" exclaimed two simultaneous voices.

"When you went off a few days ago, you expressed a wish as to where it might be, Mr. Enderleigh, didn't you?"

"What was that?" asked Myra, from whose mind the malediction had apparently faded. Her husband, on the contrary, remembered very well and he coloured at the recollection.

"I am sorry to be reminded of that," he said moodily.

"Something happened to put me out, Myra, and in a moment of irritation, without meaning it, I said that I wished the stuff at the bottom of the river. That's all."

"Yes; that's the way with you impulsive people, as we genii are always finding. You want a thing and then discover that you don't. Well, my friend, you have got your wish, willy-nilly. The stuff *is* at the bottom of the river."

"What a lark!" exclaimed the lady.

"The burglars dropped it or hid it there?" said her husband, keenly intrigued. "How on earth did you find that out?"

"The burglars had nothing to do with it, because there was no burglar—no burglary," was the reply.

"Oh, but I say! Besides, it's gone. No, Mr. Carrados! And then the side door key, you know."

"Hush!" said Carrados mysteriously. "That doesn't count. The side door key went, according to our bargain, with the shoes."

"Very well," acquiesced Myra, with something very like a giggle, "but if there was no burglar how did the silver get into the river?"

"How?" Carrados raised an accusing finger and slowly brought it dead level on his hostess. "How? Behold the culprit! You, my dear lady, threw it there!"

Moved by a common impulse Guy and Myra came slowly to their feet. Looking at Max Carrados's quietly smiling face it seemed impossible to believe that he—to doubt that he—to know what to think.

"I—threw—it—there?" articulated Myra queerly.

"You deliberately cast the 'damned stuff' in. Rising at the dead of night, without staying to put on slippers or to cover those inadequate garments that are no longer the prerogative of my sex, you crept down, carefully replaced the silver lying about, took up the burden, let yourself out by the french window in the drawing-room, crossed the lawn, reached the silent river, and with a sigh of relief at accomplishing so meritorious a task, tipped the whole bag of tricks into the water. All in a

profound sleep, of course. By the way, I hope your feet
are better to-day?"

Myra sat down again with a strange look in her eyes.

"But I could not—I could not even move the box,"
she whispered.

"Not when you are awake," he replied, becoming grave
again. "And do you know why that is? It is because you
know that you cannot, and so, your slavish body assent-
ing, you really cannot. But in your sleep you do not
know it; your unbound mind admits no limits, and so——"

"Do you know," interposed Enderleigh sagely, "I've
heard something like that several times lately. I suppose
there may be something in it after all."

"Anyway," said Mr. Carrados, "there is one thing you
can congratulate yourself on. A wife who carries out
her husband's slightest wish even in her sleep is a woman
in a thousand."

ARTHUR SOMERS ROCHE

THE JEWELED CASKET

I suppose that the same quality of imagination which lifts me above the rest of those whom society is pleased to call outlaws, is responsible for the feeling of indignation which possesses me when I look upon any brutality. Your matter-of-fact man shrugs his shoulders, tells himself that he is not responsible, and moves on. But I am not matter-of-fact; I am an artist. And the artist, more keenly in tune with what-ought-to-be than the material-minded man of business, resents any imperfection, whether it be of the body or of the spirit.

And here were both! The hunchback, imperfect of body —and the superstitious lout, imperfect of spirit, who stroked the hump.

They were standing on the curb, at the corner of Fifty-ninth Street and Fifth Avenue, waiting for a break in traffic which would permit them to cross the street. I was doing the same thing. I had walked from the snug little apartment which at the moment I was maintaining on Central Park West, across town on my way to attend an auction, on Madison Avenue. It was a balmy spring day, the sort of morning which after a blustery March revives one's faith in the miracles of Nature. Exactly as a pretty girl revives one's faith! I may admit that my faith had been revived several times this morning. It seemed to me that all the lovely girls of the universe had been placed in Central Park and on the Avenue this morning, to tantalize me with thoughts of what might have been. Not that I am overly sentimental, but in the spring—and I am a young man.

There were eyes that seemed, looking upon me, to find me personable. Glances from maidens cantering along the bridle-paths seemed to tell me that I would prove an acceptable cavalier. There were vacant seats in limousines which I might have occupied. Young ladies, shopping bent, would have found the stroll down the Avenue more enjoyable had I been by their side. At least, their eyes told me so.

And I, who hated the world, loved it this morning. Yet it was the hopeless love of one who knows that the simple joys are denied to him. I felt a moisture welling beneath my lids; my eyes were filmy. Then I laughed at my sentimentality. I had made my choice months ago when, after years of desperate struggle along the paths of honesty, I had given up the unequal battle and become one of those who prey. But when I had abandoned the paths of honesty, I had not surrendered honor. And if you do not appreciate the distinction, let it pass. Gentlemen will understand.

Suffice it that no young girl would ever be harmed by me—and even knowing me might some day cause her irreparable damage. As I have said in one of my previous memoirs, like Kipling's cat, I walk alone. Nor do I mind my solitary condition save on rare occasions, such as to-day, when spring throbbed in my veins, and for a moment I would be Darby, if only I knew a Joan.

So, because I was in a softened mood, as well as because I am an artist and a gentleman, I felt a surge of pity for the hunchback, and a surge of wrath against the man who stood beside him. For this latter person rubbed the cripple's hump.

Oddly enough, although the lout seemed none too gentle to me, the cripple did not resent the action. Perhaps, poor devil, he had become so used to the brutalities of his fellows, that his spirit had become inured to them and lost its powers of resentment.

A year or so ago, when I had been crushed by the brutalities of life, I would have felt no indignation at such a sight. I had then been unable to become angry at in-

dignities heaped upon myself. Moralists would tell you
that I had since lost my soul, but I tell you that I had
found it. A year ago, an honest man, I would have sneered
cynically; today, a thief, I took the lout by the collar
and threw him across the sidewalk.

The north- and south-bound traffic halted as the lights
flickered on the tower down the Avenue; the big policeman blew his whistle and waved the pedestrians to pass
over. It was an opportunity, and as my bewildered victim
climbed unsteadily to his feet, muttering threats, I merged
with the human tide and gained the doors of a hotel
across the street, slipped through its reception-rooms and
came out upon Fifty-ninth Street, certain that I had
avoided pursuit, and not worrying about future recognition. For my action had been so sudden that my victim
could not possibly have seen me clearly enough to know
me again. As for the hunchback, he had not glanced my
way.

And so I walked along Fifty-ninth Street toward Madison Avenue with a new justification for my career. A
world so insensitive to the miseries of others that it made
superstitious jests of them, could expect no mercy from
me.

By extreme caution, I eliminate accidents. Before I
entered the auction-rooms which were my destination, I
glanced over my shoulder to make certain that no offensively right-minded person was guiding upon my trail the
man whom I had knocked down. And if I seem like one
who strikes and flees, let me state that I will take any
fair risk in a fair fight, but when I am meting out pun-
ishment, I prefer not to take disproportionate chances. If
a policeman intervened in a street-brawl in which I was
concerned, I would be compelled to face a certain notori-
ety. It is conceivable that I might be asked my means
of livelihood, a question of obvious embarrassment.

So I entered the auction-rooms, and took a chair in the
rear. Half an hour passed before I made a bid, and then
I offered fifty dollars for a mediocre tapestry. I acquired
it at eighty-five, gave a check to an attendant, ordered

the thing sent to my apartment, and settled back in my chair to watch the rest of the proceedings. I had, so to speak, paid my entrance-fee. For I do not think it advisable that I should be merely a spectator at auctions; a connoisseur, even though in a small way, achieves an instant standing. And my acquisition of the tapestry proved that I had fair taste along with probably modest means.

Of course I had not come here solely to purchase. Indeed, the tapestry would hardly conform to the color-scheme of my rooms. Once again I felt the sentiment of springtime in my heart. I wanted a home, permanence. I wanted a place where I could put things that I had acquired for the joy of acquisition, and because they belonged in that home. Deliberately I dismissed the dangerous thoughts, drove them from my mind and heart.

No man can be a success in business if he devotes his office hours to sentimental moonings; these were my office hours, and I was here on business. For where in the world is one more likely to have opportunity to see and study those possessed of wealth than in an auction-room where articles of tremendous value are put upon the block? And the International Auction Company catered to a clientele of millionaires. Such bargains as my bit of tapestry only occurred when they were minor parts of a great collection.

Nearly everything else was priced in the thousands, and did not interest me, although occasionally I noted the names and addresses of the purchasers. And then came the Gerald jewel-box, the *pièce de résistance* of the collection which was on sale today. Gerald was a multi-millionaire of vulgar antecedents and taste who had died a few years ago. Six months later, his widow had followed him, and they had left heirs who chose to rid themselves of the miscellaneous collection which the Geralds had acquired. I could not blame the heirs for their decision, for most of the Gerald possessions were more suited to the walls or cabinets of a museum than to a private home. And I rather imagined that all of the really choice pieces had been sold at private sale; only the left-overs were offered today.

And when the auctioneer held up a golden box, studded with jewels, I felt a positive embarrassment for him, compelled as he was to declare that this article was a work of art. It was about nine inches long, six inches wide and four inches deep; and workmanship, even a high degree of craftsmanship, had been expended upon it. But the thing was too gorgeous, too flamboyant, and one readily believed the auctioneer's statement that the late Mr. Joseph Gerald had himself superintended the designing and the manufacture of the box. One also believed without hesitation that it had cost the multimillionaire over ninety thousand dollars. Certainly the precious stones that studded it were worth at least fifty thousand.

But the very idea that had given birth to the box was vulgar. It had been intended to be the receptacle for certain jewels of Gerald's wife. I could picture the poor woman. It is not difficult to imagine the sort of woman who will keep her jewels in a box that in itself is worth a fortune. Unquestionably she had been obese, stubby-nailed, thin-haired. I was certain that there had been gold used in the body of the Gerald limousine, and that the monogram upon the limousine's door had been picked out in rubies.

The thing angered me. Artists in precious metal had been debauched by Gerald's money and forced to prostitute their gifts for beauty in order to gratify a millionaire's vulgar whim. I wondered that anyone save a dealer in gold and jewels, who proposed to buy the thing for its intrinsic value, should bid upon it. But Gerald's death had not rid the world of vulgarity.

The bidding opened at ten thousand dollars, and progressed rapidly to twenty-five thousand, confined to men whom I intuitively knew were dealers. Then another man took a hand. His clothing alone stamped him for what he was, a newly enriched vulgarian. For his coat was cut in the extreme of Broadway fashion; his neckwear was an offense to a gentleman, and the solitaire diamond that gleamed from its silken folds must have weighed a dozen carats. He had not been born to money; long acquaintance with it would have inculcated in him a few, at least, of the fundamentals of correct attire. His nose was a mere blob, piglike. His eyes, peeping over rolls of fat, were also porcine. His forehead slanted back, and his heavy jaws and jutting chin made him animal-like. Another of those filthy profiteers who had grown fat upon the sufferings of the world! Another of those persons who have risen from the depths during civilization's great convulsion. As a seismic disturbance casts strange monsters upon the surface of the sea, so the great war hurled strange people from their degraded levels to the top of a society which they pollute.

Even as I was able to visualize the departed Mrs. Gerald, so I could picture the wife of this man: as loathsome as himself, doubtless. But also I could picture the priceless jewelry that would go into that box. For if a man would give sixty-five thousand dollars—it was knocked down to him at that price—for a place in which to put his jewels, what were the jewels themselves worth?

The mere thought made me dizzy. If I could get my hands upon that box when it was filled, the fancies that spring had put into my mind today, and which I had dismissed as hopeless, might be possible to me. One of those young girls whose eyes had seemed inviting on the Avenue today—

"Sold to Mr. Marcus Anderson," said the auctioneer. There was justifiable triumph in his voice. He had done well by the Gerald heirs.

Slumped down in my chair, fuming with hatred toward Anderson, I straightened up when I heard his name. For there were few people who had not heard of Anderson. He was supposed to have become, during the war, one of the richest men in the world. My appraisal of him had been absolutely correct, and my vanity was tickled that, even in so slight a matter, I had not erred.

I watched him go to a desk and write a check. My eyes

followed him as he came down the aisle formed by blocks of seats and passed through the door. He came so close to me that the skirt of his coat brushed my knees. Mr. Anderson, as he climbed into his enormous town-car, did not know how nearly he had escaped a violent attack.

I stayed awhile longer, watching less valuable things as they were auctioned off, but I noticed no one present who seemed to offer me a chance of future profit. They were all decent, well-bred folk, and it is not upon these that I wage my warfare. No gentleman or lady need ever fear the activities of John Ainsley. There are enough vulgarians in the world for me to prey upon.

So I left and strolled down the Avenue. I dismissed Anderson from my mind. After all, I need an opportunity for the exercise of my talent, and there was no opportunity here.

It was sheer accident that made me lunch that day at the Mirabeau. The winelike air and the bright sun made me continue down the Avenue as far as Washington Square, and then I discovered that I was hungry. The Mirabeau, that resort of lovers of good food, and where one may rely on finding, sooner or later, every Frenchman who comes to New York, was the nearest place. I dropped in there, surrendered myself to the discretion of the voluble French waiter who attended me, and began a hearty meal.

I paid little attention to my fellow-guests, an almost evenly divided mixture of Bohemians, business men and Frenchmen. I notice that those who scrutinize their neighbors in public places invite an equal scrutiny, and so I keep my eyes upon my plate. I am content that few people know me by sight, and that still fewer know me by the name under which I choose to masquerade.

But a waiter stumbled against me, and in acknowledging his quick apology, I looked up. Just beyond him I saw two people. One was the hunchback whose humiliation—although he had not at the time seemed aware of it—I had resented today. The other, towering above him, was the most dangerous man in Europe, the man whom I had outwitted on an occasion months ago, Monsieur Armand Cochet, known to the underworld and the police of Europe as the master criminal leader of the world, the White Eagle.

Myself? Ah, I say that Cochet is the greatest criminal *leader*. I work alone, needing no gangsters to carry out my orders, using no machinery save my own hands and mind in the achievement of my triumphs. Also, if more need be said on the question of the relative abilities of the White Eagle and myself, you who have read my memoirs will remember the affair of the Club of One-eyed Men, and will not have forgotten that I scored off the White Eagle in that instance.

For that matter, I knew that the White Eagle had not forgotten it, and while I may lay claim to at least an ordinary courage, I will confess that, as I met those fierce blue eyes, panic assailed me. The great curved beak which was his nose and which, in conjunction with his white hair, had given him his nickname; the wide mouth, thin-lipped, with a sneering droop at one corner; and the lithe body, still powerful despite his years— these filled me with a fear that I had never known before. And I have seen the gray-clad boche leaping down into the trench where I was standing.

And then I was able to banish fear. For I remembered that the White Eagle did not know the face of the man who had tricked him months ago. True, one of his followers knew me, but men are rarely recognized by descriptions. And even as I gave myself this assurance, the White Eagle glanced carelessly away, and he and his companion followed the waiter to a table.

I heard them state that they were expecting a third person, and I took the chance that that third person was not the one-eyed follower of the White Eagle who knew me by sight. For where the White Eagle flew, there must be prey. I had robbed him of his quarry before; I might do it again.

And this was a game worthy of my talent. Robbing

stupid profiteers hardly gave me excitement. But snatching meat from the talons of the White Eagle was a man's sport. I smiled as I thought of the elaborate organization ruled by M. Cochet. What a triumph if once again I could make that organization work, not for its master, but for myself.

Fear counseled me to pay my check and quietly depart. Pride told me that if I continued the easy road, my genius would desert me. I called myself an artist; in my heart I knew that I was worthy of that title. But the artist who of deliberate choice paints pot-boilers ceases to be an artist. I had wished to rob Anderson, a gross, stupid man without wit to cope with me if I decided to assail his security. Had I snatched Anderson's box, it would have been an act of common robbery.

Yet I had for a moment considered doing that very thing. Why? Because my wits were growing rusty from disuse. Here was a chance to sharpen them. And even as I said this to myself, I realized that I had spoken the truth. For into the restaurant came Marcus Anderson, and he joined the White Eagle and his hunchback companion.

"My dear Duke!" cried Anderson.

So Monsieur Armand Cochet, the White Eagle, was a duke! I smiled gayly to myself. The sentimentalities that April had brought to me left me for good.

Beyond Anderson's salutation to the couple who awaited him, I could hear no more of their speech. Only the multimillionaire's snobbish delight at knowing a gentleman of title had enabled me to hear his greeting. Anderson had deliberately spoken loudly in order that the patrons of the restaurant might know that aristocracy was here. Now, content that attention had been attracted, Anderson did not raise his voice. But stealing an occasional glance at him through the medium of a mirror on the wall, I could see that the man was overcome with snobbish gratification. He was as self-conscious as a pretty débutante, looking around to see who noticed him, stroking his silly little mustache, absurd on so gross a face, and touching his tie and the huge diamond gleaming from it.

But one does not need to hear—if one is John Ainsley—in order to know what is being said. I could follow the course of their conversation easily. First there were the pleasant inquiries concerning each other's health. Then there was a reminiscent anecdote by the White Eagle. The pale-faced hunchback capped his leader's story. Anderson delivered himself of a heavy jest. Encouraged, he began to brag. The White Eagle led him on, ably assisted by the cripple.

I could tell that the two criminals—the hunchback must necessarily be a criminal, inasmuch as he was the White Eagle's companion—were grossly flattering their guest. And Anderson was lapping it up like a greedy pup.

Now, Armand Cochet did nothing, I judged, without a purpose. The man was a gentleman, fallen, it is true, from his high estate, but a man of fine intuitions and delicate instincts. Such a one could take no pleasure in the society of Anderson. This was business upon which the White Eagle was engaged; nothing less would have made him tolerate the society of the profiteer.

But what was his business? I meant, when I put the question to myself, the exact nature of the scheme which the White Eagle must be planning. Robbery, of course; but what, when and how?

I lingered over my coffee until the others paid their check and passed by my table. I stole another glance at the hunchback. He was a fit companion for his master, for despite his slight and deformed physique, there was upon his face a ruthlessness equal to that of the White Eagle. His delicate features and pale skin would have made the unobservant class him as a poetic-minded youth. Most of us, when delicacy is coupled with deformity, ascribe spirituality to the partnership. But I, who must know criminals, understood that the clean-cut mouth was vicious, and that the brown eyes flashed hate more often than mirth.

Leisurely I followed them. I saw them step into An-

derson's town-car and start uptown. I followed in a taxi.
I was not foolish enough to tell my driver to follow the
car ahead, but I told him to go slowly, that I wished to
enjoy the spring air; and when the town-car turned a
corner, I suggested to my driver that he do the same
thing. So without arousing the chauffeur's curious suspicion, I saw the town-car stop before a modest private
residence on a side-street in the upper East Side, and
noted the number of the house into which the White
Eagle and his companion entered. As for Anderson, his
address was easy to find. A telephone-book—or if his telephone was not listed, there were a hundred other ways to
find where he lived. I did not wish to follow him farther.

I dismissed my taxi at Madison Avenue, and entered a
grocery store. It was an expensive-looking shop, the sort
that would have a fashionable patronage. I asked for the
proprietor, told him that I wanted five minutes of his
time, and went directly to the point.

"I'm in the automobile accessory business," I said. "I
have an automatic windshield-cleaner that I manufacture.
It's an article that's hard to find. People won't be convinced by a demonstration. They think it won't wear. So I
have to let them use it for a couple of weeks. Now,
social position and bank references mean nothing to me.
I've found out that the richer people are, the less inclined they are to pay little bills in a hurry. I've only
a small capital and I need cash. The people in this neighborhood trade with you. You know the ones that pay by
the fifth of the month."

The grocer grinned. "It ain't hard to remember them,"
he said.

"That's exactly my point," I told him. "You give me
a list of your customers who pay their bills promptly,
and I'll give you five per cent on every sale I make. And
for your trouble, so you'll know your time isn't wasted,
I'll give you twenty dollars right now."

"Fair enough," said the grocer enthusiastically. And he
took me into his office.

An hour later I left him, armed with a list that would

have been worth money to a yellow newspaper. For the great public would have been interested to know that some of its fashionable idols never paid a bill, even a food-bill, until a court summons was served upon them. For the grocer, a simple-minded soul, had given me the names of those to avoid as well as those to visit. He would have been surprised had he seen me, in my own apartment a little later, carefully destroying his list. For I wanted none of its details. What I wished to find out from my friend the grocer was the personnel of the household before which Anderson's town-car had stopped. And who should know that personnel better than the tradesman who supplied the house with food? And this I had learned in casual conversation without seeming to ask for information.

The Duc de Montarlier, then, was the gentleman who had rented furnished for a term of twelve months the private house on the side-street near the Avenue. He was a distinguished-looking Frenchman. Ah, how well I knew that! His secretary, Raoul Lotier, a hunchback, paid all his bills, and paid them every week. The Duc had no other French servants. He had acquired a staff of Japanese help from an employment agency, and so far as my friend the grocer knew, the Japs not only did the ordering but ran all the domestic machinery. There were no women employed in the house. Visitors? My grocer did not know.

I spent that evening in the public library, going over the files, for the past winter, of that New York paper which devotes most space to the chronicling of social events. Yet, carefully as I studied the so-called society columns, I never ran across the name of the Duc de Montarlier.

The White Eagle, then, had acquired no social prominence. That meant one of two things—that he dared not risk recognition, or that he was working with a definite objective and not merely making the acquaintance of numbers of rich persons whom he hoped to rob. It was then safe to assume that Marcus Anderson was his definite

objective. Certainly Anderson was rich enough to be legitimate game for the Frenchman, and despite his wealth,
stupid enough to make the White Eagle feel certain of
success.

But he had not robbed Anderson yet. That was obvious. The White Eagle was not the sort to linger on after
the carcass was eaten. In bed that night I asked myself
again the question: what, when and how?

The morning papers answered me. For they chronicled
yesterday's auction, and in mentioning the purchase of
the gold box by Marcus Anderson, added the illuminating
line, "who sails for South America on Thursday to settle
the final details in the amalgamation of various cattle-
interests of the Argentine."

Today was Wednesday. The White Eagle cultivated no
acquaintance without reason. He was friendly with Anderson because he intended to rob him. That robbery
had not occurred up to yesterday. If it had not occurred
last night, it would occur today or tonight. And how
would I turn this knowledge—for it *was* knowledge; I
knew criminals, and more than others I knew the White
Eagle—to my own profit?

Frantically I studied the situation. The White Eagle,
by posing as a nobleman, had ingratiated himself with
Marcus Anderson. Doubtless he had flattered the millionaire by refusing to meet Anderson's friends. He must
have told his prospective victim that he did not care to
know many Americans. For if a French duke met many
people, attended many dinners, his presence in this country could not be kept from the papers. The White Eagle
had been very friendly with Anderson at luncheon at
the Mirabeau. They were, seemingly, intimates. Some time
today, then, the Frenchman would call upon Anderson
to say farewell, and then the robbery would take place.
And there would be no other guests present when the
White Eagle made that call. I could be sure of that.
My reasoning told me that, anxious as Anderson might
be to advertise his friendship with the Duc, the White
Eagle would have forbidden such exploitation. There

would be no others present at the White Eagle's last call.

I rid myself of my excitement. If my logic was correct, the thing for me to do was to watch Anderson's house. It was one of the few occasions when I have regretted the lack of assistants. A few spies to report the situation, to map out the ground—but a single link is more powerful than a chain, because it has no joints. If I failed because I lacked followers, I could console myself by thinking of the hundreds, aye, thousands, of men who have gone to jail because their confederates betrayed them.

But I hated to fail. From the first moment when in a Paris dance-hall I had seen Cochet, the memory of his arrogant conceit had lingered with me. I would rather rob him than have access to the vaults of the Treasury. And if one man could outwit him, I would be that man. So I lingered that Wednesday night in the basement areaway of a house opposite the mansion of Anderson. Yesterday's balmy atmosphere had not lingered until tonight. It was bitterly cold; yet excitement and the fear of being discovered by a passing policeman kept me warm. And when I saw the White Eagle and his secretary alight from an automobile and enter that garish palace, I knew that my reasoning had thus far been correct.

Now, I had made no definite plan. Suddenly it occurred to me that even if the White Eagle and his companion descended the Anderson steps carrying the fruits of crime in their hands, it would be no easy matter for me to deprive them of those fruits. After all, I was no highwayman; I relied on wit and surprise for my success. Why, then, was I lurking in this areaway? Before I answered this question, I tried to put myself in the White Eagle's place.

He had cultivated Anderson's acquaintance for the purpose of robbing the millionaire. That robbery must occur tonight or be indefinitely postponed. It would be a robbery of finesse and subtlety; the White Eagle would not resort to violence save in the last extremity. Now, if the robbery were one of violence, the White Eagle's departure from Anderson's house would be a pellmell affair. Into such an affair I would not thrust myself.

On the other hand, if finesse and subtlety won the battle, the two criminals would leave their host in leisurely fashion. In that case, where would they go?

I could not believe that the White Eagle had brought with him many of his Parisian followers. To do so would be to court suspicion. The French police keep in fairly close touch with the detective bureaus of other countries. It might be possible for the White Eagle and one or two companions to slip quietly out of France without attracting notice. But if he took many of his followers with him, he would be running an unnecessary risk.

It was fair to assume, then, that in this American venture of his, he was working practically alone—in which case he would not have many different rendezvous where he and his followers could meet. Also, the White Eagle, like any great general,—and he was that,—prepared in advance for defeat. He would not wish to flee blindly in the event of victory; and in case of defeat it would not perhaps be necessary to flee. In other words, if the White Eagle did not succeed in robbing Anderson, he would return quietly to the house which he had rented. And if he succeeded in robbing the millionaire, he would probably return to that house. In his stay of several months in New York he must have acquired certain things of value and of bulk, which he would wish to take with him in the event of flight. And probably, unquestionably, if I knew the man, he would accomplish his purpose so subtly that he would have a start of at least an hour or two before his crime was discovered.

Having no followers here to guard other rendezvous, it was almost inevitable that he would return to his house. I was cooling my heels to no purpose here.

So I went to the side-street on which the White Eagle lived. Arrived in the neighborhood of his house, and following the same train of reasoning which had brought me here, I decided that he must have let his servants go for the night, if he had not, indeed, discharged them. Nothing venture, nothing gain! I boldly rang the bell at the servants' entrance slightly below the street level. I rang it half a dozen times. And then I did something which I rarely do, but at which I am extremely capable. I picked the lock and entered the house.

I went over that house from cellar to servants' quarters on the top floor. In these latter rooms I found no clothing. The servants had been discharged and had left with all their belongings. Two floors below, I entered a study. Behind it was the chief bedroom of the house. I knew that it must belong to the White Eagle. And in that bedroom were packed suitcases. To that room, then, the White Eagle would unquestionably come. But in the study was a decanter of wine and cigarettes. If I knew my Cochet, there would be at least one cigarette smoked and one glass of wine drunk in celebration of his latest *coup*. In this room, then, behind a great leather couch, I ensconced myself.

But before I went into hiding I took half a dozen towels from the bathroom adjoining the bedchamber, and from the latter room took a score of apparently discarded cravats. I tested each one of these and found them satisfactory. They were no longer beautiful, but I was certain that they would prove serviceable. And behind the leather couch I knotted them into four stout thongs. I had finished when I heard the front door open.

Cochet bounded up the stairs with an activity which I envied. I hoped that I, when I attained his years, would be as supple. He entered the room where I was hidden, snapped on the lights, filled two glasses from the decanter on the table, and lifted one high above his head. The hunchback, less active, now entered the room. Cochet greeted him loudly.

"Drink, *mon brave!*" he cried. "Drink to the genius of the White Eagle, who sees and swoops and rises triumphant!"

"Genius is too weak a word," said the hunchback.
"You work miracles, my master."

He took the other glass from the table and drank
eagerly. Cochet filled the glasses again.

"And of a simplicity, Raoul," boasted the White Eagle.
"This pig-dog of a profiteer shows us his priceless
box, opens it and lets us behold the richest jewels
of his so vulgar wife that gleam within it. And then,
as he closes the safe door, I distract his attention
and you snatch the box even as the door is being
closed."

In my hiding-place I nodded approvingly. This was
sleight of hand that might be matched against my own
gift of legerdemain.

The hunchback's voice was deprecating. "I have the
trick of the fingers, monsieur, but what are the mechanic's
hands without the artist's brains? To you goes all the
credit."

Cochet laughed merrily. "But the profits, eh, *mon
vieux?* They are more important than the glory, and you
will have your share of those. But we must not stay
here. That lady whom you have so justly termed vulgar
may desire to see her jewels once again this evening.
One never knows in what direction a woman's whim may
lead her."

"As always, my master, you are right," said the cripple.
"I will telephone for a taxicab; we shall disappear. In a
fortnight we shall land in *la belle France*——"

"But so much may happen in a fortnight."

I flatter myself that it was a line worthy of the
situation. Certainly Cochet and Lotier greeted it with that
stark amazement which a dramatic speech should arouse.
I assure you that I have never enjoyed a moment as
much as I enjoyed this one now as, an automatic pistol
in my hand, I followed my words into the room from
behind the couch.

Cochet recovered his self-possession first.

"This is an unexpected honor, monsieur," he said.

I shrugged. "The more honor, the more surprise to a

modest man," I grinned. "Messieurs will kindly elevate their hands and keep them in the air."

The hunchback flashed a lightning glance of question at the White Eagle. But Cochet knew that behind my levity lurked grimness.

"Obey, Raoul," he ordered. He looked at me. "Does monsieur care to explain?"

I doubt if I could have carried myself any better than he, in such a situation.

"The Anderson jewel-box and its contents, monsieur," I said. "If monsieur will kindly give that to me, I shall bid him *bon soir* and *bonne chance*." I held out my left hand.

The White Eagle simulated amusement. I cut short his laugh.

"I have overheard your conversation," I reminded him.

"Monsieur lacks a sense of humor," he retorted blandly. "He accepts idle jests as solemn truths."

"The box, please," I insisted.

"If monsieur's sad lack of humor persists, what can we do?" asked Cochet.

"Nothing," I snapped. "But I can do something. I can search you."

The cripple was ready to fight, but the White Eagle was a wary old campaigner. He believed that I would fire, and so he sharply again ordered the hunchback to obey. At the muzzle of my pistol Lotier bound, with the impromptu ropes that I had manufactured from the neckties, the hands and feet of his master. Then I made the cripple insert his wrists through a slip-noose. I drew it tight, and the rest was easy. The use of the towels as gags was unnecessary.

And a few minutes later I decided that it had not been necessary even to bind them. In fact, my presence here was unnecessary. For the Anderson jewel-box could not be found in the expansive overcoat pockets of either of them. Nor had they left it in the hall downstairs, or in the drawing-room, or anywhere else in the house.

It must have been delivered to a confederate waiting outside the millionaire's house. Yet this I did not believe. The White Eagle was not the sort who lets some one else take charge of the spoils of his warfare against society.

"Perhaps," said Cochet as I returned from my fruitless search of the premises, "monsieur is ready to apologize."

In truth, I was. From my pocket I drew a jackknife. I opened it and placed it on the floor.

"It will take you perhaps fifteen minutes to saw your bonds," I told Cochet. "And despite monsieur's affable manner, I feel that I need a quarter of an hour in which to disappear."

Cochet smiled; but behind that smile lay deadly menace. Always, from now on, a more dangerous enemy than the police would be at my heels. Though he smiled, Cochet would never forgive this indignity.

"Bon soir, messieurs," I said. I had failed, but I tried to carry off my failure with a good grace. I am not your vulgar crook who descends to threat or torture. My reasoning had not been sound. I did not believe that the box had been surrendered to a confederate, but what is belief in the face of fact?

"You will have time to escape from this house," I said, "before the police arrive here, provided that there is some element of truth in the jests I heard you exchange. Because I have been unfortunate is no reason that I should wish you ill fortune. Again, good evening, gentlemen."

And then I saw a gleam of triumph on the delicate face of the hunchback. Now, one cannot succeed at my profession unless one has the quick intuition of a woman. And to that intuition must be coupled the logic of a man —not of an ordinary man, but the sort of man that I am.

I remembered how insensitive the cripple's hump had seemed to the rough touch of the bully whom I had knocked down. I tried to visualize the sleight of hand by which the box had been extracted from Anderson's safe even as the millionaire locked its door. Where had the box been hidden?

I remembered the affair of the one-eyed men, and how

a pearl had been secreted in a glass eye. The jewel-box was too bulky to be placed in the pocket of a dinner jacket, and both of these men wore evening clothes. And the cripple wore a look of triumph. Also, his hump was not sensitive.

Oh, Armand Cochet is the White Eagle, but I am John Ainsley! Shall I add more, or shall I let the modest narration of my deeds speak for me? I bent over, tore the dinner jacket from the body of Lotier, exposed the carefully contrived false hump, and from that artificial deformity I took the jewel-box.

I waved them a mocking good-by. With the box under my arm beneath my coat, I sauntered out of the house, over to Fifth Avenue, and taxied, like any law-abiding citizen, to my apartment overlooking the Park.

Five minutes later I was examining the contents of the casket. I was rich. I could abandon forever the life to which necessity had driven me. At least, on that April evening I thought that I could. I did not know that sometimes there is truth in old saws. I had forgotten one of them. My readers may remember it. "Once a thief——"

ARTHUR SOMERS ROCHE

THE CLUB OF ONE-EYED MEN

IT was time for me to go to work. Seated at my table just removed from the throngs on the sidewalk, sipping my vermouth, I arrived reluctantly at this conclusion. Not that poverty pressed me! On the contrary, from the proceeds of a certain bit of legerdemain there remained to me, after paying my passage across the Atlantic, my expenses in Paris these last three months, and restoring my wardrobe to its present satisfactory condition, some ten thousand dollars. Certainly, benefited by the exchange, I could hope to live decently for another six months at least.

Not so long ago, I would have been overjoyed at assurance of financial security for six weeks, or even six days. Indeed, sufficient food in my stomach to keep hunger away for six hours was a rare condition with me. But our ideas change with our changing prosperity. Let those who think that the mind governs material things ponder this obvious reverse.

I am, I think, one who makes up his mind quickly, and acts immediately. Certainly when I had decided that I would rather live a thief than starve an honest man, I had acted instantly. Let me say, in parenthesis, that I had not yet arrived at regret for that decision. I acted, in this perhaps less important matter, as suddenly as I had acted on that evening when I had kissed an airy farewell to the traditions of all the Ainsleys, of whom I, John, was the first to turn to crime.

I raised my finger, and an attentive *garçon* leaped to my table. I paid him for my *apéritif*, rose, and with one stride was mingled with the crowd that surged from the Place de l'Opéra up the Boulevard des Capucines. It was an observation of the individuals who made up the crowd that had brought me to decision.

For it was springtime, and the world had come to Paris. From my place at the table I had seen fortunes in furs and jewels pass by. The profiteers of all the world were here; and their wives and daughters and mistresses flaunted the success of their males before the others of their kind.

Swarthy Argentinians grown rich in beef and hides, shining-eyed Spaniards who had traded while Europe bled, munitions-makers from England and America—they rode and walked the streets of Paris, gross, vulgar and overfed. As, after a terrific storm, strange carcasses arise from the depths and float offensively upon the surface of the sea, so now upon the surface of society drifted weird carrion.

The sight of them, obese and opulent, made me realize that it was time for me to set about the acquisition of some of their more merchantable gauds. Not that I intended to prey directly upon these *nouveaux riches!* But where the carrion lies, the vulture flies. It was toward the vulture, his talons gripping choice morsels, that I would bend my energies. I would let the vulture do all the unpleasant work, and I would reap his profit.

For do not think that I had spent these months in Paris in mere stupid gratification of appetites that had been balked so long by poverty. It is true that I had indulged in sundry luxuries and pleasures, that I had lived once more as a gentleman should live, unharassed by soiling economies; but I had devoted myself studiously to thought of the future.

That that future must be outside the law I had determined. My first venture into crime had yielded me a profit so great, for such slight effort and risk, that I never for a moment considered anything but continuing upon the career that the needs of existence had made me choose. For understand that these are not the penitent confessions of a paltry pickpocket: they are the narratives of an artist.

In the apartment which I had rented, on the Rue Daunou, I had deliberately studied my problem. I had acquired all the literature dealing with criminals that I could find. And I came to the inevitable conclusion that the so-called supercriminal had never existed. For always the histories of these persons ended with the accounts of their arrests and convictions to punishments too unpleasant to contemplate. A supercriminal should be one who escaped the law completely, who died, when his time came, full of riches as well as sin.

Yet some of these men had shown a talent for crime that approached genius. I asked myself why they had finally failed, why, at the end, in the dock, they had heard the judgment of society.

The answer was obvious: no man can be stronger or cleverer than all the forces of all society. The man, then, who antagonizes these forces is a fool. A fool must fail in whatever he attempts. But the man who recognizes the difficulties before him, and takes precautions that will minimize these difficulties, increases his chance of success.

I had seen one sample of the species termed supercrook, and I knew myself to be, in every possible way, more capable of success in his profession than he. If, then, I had more ability than he, and if I so directed my energies and efforts that I would run the least risk of antagonizing the police, it seemed to me that, with a bit of luck, there was no reason why I should not prove the exception to the rule, and forever avoid exposure.

Study, in the seclusion of my Paris apartment, informed me that while I could hardly hope to improve upon the methods of some of the more famous of the historical supercrooks, I could, by applying their methods in a different fashion, avoid their errors. For the crook has no friends; neither has he any of the ordinary recourses of the law-abiding citizen. If your reputable merchant is robbed, he can complain to the nearest authority, and immediately all of society's complicated legal machinery is set to work in his behalf. But if the thief is robbed, where may he look for redress?

To prey upon thieves: that should be my career. To wait until the vulture rose from the carrion and then to take from him his tidbits: that was my plan. I would work alone, having neither confederates nor confidants.

And now the sight of all this wealth paraded before me spurred me to action. Crooks were battening upon these parvenus. Every day the Paris papers told of robberies. The New York papers, which I received regularly, told of the continuance of the crime-wave there. Everywhere in the world thieves were plying their trade. I had mapped out my course of action; good living had restored my muscles and nerves to their former vigor; it was time for me to go to work.

I walked across the Place de l'Opéra and entered a steamship agency. By great good fortune a room and bath had been surrendered half an hour ago, and it was possible for me to obtain it. So I left there in twenty minutes, the possessor of a ticket which entitled me to sail three days later from Cherbourg on the *Altaria*.

For of course it was necessary for me to ply my trade in my own country. It is true that I had a smattering of French, but I did not converse easily in that language. I would be handicapped at the outset, if I dealt with French criminals.

There was, it is true, a certain risk in returning to New York. My first venture into theft had been at the expense of Daragon, the Fifth Avenue jeweler. But it was not a certainty that Daragon knew who had robbed him. Moreover, looking at myself in the gilt-bordered mirror in my bedroom on the Rue Daunou, I seriously doubted if Daragon would be able to recognize me. On the evening that I had abstracted from his pocket the ring which had brought me funds wherewith once again to live like a gentleman, my hair had been long and unkempt, my cheeks sunken and ghastly white. Now there were no hollows under my eyes; my flesh was firm, and my skin was red with health. Then I had looked like a consump-

tive; now I looked like an athlete. I could discount any
fears of recognition by the jeweler.

And there were just as many persons of ill-gotten
wealth in New York as there were in Paris. I was not
narrowing my opportunities by returning to a country
with which I was familiar. Indeed, as I contemplated
my return, I wished that I had never left New York.
For now that I planned activity, it did not seem as
feasible, as simple as it had seemed when I was merely
studying the careers of masters of crime. I suddenly wondered, as I sat in my window, just when, where and how
I would begin my operations.

For it is easy enough to speculate idly, to ascertain
the weaknesses whereby others have failed, to survey the
future, to state that one will do this and avoid that; but
actuality differs from speculation. After all, a client must
come to a lawyer before the attorney can demonstrate
that other lawyers err in their handling of cases; the
patient must come to the doctor before the physician can
prove his new theory of diagnosis; and opportunity must
come to me before I could begin the practice of my new
profession.

Up to now, living comfortably and lazily, I had not
given much thought to practice; I had devoted myself to
theory. But the sight of all the wealth exhibited in the
Place de l'Opéra this spring afternoon had given a fillip
to ambition. I had acted immediately. But having acted,
to the extent of purchasing transportation to New York,
I began to wonder to what purpose.

I couldn't watch the papers, ascertain when a crime
had been committed, and then rob the perpetrators. No
one but a detective genius could hope to find out who
committed the crimes in the first place. And having decided that my only safety lay in working alone, I could
hardly cultivate the acquaintance of criminals, and learn
their plans in advance. What had seemed, for several
weeks, a most excellent theory, became suddenly almost
impossible of practice.

And yet the theory was sound. I assured myself of

this. Because I did not see immediately how to put it into working practice proved nothing against the theory. Still, though I cheered myself with the reflection that Opportunity is never so disguised but that keen eyes may learn her identity, I was rather depressed as, dressed for dinner, I left my apartment in order to keep an engagement with some casual acquaintances met at Maxim's bar.

They were Americans, like myself, who were in Paris on business, and who had, in return for some little courtesies that I had shown them, expressed a desire that I should be their guest on a tour of Montmartre.

I met them at the appointed time. I had seen before, all that Montmartre offered, but these were pleasant chaps, gentlemen both, and it was a pleasure to associate, however casually, with one's own kind. And they could get something of a thrill from visiting the tawdry dives with which Paris is infested.

We wound up, late at night, at the Jardin des Nymphes. I would rather have said good night at the door of this place, but did not wish to seem unappreciative of my compatriots' hospitality. Vowing that I could not hold another glass of wine, I yielded to their importunities and entered the notorious dance-hall.

All Tenderloins are alike; the Jardin des Nymphes has its parallel in New York, in San Francisco; I presume that India and China could offer the vice-hungry visitor something similar. The underworld must make its contacts, somewhere, with the upper world on which it feeds.

And nowadays these contacts are franker than they were a dozen years ago. The so-called upper world has been invaded and conquered by barbarians; these outlanders bring to the circles to which their money has admitted them the crude tastes of the uncultured. So long as they are amused, they care not who furnishes their pleasure.

Tonight I saw pillars of finance embracing in the dance, women whose faces told their trade. I saw slant-browed

youths, but yesterday from the gutter, one-stepping with
women of assured social position. A philosopher, noting
how assiduously the upper world courted the lower, might
wonder at the pretense of difference between the two.
But I was no philosopher; I was merely a very bored and
tired gentleman who wished that his friends would permit
him to retire to his bed.

One of my hosts ordered champagne. A moment later
a bold-eyed girl smiled from an adjoining table. My
friends rose gallantly to the occasion; in a moment the
smiling fair one had acquired two other friendly maidens,
and they had crowded about our table at the edge of the
dancing space. More champagne was brought, and in another few moments my two hosts were dancing with their
newly acquired charmers.

I pleaded fatigue. The lady who had selected me as her
gallant sighed with relief.

"Me, I 'ave dance' my shoes almos' off," she said. "I
am glad that Monsieur feels not too gay."

I looked at her; I did not even wish to talk to her. But
after all, my friends had practically invited her to join
us; common courtesy demanded speech. So we talked at
random. Little by little I drew from her bits of information about the habitués of the place. She had a brutally
droll humor, and was not sparing in its use. A writer for
one of the scandal papers would have reveled in the gross
gossip, concerning the great and the near-great, which
poured from her lips. For she knew which matron had
compromised herself, which man had succumbed to harpy
charms.

And then she emitted a whistle of surprise. She had
become intimate with me by now. She gripped my arm,
and pointed at a tall, white-haired man who was entering
a box on the other side of the floor. In the bright lights
that illumined the room I could see him quite clearly.
Well groomed, with an easy, assured manner, a certain
droop at one corner of his wide mouth seemed to indicate
that of the two worlds represented here, the lower had
spawned him.

"That," said my fair informant, "is the White Eagle. Monsieur has heard of him? No?"

"Who is he?" I asked.

She shrugged her powdered shoulders. "He is the White Eagle, monsieur. If the name means nothing—" She shrugged again.

I looked again at the box across the floor. The White Eagle had sat down now, and had accepted champagne from the gentleman already there. I observed that gentleman. Gross, vulgar-seeming, his ostentation of dress and manner was only equaled by the painted and bejeweled fat old woman who was his companion. I set them down immediately as persons of immense and recent wealth.

The White Eagle turned his head, and even at that distance I understood why he bore his picturesque appellation. For his nose was a great curved beak. In profile one could not avoid noticing it. That, with his white hair, sufficiently explained his nickname.

"Who is he?" I asked of my companion again.

"Monsieur evidently does not read the Paris papers," she commented.

"With difficulty, mademoiselle," I admitted. "And I have been in Paris only a few months."

"Ah, that explains." She lowered her voice. "The White Eagle, monsieur, was tried for the theft of the Lagan jewels. He was what you call acquit', as he has always been acquit', every time the police try to put him in prison."

"A criminal?" I said with interest.

She shrugged again. "It has never been prove'," she smiled.

I nodded understandingly; I felt a thrill chase up and down my spinal column. Here, perhaps, was that opportunity which I needed. For the White Eagle was hovering around that vulgar couple in the box opposite for reasons, I shrewdly surmised, connected with his profession. I was looking, then, at another of the so-called supercrooks, the class upon which I had determined to prey.

I turned to my companion. "Shall we dance?" I asked.

She was tired, but could not afford to offend. We went together upon the floor, and it was not difficult so to maneuver that we remained for fully five minutes close to the box where sat the White Eagle and his prey.

He seemed on familiar terms with his quarry. Indeed, it seemed that he and the other man were discussing some matter of business. I would have given a great deal to overhear their conversation. Some cunning swindle was in the air, I felt assured. And I was confident that I could make that swindle inure to my own profit if I could but learn its nature.

But that was impossible. I returned with my partner to our table. As I sat down, I saw the White Eagle rise, kiss with great manner the pudgy hand of the overfed woman opposite, shake hands with her gross husband—the other two must have been married; certainly nothing but that inexorable relation would make them endure each other's company—and leave the box.

A moment later the other two rose. The man draped about the fat and wrinkled shoulders of his companion a cape of ermine that must have cost two hundred thousand francs. He handed a bank-note to his waiter, and the servant's forehead almost touched the floor in the excess of his gratitude.

I too rose abruptly. I pleaded a sudden headache of a severity too great to be endured. I refused, almost harshly, the offers of my two hosts to escort me home. I would not dream, I told them, of cutting short their evening's entertainment. And so they let me go.

I gained my hat and coat from the cloak-room, and raced out into the lobby of the dance-hall in time to see the couple whom I was following enter a limousine. I hailed a taxi and bade the driver follow the car ahead. I did not wish to do anything so crude as this, but I could not follow on foot, and I wished to know where the friends of the White Eagle were stopping.

I found out in a few minutes, when their car stopped

before the Meurice. I dismissed my taxi and entered into conversation with the hotel porter. From him, without difficulty, and without arousing his suspicion, I learned the name of the couple who had just entered the hotel. Then I turned and walked to my apartment in the Rue Daunou.

I find that one thinks better in bed than any other place. Undressed, then, with cigarettes on a stand beside me, I pondered the strange relationship which I had seen evidenced tonight.

What was the basis of the acquaintance between the White Eagle, a notorious though unpunished criminal, and Mr. and Mrs. Josiah Higgins, of Cincinnati, Ohio?

I wondered that I had not recognized the Higginses at first glance. Still, the photographs of them, which had appeared in the American and European press, had evidently been retouched to a degree. And if I had not instantly recognized the faces, I paid proper tribute to the Higgins glory by immediately identifying their names.

Who in the newspaper reading world had not heard of Josiah Higgins, who had been a multimillionaire before the war, and who was now popularly reputed to be worth at least a billion? Statisticians had estimated how many times his fortune, if reduced to dollar bills, would girdle the globe, how many times it would rebuild the Pyramids if reduced to silver coins. And other statisticians had solemnly affirmed that it cost thirty thousand dollars to dress Mrs. Higgins for breakfast, and at least a million and a quarter properly to clothe and ornament her for dinner.

Their extravagances had become a matter of international awe. Also, the queer parsimony that accompanied their extravagance was known to all the world. Higgins proudly boasted that he never gave a dollar to charity, and that he never lent money. They tipped outrageously, but Higgins haggled with his workmen, and was probably the most cordially hated employer in America.

They had assailed the gates of fashion in New York, and their rebuffs had become historic. They had failed

to impress Mayfair and the Faubourgs as well as Fifth
Avenue, but they did not lack for satellites. They were in
a fair way toward creating a fashionable society of their
own, if fashion be judged, as it frequently is, by the
amount of newspaper space accorded it.

And this couple talked confidentially with such a person as the White Eagle! The thought of blackmail entered my mind, but I dismissed it at once. If the White
Eagle had been threatening the millionaire, the manner
of each of them would have partaken of strain. No, they
had been talking business.

What business? What possible business could exist between the White Eagle and Josiah Higgins? If Higgins
had had a son or daughter who could have become en-
tangled in some underworld affair, I could understand
that the White Eagle had been called upon for aid. But
the couple were childless.

If Higgins were as foolish as he was unadmirable, I
could have guessed at a solution of the problem that
puzzled me. I could have imagined that the White Eagle
was surreptitiously disposing of stolen goods to the millionaire. But Higgins was too sane to indulge in that sort
of shady barter, if he were not too honest.

I tossed upon the bed; I fumed and fretted and
smoked a score of cigarettes. Somewhere in this relation
between the criminal and the millionaire lay an opportunity for me, if only I had eyes wherewith to see it.

For whatever the relation between Higgins and the
White Eagle, it must be something underhanded, even
though I could not guess why the millionaire should
descend to such a matter. The White Eagle was a crook;
a crook does only crooked business, whether his partner
be honest or otherwise. That is axiomatic. But where in
the axiom lay a profit for me?

I awoke with a headache; I had slept little, and that
little had been interrupted by dreams in which the White
Eagle took a fortune from Josiah Higgins, while I looked
on, powerless to abstract the fortune from the so-called
supercrook.

I tried to eat breakfast; but the combination of too much wine and too little sleep had killed my appetite. I was nervous, restless, and so I went for a walk. I crossed to the Left Bank, wandering aimlessly, my mind intent on the puzzle, solution of which I felt meant profit to me, and finally found myself in the neighborhood of the Luxembourg. The walk had cleared my head, and appetite had come to me. I walked on to Foyot's and ordered breakfast. Food put me in a more philosophical frame of mind. After all, I might be deluding myself; Higgins might have made the acquaintance of a notorious crook simply for the sake of the thrill that some people gain from such an acquaintance. At any rate, it did not behoove me to wear out my nerves in imagining problems that, having no existence, could have no solution.

And yet I was ashamed of these reflections; for after all, they were simply confessions of my own inability to meet a situation and make it yield a profit.

Despite my resolutions, then, to think no more of Higgins and the White Eagle, they were both in my mind as, turning a corner into the Rue des Saints Pères, I collided with a group of people standing before a doorway. I muttered an apology, stepped back, and noted that the person of the group with whom I had come into most violent contact—he had fallen to the ground—was blind in one eye.

I bent over swiftly, and helped him to his feet. My perfunctory apology became profuse and sincere. Seeing that he was poorly dressed, I ventured to offer him a coin. He seized it greedily, and I would have passed on, only that I noticed that the rest of the group were all blind in one eye.

Other groups stood across the street, in the street, and farther down the narrow sidewalk on which I stood. And I noticed that every single one of them suffered the same affliction: they were all blind in one eye.

I suppose that my amazed horror was reflected in my face. For the man to whom I had presented the gratuity laughed at me.

"Monsieur is amazed, yes? To see so many of us is strange?"

"Is this a hospital here?" I asked, pointing at the building before which we stood.

He shook his head. "No, monsieur, it is the home of a patron of all afflicted such as we. Monsieur has not read this morning's *Cri de Paris?*"

I shook my head, and he thrust into my hand a copy of the paper, folded back to expose an advertisement. I read it lamely in my faltering French. Translated, it ran:

"A gentleman whose son, having lost an eye for France, bore his wound proudly, despite his affliction, until his death by accident recently, wishes to honor the memory of that noble son by kindnesses to those similarly afflicted. The gentleman will devote part of his large fortune to the founding and maintenance of a club for one-eyed men. It will not be limited only to those who lost their sight in the war against the cursed Boche. All men who are without the sight of one eye are eligible to the privileges of the Club. Those interested are requested to apply to Number —, Rue des Saints Pères, between the hours of nine and twelve on Wednesday."

I read this amazing advertisement, so typically French in sentiment, and my eyes filled with tears. It was a charity a trifle too bizarre for American taste, but its kindness would appeal to the generosity of any country. I placed another coin in my informant's palm, and hurried away from the grotesque scene.

But at the first corner I stopped, turned, and stared after a man who had passed me. It was the White Eagle; and all my interest in him, which had evaporated while I read the strange advertisement, condensed and flowed back into my brain.

And then interest became amazement, for he entered the house before which the groups of blind men stood. Immediately upon his entrance a servant came to the door and beckoned to the unfortunates. Five minutes later they were all within the house.

I waited outside, at a convenient corner. Somehow or

other I could not believe that this grotesque advertisement contained all that was of interest. Of course, crooks are notoriously impulsive, given to streaks of extravagant generosity. Nevertheless, I waited.

One by one, the blind men began to emerge from the house. All of them seemed happy, as though incredible good fortune had come to them. Finally the man whom I had tipped appeared. I accosted him, and he beamed upon me.

"Ah, it is my generous American!"

"Well, did you join the Club?" I asked.

"But yes, monsieur!" He almost capered in delight. As I have said, my French is feeble. Yet I managed to gather from his excited speech that all the applicants had been admitted to Club membership, that not only were there no dues, but that those members who were in need were to be granted annuities, that the Club was to have an outing upon a river steamer next week, on which occasion detailed plans were to be submitted to the membership by its benefactor.

"Did you meet the patron himself?" I asked.

"M. Armand Cochet? But surely, monsieur. A noble gentleman, white of hair, and with a manner of a prince."

"I think I saw him enter, then," said I. "A man with a great nose?"

"Monsieur is correct," said the man. "And with an eye like an eagle, and the heart of a dove. Of a truth, a great man."

"But certainly," I agreed.

I congratulated my friend, parted from him with mutual expressions of esteem, and walked toward the river. And the farther I walked, the more incredible it seemed to me that the White Eagle, or M. Armand Cochet, could be engaged in such an astounding philanthropy as that in which I had discovered him this morning. And yet, battling against my disbelief, was my knowledge of the impetuous kindnesses of those who live by their wits. Perhaps the White Eagle pacified his conscience by such a typically Gallic charity.

But criminals do not ordinarily invite public attention. Of course, though, I must not forget, that according to my fair companion of last night, the White Eagle had never yet been convicted of crime. Perhaps he did not fear public interest in him.

But it was among the ordinary probabilities that one or more of the applicants attracted by his bizarre advertisement should be of the criminal class. One would expect the White Eagle to be fearful of recognition by such a one. Still, beggars can't be choosers, and I suppose the White Eagle felt that those in need of charity, for the Club was obviously a charitable affair, would not be inclined to question the source of the revenues which were to be applied to their wants.

But I had given altogether too much of my thought to the White Eagle and his affairs. I confessed myself, finally, beaten. I could neither understand what could be the relation between the supercrook and the millionaire, nor why the White Eagle should institute a philanthropy. I vowed that I would think no more on these matters. If in the dealings between Higgins and the white-haired man there lay opportunity for me, I would forgo it. I would not drive myself to distraction by futile speculation. Nor would I be ashamed of my inability to strip the disguise from the figure of Opportunity. I would await her next passing, hoping that she would be more easy of recognition then.

Even though one has rented a furnished apartment, and has lived in it only a few months, one finds that little by little one has acquired a considerable quantity of possessions. I was sailing in two days; I could not afford to be willfully extravagant; so I spent the rest of this day in dealings with secondhand merchants, realizing a few thousand francs. The next day I spent in packing and shipping my trunks and in purchasing some necessaries for the trip. And the next morning, promptly at nine o'clock, I passed through the train gates at the Gare du Nord, and entered a first-class carriage.

Having seen to it that my bags were safely deposited

in a corner of the carriage, I walked to the platform to watch the rest of the travelers. I strolled as far as the train gates, puffing at a cigarette. I was about to turn back when I saw, accompanied by a maid, a valet and an obsequious-seeming youth who was unquestionably the millionaire's secretary, Mr. and Mrs. Higgins.

I had not examined the passenger-list, and so was surprised at their arrival. But beyond a natural interest at the coincidence, I should have thought very little about it, had not they been followed through the gates by a man who was blind in one eye. Not merely that, but he was indisputably one of the group with which I had collided on a corner of the Rue des Saints Pères!

I could not be mistaken; the fact that his dress was much improved, that he had been to a barber, made no difference. In that first moment of shock, when I had realized that all these loiterers on the sidewalk were blind, the features of those whom I beheld were ineradicably impressed upon my memory.

All my resolutions, that I would worry no more about Higgins and the White Eagle, left me. Indeed, I watched eagerly for the arrival of the supercrook. But he did not come, though I waited until the last moment before the train started.

I strolled through the train shortly after we pulled out from the station. The Higgins party occupied two private compartments, as I could tell from the half-opened doors. The one-eyed man shared a compartment with three other people, American tourists.

The one-eyed man, then, was not part of the Higgins entourage. He had exchanged no signs of recognition with the millionaire as they passed through the train gates, although they had been close enough to touch each other.

Puzzled, bewildered, almost frantic because I could not peer through curtains behind which, I was convinced, a play of vital significance to me was being performed, I rode to Cherbourg. I was no wiser at the end of the railway journey. Indeed, I was no wiser six days later when the *Altaria* was only a night out from her dock in New York.

During those six days I had observed, as closely as I could without drawing attention to myself, Higgins and the one-eyed man. But, although nearly every one of the first-class passengers, including myself, exchanged words, at some time or other, with the millionaire, the one-eyed man never, to my knowledge, even exchanged a look with Higgins. The one-eyed man kept to himself; whenever he walked the deck, he was alone; he never seemed to utter more than monosyllables to his table-mates in the saloon; he neither offered nor accepted hospitality in the smoke-room, but drank alone.

On the night before we landed, I attended the concert in the lounge. I sat with a couple of chance acquaintances near the door, where we watched the various arrivals, exchanged banter with them, and gossiped, after the fashion of travelers, about their manners, appearances, probable income, and flirtations during the voyage. Then, as Mr. and Mrs. Higgins passed through the wide doors, we all three gasped.

Higgins was worthy of note. His white waistcoat was fastened with emerald buttons; he wore a solitaire diamond on one hand that must have weighed a dozen carats and been worth a fortune. A solid rope of diamonds hung from his watch pocket, supporting a ruby fob.

His vulgarities had formed the basis of half the smoke-room talk during the trip, but this ostentation, in excessively bad taste, outdid anything else. But he was diffident as compared with his wife.

It was not alone that her gown was cut so low that one blushed with vicarious shame, wondering that so ill-formed a woman should care to expose her muddy flesh. It was not that her jewels were so expensive, even; it was that she wore such an unbelievable number of them. She seemed plastered with precious stones, until one forgot how low her dress was cut. I had read of her jewels, but had assumed that the newspaper writers had been guilty of the usual Sunday supplement exaggeration. Now I knew that they had been restrained.

And one jewel, a pearl hanging from a chain until it rested like a round white grape upon her bosom, held my fascinated eyes. It drew my companions' attention too, for one of them, Brokaw by name, mentioned it.

"Get the pearl?" he whispered. "Got any idea what that thing's worth?"

I shook my head. "I know," he said. "I was in Maret's on the Rue de la Paix, the day they bought it. Me," he chuckled, "buying a thousand-franc brooch to take home to the Missus, and thinking what a hit I'd make with her! And in comes Higgins and his wife, and at the top of his lungs old Josiah declares that he's come for the Ranee's Pearl, and that he's brought his check for a million francs with him. Believe me, friends, I almost died with shame to think how I'd been haggling over my little brooch. I paid what they asked, apologized for annoying them, and sneaked out. One million francs, and no matter what the exchange is, that's *money!*"

I admitted that it was. "But it's not extremely large," I said.

"It's as big as your eye," he declared. "And it's the most perfect pearl of its size in existence. I heard Maret jabbering about it. Some Indian princess went bust and sold it." He whistled. "He'll have to pay another chunk of money to-morrow, at the Customs, when he shows them that bit of junk. That'll break his heart. He sure hates to spend a nickel where it won't show, the old tight-wad."

I agreed with him, sighing as I did so, thinking how well I could use the money represented by that pearl. Indeed, the thought was so agonizing that I left the lounge long before the concert was over, seeking solace in the smoke-room.

The room was deserted, save for the one-eyed man. Unwilling to arouse any latent suspicion in him, I had hitherto refrained from accosting him. But now I nodded pleasantly to him. It was my last chance to make his acquaintance, and I had not yet given up the idea that here was opportunity.

But when I followed my nod with an invitation to join me in a pint of champagne, he brusquely refused. His one good eye shot a suspicious glance at me. I noted that that eye was gray, and that his glass eye matched the other.

Rebuffed, I made no further effort. I drank my wine, rose, took a turn around the deck, and went to my stateroom. I immediately undressed and went to bed, finally convinced that whatever the mystery of Higgins, the White Eagle and the one-eyed man, it was beyond my power to solve and profit by it.

Somewhere along toward dawn, I was aroused by pounding at my door. I climbed from my bed, threw a dressing-gown over my pajamas, and opened the door. A ship's officer stood there.

"Sorry, sir," he said, "but would you mind coming to the lounge?"

"What's the idea?" I asked. "Ship on fire or something?"

He smiled deprecatingly. "Nothing like that, sir, but one of the passengers has lost some jewelry. Rather a valuable trinket."

"Well, what's that to do with me?" I demanded.

"Nothing, sir, I hope," he replied. "But the gentleman insists that all persons who passed by the door of his cabin to-night submit to a search. It's Mr. Higgins, sir—his wife's pearl; you and three other gentlemen have cabins in this corridor. To reach your rooms you have to pass by the Higgins' suite. The steward on watch swears that no other people have entered the corridor since Mr. and Mrs. Higgins retired."

"And because I happen to have a cabin in the same quarter of the ship with Higgins, I'm to be insulted by that swine, am I?" I cried.

The officer became more apologetic. "Swine is right, sir, but I hope you'll make it easy for us. Of course, you have a right to refuse, but that will only cause trouble on the dock. The captain presents his compliments, sir, and hopes that you will waive your rights, and help him to avoid scandal for the ship's sake."

"If you put it that way, to oblige the captain—certainly," said I.

I followed him down the corridor, across an open space and into the lounge. There were Mr. and Mrs. Higgins and their servants; also there were two Englishmen, with whom I had struck up a casual acquaintance, and to whom I nodded now. And then I saw the third of the gentlemen to whom the ship's officer had referred. It was the one-eyed man.

We all submitted to a search. We handed over the keys of our baggage to an officer. Half an hour later he returned with the statement that he had searched all our effects and found no trace of the missing pearl. Then one of the Englishmen did what I had been wanting to do. He walked over to Higgins.

"We've heard your story," he said "You returned from the concert, you and your wife. She took off her jewels and laid them on a table in her cabin. She then went into your cabin, to talk to you. When she returned to her own room, five minutes later, the Ranee's Pearl was gone. Some one had opened the door and stolen it."

"And it must have been some one in one of the cabins on the corridor," cried Higgins.

"That's what you say," said the Englishman. "It doesn't matter to a vulgar beast like you that you insult your betters. Now, we've all been searched, and none of us has your filthy pearl. I merely want to tell you that I'm glad you lost it, and that I hope the loss teaches you and your wife the vulgarity of ostentation. Good evening, sir."

He turned on his heel, followed by his compatriot, and stalked, with what dignity a man in a bathrobe may achieve, from the lounge.

The one-eyed man came close to Higgins, and in rapid French assailed him. And then, suddenly, I understood. Not Higgins' manner told me; the plutocrat acted his part too well. But the light of one of the electric lamps flashed

on the Frenchman's face, and the mystery that had been
puzzling me for a week was solved at last.

I went back to bed, neither reproaching Higgins, nor
paying any attention to his perfunctory apologies. I slept
soundly, happily, as one should who knows that on the
morrow he will acquire a fortune.

With the other passengers I disembarked next day. I
submitted to the usual examination of my baggage. I saw
the reporters buzzing about the Higginses, and knew that
the afternoon headlines would be devoted to the loss of
the precious Ranee's Pearl. I chuckled as I thought of the
story that could be written, but would not be printed in
the newspapers. You see, I had no doubt as to my success.
I had pierced the disguise of Opportunity.

Outside the Customs shed I followed the porter with
my baggage to a taxi. I told the chauffeur to drive my
things to the Hotel Regina, took his number to assure myself of his honesty, and then waited. In a few minutes the
one-eyed man arrived. His porter handed his bags to a
taxi driver. The one-eyed man climbed into the cab.

And I climbed in after him. He would have expostu-
lated, save that I pressed something against his ribs, the
something being the muzzle of an automatic pistol. The
driver did not see this byplay, and when I told him that I
would accompany his passenger, made no objection. He
closed the door upon us, climbed into his seat and started
the cab.

"What do you want?" demanded the one-eyed man.

I smiled cheerfully at him. "Your right eye," I told
him. I pressed the pistol muzzle harder against his chest.
"No use in crying out; it would be jail for you even if
you lived," I warned him.

There, in the center of crowded West Street, he removed his glass eye and handed it to me. At the next
corner I knocked on the window, and the chauffeur
stopped. I alighted, waved an airy adieu to my one-eyed
friend, and strolled blithely across town, a little later to
pick up a taxi and drive to the Regina.

Afraid of pursuit? Had I not already conquered the

one-eyed man? Afraid of the police? Would Higgins, who had conspired at the simulation of a robbery, in order to avoid the payment of a tremendous duty, confess his own attempt at crime?

For the minute that I had discovered the whereabouts of the Ranee's Pearl, I understood why Higgins had discussed business with the White Eagle. The millionaire's notorious parsimony had caused him to invoke the super-crook's aid at defrauding the Customs. That was the only possible explanation of all that had bewildered me.

How had I discovered the whereabouts of the pearl? Simply enough: the one-eyed man's glass eye had been gray in the smoke-room; it was green when the electric light flashed upon it in the lounge. Instantly I understood why the White Eagle had printed his bizarre advertisement. Among the applicants for membership in his club, he had found the criminal willing to aid him, in his furtherance of the desire of Josiah Higgins to defraud his government.

Would the one-eyed man have returned the pearl to Higgins later on, or would he have delivered it to the White Eagle? Would there have been honor among these thieves?

Ask me some easier question. Ask me, for instance, what I did when I arrived at my room in the Regina. I will tell you: I deftly took apart the two halves of the green glass eye which had been surrendered to me, and I kissed the Ranee's Pearl.

I had been right in my theory. Where the carrion lies, the vulture flies.

SAX ROHMER

THE PIGTAIL OF HI WING HO

I

HOW I OBTAINED IT

LEAVING the dock gates behind me I tramped through the steady drizzle, going parallel with the river and making for the Chinese quarter. The hour was about half-past eleven on one of those September nights when, in such a locality as this, a stifling quality seems to enter the atmosphere, rendering it all but unbreathable. A mist floated over the river, and it was difficult to say if the rain was still falling, indeed, or if the ample moisture upon my garments was traceable only to the fog. Sounds were muffled, lights dimmed, and the frequent hooting of sirens from the river added another touch of weirdness to the scene.

Even when the peculiar duties of my friend, Paul Harley, called him away from England, the lure of this miniature Orient which I had first explored under his guidance, often called me from my chambers. In the house with the two doors in Wade Street, Limehouse, I would discard the armour of respectability, and, dressed in a manner unlikely to provoke comment in dockland, would haunt those dreary ways sometimes from midnight until close upon dawn. Yet, well as I knew the district and the strange and often dangerous creatures lurking in its many burrows, I experienced a chill partly physical and partly of apprehension to-night; indeed, strange though it may sound, I hastened my footsteps in order the sooner to reach the low den for which I was bound—Malay Jack's—a spot marked plainly on the crimes-map and which few respectable travellers would have regarded as a haven of refuge.

But the chill of the adjacent river, and some quality of utter desolation which seemed to emanate from the deserted wharves and ramshackle buildings about me, were driving me thither now; for I knew that human companionship, of a sort, and a glass of good liquor—from a store which the Customs would have been happy to locate—awaited me there. I might chance, too, upon Durham or Wessex, of New Scotland Yard, both good friends of mine, or even upon the Terror of China-town, Chief Inspector Kerry, a man for whom I had an esteem which none of his ungracious manners could diminish.

I was just about to turn to the right into a narrow and nameless alley, lying at right angles to the Thames, when I pulled up sharply, clenching my fists and listening.

A confused and continuous sound, not unlike that which might be occasioned by several large and savage hounds at close grips, was proceeding out of the darkness ahead of me; a worrying, growling, and scuffling which presently I identified as human, although in fact it was animal enough. A moment I hesitated, then, distinguishing among the sounds of conflict an unmistakable, though subdued, cry for help, I leaped forward and found myself in the midst of the *mêlée*.

This was taking place in the lee of a high, dilapidated brick wall. A lamp in a sort of iron bracket spluttered dimly above on the right, but the scene of the conflict lay in densest shadow, so that the figures were indistinguishable.

"Help! they're strangling me——"

From almost at my feet the cry arose and was drowned in Chinese chattering. But guided by it I now managed to make out that the struggle in progress waged between a burly English sailorman and two lithe Chinese. The yellow

men seemed to have gained the advantage and my course
was clear.

A straight right on the jaw of the Chinaman who was
engaged in endeavouring to throttle the victim laid him
prone in the dirty roadway. His companion, who was
holding the wrist of the recumbent man, sprang upright
as though propelled by a spring. I struck out at him
savagely. He uttered a shrill scream not unlike that of a
stricken hare, and fled so rapidly that he seemed to melt
in the mist.

"Gawd bless you, mate!" came chokingly from the
ground—and the rescued man, extricating himself from
beneath the body of his stunned assailant, rose unsteadily
to his feet and lurched toward me.

As I had surmised, he was a sailor, wearing a rough,
blue-serge jacket and having his greasy trousers thrust
into heavy seaboots—by which I judged that he was but
newly come ashore. He stooped and picked up his cap. It
was covered with mud, as were the rest of his garments,
but he brushed it with his sleeve as though it had been
but slightly soiled and clapped it on his head.

He grasped my hand in a grip of iron, peering into my
face, and his breath was eloquent.

"I'd had one or two, mate," he confided huskily (the
confession was unnecessary). "It was them two in the
Blue Anchor as did it; if I 'adn't 'ad them last two, I
could 'ave broke up them Chinks with one 'and tied
behind me."

"That's all right," I said hastily, "but what are we
going to do about this Chink here?" I added, endeavouring
at the same time to extricate my hand from the vise-like
grip in which he persistently held it. "He hit the tiles
pretty heavy when he went down."

As if to settle my doubts, the recumbent figure suddenly arose and without a word fled into the darkness and
was gone like a phantom. My new friend made no attempt to follow, but:

"You can't kill a bloody Chink," he confided, still
clutching my hand; "it ain't 'umanly possible. It's easier

to kill a cat. Come along o' me and 'ave one; then I'll tell you somethink. I'll put you on somethink, I will."

With surprising steadiness of gait, considering the liquid cargo he had aboard, the man, releasing my hand and now seizing me firmly by the arm, confidently led me by divers narrow ways, which I knew, to a little beerhouse frequented by persons of his class. My own attire was such as to excite no suspicion in these surroundings, and although I considered that my acquaintance had imbibed more than enough for one night, I let him have his own way in order that I might learn the story which he seemed disposed to confide in me. Settled in the corner of the beerhouse—which chanced to be nearly empty— with portentous pewters before us, the conversation was opened by my new friend:

"I've been paid off from the *Jupiter*—Samuelson's Planet Line," he explained. "What I am is a fireman."

"She was from Singapore to London?" I asked.

"She was," he replied, "and it was at Suez it 'appened —at Suez."

I did not interrupt him.

"I was ashore at Suez—we all was, owin' to a 'itch with the canal company—a matter of money, I may say. They make yer pay before they'll take yer through. Do you know that?"

I nodded.

"Suez is a place," he continued, "where they don't sell whisky, only poison. Was you ever at Suez?"

Again I nodded, being most anxious to avoid diverting the current of my friend's thoughts.

"Well, then," he continued, "you know Greek Jimmy's —and that's where I'd been."

I did not know Greek Jimmy's, but I thought it un- necessary to mention the fact.

"It was just about this time on a steamin' 'ot night as I come out of Jimmy's and started for the ship. I was walkin' along the Waghorn Quay, same as I might be walkin' along to-night, all by myself—bit of a list to port but nothing much—full o' joy an' happiness, 'appy an' free—'appy an' free. Just like you might have noticed to-night, I noticed a knot of Chinks scrappin' on the ground all amongst the dust right in front of me. I rammed in, windmillin' all round and knocking 'em down like skittles. Seemed to me there was about ten of 'em, but allowin' for Jimmy's whisky, maybe there wasn't more than three. Anyway, they all shifted and left me standin' there in the empty street with this 'ere in my 'and."

At that, without more ado, he thrust his hand deep into some concealed pocket and jerked out a Chinese pigtail, which had been severed, apparently some three inches from the scalp, by a clean cut. My acquaintance, with somewhat bleared eyes glistening in appreciation of his own dramatic skill—for I could not conceal my surprise—dangled it before me triumphantly.

"Which of 'em it belong to," he continued, thrusting it into another pocket and drumming loudly on the counter for more beer, "I can't say, 'cos I don't know. But that ain't all."

The tankards being refilled and my friend having sampled the contents of his own:

"That ain't all," he continued. "I thought I'd keep it as a sort of relic, like. What 'appened? I'll tell you. Amongst the crew there's three Chinks—see? We ain't through the canal before one of 'em, a new one to me—Li Ping is his name—offers me five bob for the pigtail, which he sees me looking at one mornin'. I give him a punch on the nose an' 'e don't renew the offer: but that night (we're layin' at Port Said) 'e tries to pinch it! I dam' near broke his neck, and 'e don't try any more. To-night"—he extended his right arm forensically—"a deppitation of Chinks waits on me at the dock gates; they explains as from a patriotic point of view they feels it to be their dooty to buy the pigtail off of me, and they bids a quid, a bar of gold—a Jimmy o' Goblin!"

He snapped his fingers contemptuously and emptied his pewter. A sense of what was coming began to dawn on me. That the "hold-up" near the riverside formed part of the scheme was possible, and, reflecting on my rough treatment of the two Chinamen, I chuckled inwardly. Possibly, however, the scheme had germinated in my acquaintance's mind merely as a result of an otherwise common assault, of a kind not unusual in these parts, but, whether elaborate or comparatively simple, that the story of the pigtail was a "plant" designed to reach my pocket, seemed a reasonable hypothesis.

"I told him to go to China," concluded the object of my suspicion, again rapping upon the counter, "and you see what come of it. All I got to say is this: If they're so bloody patriotic, I says one thing: I ain't the man to stand in their way. You done me a good turn to-night, mate; I'm doing you one. 'Ere's the bloody pigtail, 'ere's my empty mug. Fill the mug and the pigtail's yours. It's good for a quid at the dock gates any day!"

My suspicions vanished; my interest arose to boiling-point. I refilled my acquaintance's mug, pressed a sovereign upon him (in honesty I must confess that he was loath to take it), and departed with the pigtail coiled neatly in an inner pocket of my jacket. I entered the house in Wade Street by the side door, and half an hour later let myself out by the front door, having cast off my dockland disguise.

II

HOW I LOST IT

It was not until the following evening that I found leisure to examine my strange acquisition, for affairs of more immediate importance engrossed my attention. But at about ten o'clock I seated myself at my table, lighted the lamp, and taking out the pigtail from the table drawer, placed it on the blotting-pad and began to examine it with the greatest curiosity, for few Chinese affect the pigtail nowadays.

I had scarcely commenced my examination, however, when it was dramatically interrupted. The door bell commenced to ring jerkily. I stood up, and as I did so the ringing ceased and in its place came a muffled beating on the door. I hurried into the passage as the bell commenced ringing again, and I had almost reached the door when once more the ringing ceased; but now I could hear a woman's voice, low but agitated:

"Open the door! Oh, for God's sake be quick!"

Completely mystified, and not a little alarmed, I threw open the door, and in there staggered a woman heavily veiled, so that I could see little of her features, but by the lines of her figure I judged her to be young.

Uttering a sort of moan of terror she herself closed the door, and stood with her back to it, watching me through the thick veil, while her breast rose and fell tumultuously.

"Thank God there was someone at home!" she gasped.

I think I may say with justice that I had never been so surprised in my life; every particular of the incident marked it as unique—set it apart from the episodes of everyday life.

"Madam," I began doubtfully, "you seem to be much alarmed at something, and if I can be of any assistance to you——"

"You have saved my life!" she whispered, and pressed one hand to her bosom. "In a moment I will explain."

"Won't you rest a little after your evidently alarming experience?" I suggested.

My strange visitor nodded, without speaking, and I conducted her to the study which I had just left, and placed the most comfortable arm-chair close beside the table so that as I sat I might study this woman who so strangely had burst in upon me. I even tilted the shaded lamp, artlessly, a trick I had learned from Harley, in order that the light might fall upon her face.

She may have detected this device; I know not; but as if in answer to its challenge, she raised her gloved hands and unfastened the heavy veil which had concealed her features.

Thereupon I found myself looking into a pair of lustrous black eyes whose almond shape was that of the

Orient; I found myself looking at a woman who, since she was evidently a Jewess, was probably no older than eighteen or nineteen, but whose beauty was ripely voluptuous, who might fittingly have posed for Salomé, who, despite her modern fashionable garments, at once suggested to my mind the wanton beauty of the daughter of Herodias.

I stared at her silently for a time, and presently her full lips parted in a slow smile. My ideas were diverted into another channel.

"You have yet to tell me what alarmed you," I said in a low voice, but as courteously as possible, "and if I can be of any assistance in the matter."

My visitor seemed to recollect her fright—or the necessity for simulation. The pupils of her fine eyes seemed to grow larger and darker; she pressed her white teeth into her lower lip, and resting her hands upon the table leaned toward me.

"I am a stranger to London," she began, now exhibiting a certain diffidence, "and to-night I was looking for the chambers of Mr. Raphael Philips of Figtree Court."

"This is Figtree Court," I said, "but I know of no Mr. Raphael Philips who has chambers here."

The black eyes met mine despairingly.

"But I am positive of the address!" protested my beautiful but strange caller—from her left glove she drew out a scrap of paper, "here it is."

I glanced at the fragment, upon which, in a woman's hand, the words were pencilled: "Mr. Raphael Philips, 36-b Figtree Court, London."

I stared at my visitor, deeply mystified.

"These chambers are 36-b!" I said. "But I am not Raphael Philips, nor have I ever heard of him. My name is Malcolm Knox. There is evidently some mistake, but" —returning the slip of paper—"pardon me if I remind you, I have yet to learn the cause of your alarm."

"I was followed across the court and up the stairs."

"Followed? By whom?"

D. S.—VIII—10

"By a dreadful-looking man, chattering in some tongue I did not understand!"

My amazement was momentarily growing greater.

"What kind of a man?" I demanded rather abruptly.

"A yellow-faced man—remember I could only just distinguish him in the darkness on the stairway, and see little more of him than his eyes at that, and his ugly gleaming teeth—oh! it was horrible!"

"You astound me," I said; "the thing is utterly incomprehensible." I switched off the light of the lamp. "I'll see if there's any sign of him in the court below."

"Oh, don't leave me! For heaven's sake don't leave me alone!"

She clutched my arm in the darkness.

"Have no fear; I merely propose to look out from this window."

Suiting the action to the word, I peered down into the court below. It was quite deserted. The night was a very dark one, and there were many patches of shadow in which a man might have lain concealed.

"I can see no one," I said, speaking as confidently as possible, and relighting the lamp, "if I call a cab for you and see you safely into it, you will have nothing to fear, I think."

"I have a cab waiting," she replied, and lowering the veil she stood up to go.

"Kindly allow me to see you to it. I am sorry you have been subjected to this annoyance, especially as you have not attained the object of your visit."

"Thank you so much for your kindness; there must be some mistake about the address, of course."

She clung to my arm very tightly as we descended the stairs, and often glanced back over her shoulder affrightedly, as we crossed the court. There was not a sign of anyone about, however, and I could not make up my mind whether the story of the yellow man was a delusion or a fabrication. I inclined to the latter theory, but the object of such a deception was more difficult to determine.

Sure enough, a taxicab was waiting at the entrance to

the court; and my visitor, having seated herself within, extended her hand to me, and even through the thick veil I could detect her brilliant smile.

"Thank you so much, Mr. Knox," she said, "and a thousand apologies. I am sincerely sorry to have given you all this trouble."

The cab drove off. For a moment I stood looking after it, in a state of dreamy incertitude, then turned and slowly retraced my steps. Reopening the door of my chambers with my key, I returned to my study and sat down at the table to endeavour to arrange the facts of what I recognized to be a really amazing episode. The adventure, trifling though it seemed, undoubtedly held some hidden significance that at present was not apparent to me. In accordance with the excellent custom of my friend, Paul Harley, I prepared to make notes of the occurrence while the facts were still fresh in my memory. At the moment that I was about to begin, I made an astounding discovery.

Although I had been absent only a few minutes, and had locked my door behind me, the pigtail was gone!

I sat quite still, listening intently. The woman's story of the yellow man on the stairs suddenly assumed a totally different aspect—a new and sinister aspect. Could it be that the pigtail was at the bottom of the mystery?—could it be that some murderous Chinaman who had been lurking in hiding, waiting his opportunity, had in some way gained access to my chambers during that brief absence? If so, was he gone?

From the table drawer I took out a revolver, ascertained that it was fully loaded, and turning up light after light as I proceeded, conducted a room-to-room search. It was without result; there was absolutely nothing to indicate that anyone had surreptitiously entered or departed from my chambers.

I returned to the study and sat gazing at the revolver lying on the blotting-pad before me. Perhaps my mind worked slowly, but I think that fully fifteen minutes must have passed before it dawned on me that the explanation

not only of the missing pigtail but of the other incidents
of the night, was simple enough. The yellow man had
been a fabrication, and my dark-eyed visitor had not
been in quest of "Raphael Philips," but in quest of the
pigtail: and her quest had been successful!

"What a hopeless fool I am!" I cried, and banged my
fist down upon the table, "there was no yellow man at
all—there was——"

My door bell rang. I sprang nervously to my feet,
glanced at the revolver on the table—and finally dropped
it into my coat pocket ere going out and opening the door.

On the landing stood a police constable and an officer
in plain clothes.

"Your name is Malcolm Knox?" asked the constable,
glancing at a note-book which he held in his hand.

"It is," I replied.

"You are required to come at once to Bow Street to
identify a woman who was found murdered in a taxi-cab
in the Strand about eleven o'clock to-night."

I suppressed an exclamation of horror; I felt myself
turning pale.

"But what has it to do——"

"The driver stated she came from your chambers, for
you saw her off, and her last words to you were 'Good
night, Mr. Knox, I am sincerely sorry to have given you
all this trouble.' Is that correct, sir?"

The constable, who had read out the information in an
official voice, now looked at me, as I stood there stupefied.

"It is," I said blankly. "I'll come at once."

It would seem that I had misjudged my unfortunate
visitor: her story of the yellow man on the stair had
apparently been not a fabrication, but a gruesome fact!

III

HOW I REGAINED IT

My ghastly duty was performed; I had identified the
dreadful thing, which less than an hour before had been

a strikingly beautiful woman, as my mysterious visitor. The police were palpably disappointed at the sparsity of my knowledge respecting her. In fact, had it not chanced that Detective Sergeant Durham was in the station, I think they would have doubted the accuracy of my story.

As a man of some experience in such matters, I fully recognized its improbability, but beyond relating the circumstances leading up to my possession of the pigtail and the events which had ensued, I could do no more in the matter. The weird relic had not been found on the dead woman, nor in the cab.

Now the unsavoury business was finished, and I walked along Bow Street, racking my mind for the master-key to this mystery in which I had become enmeshed. How I longed to rush off to Harley's rooms in Chancery Lane and to tell him the whole story! But my friend was a thousand miles away—and I had to see the thing out alone.

That the pigtail was some sacred relic stolen from a Chinese temple and sought for by its fanatical custodians was a theory which persistently intruded itself. But I could find no place in that hypothesis for the beautiful Jewess; and that she was intimately concerned I did not doubt. A cool survey of the facts rendered it fairly evident that it was she and none other who had stolen the pigtail from my rooms. Some third party—possibly the "yellow man" of whom she had spoken—had in turn stolen it from her, strangling her in the process.

The police theory of the murder (and I was prepared to accept it) was that the assassin had been crouching in hiding behind or beside the cab—or even within the dark interior. He had leaped in and attacked the woman at the moment that the taxi-man had started his engine; if already inside, the deed had proven even easier. Then, during some block in the traffic, he had slipped out unseen, leaving the body of the victim to be discovered when the cab pulled up at the hotel.

I knew of only one place in London where I might hope to obtain useful information, and for that place I was

making now. It was Malay Jack's, whence I had been
bound on the previous night when my strange meeting
with the seaman who then possessed the pigtail had led
to a change of plan. The scum of the Asiatic population
always come at one time or another to Jack's, and I
hoped by dint of a little patience to achieve what the
police had now apparently despaired of achieving—the
discovery of the assassin.

Having called at my chambers to obtain my revolver,
I mounted an eastward-bound motor-bus. The night, as I
have already stated, was exceptionally dark. There was
no moon, and heavy clouds were spread over the sky;
so that the deserted East End streets presented a sufficiently uninviting aspect, but one with which I was by
no means unfamiliar and which certainly in no way
daunted me.

Changing at Paul Harley's Chinatown base in Wade
Street, I turned my steps in the same direction as upon
the preceding night; but if my own will played no part
in the matter, then decidedly Providence truly guided
me. Poetic justice is rare enough in real life, yet I was
destined to-night to witness swift retribution overtaking
a malefactor.

The by-ways which I had trodden were utterly deserted; I was far from the lighted high road, and the only
signs of human activity that reached me came from the
adjacent river; therefore, when presently an outcry arose
from somewhere on my left, for a moment I really believed that my imagination was vividly reproducing the
episode of the night before!

A furious scuffle—between a European and an Asiatic—
was in progress not twenty yards away!

Realizing that such was indeed the case, and that I was
not the victim of hallucination, I advanced slowly in the
direction of the sounds, but my footsteps reëchoed hol-
lowly from wall to wall of the narrow passage-way, and
my coming brought the conflict to a sudden and dramatic
termination.

"Thought I wouldn't know yer ugly face, did yer?"

yelled a familiar voice. "No good squealin'—I got yer!
I'd bust you up if I could!" (a sound of furious blows
and inarticulate chattering) "but it ain't 'umanly possible
to kill a Chink——"

I hurried forward toward the spot where two dim figures were locked in deadly conflict.

"Take that to remember me by!" gasped the husky
voice as I ran up.

One of the figures collapsed in a heap upon the ground.
The other made off at a lumbering gait along a second
and even narrower passage branching at right angles from
that in which the scuffle had taken place.

The clatter of the heavy sea-boots died away in the
distance. I stood beside the fallen man, looking keenly
about to right and left; for an impression was strong
upon me that another than I had been witness of the
scene—that a shadowy form had slunk back furtively at
my approach. But the night gave up no sound in
confirmation of this, and I could detect no sign of any
lurker.

I stooped over the Chinaman (for a Chinaman it was)
who lay at my feet, and directed the ray of my pocket-
lamp upon his yellow and contorted countenance. I suppressed a cry of surprise and horror.

Despite the human impossibility referred to by the
missing fireman, this particular Chinaman had joined the
shades of his ancestors. I think that final blow, which
had felled him, had brought his shaven skull in such
violent contact with the wall that he had died of the
thundering concussion set up.

Kneeling there and looking into his upturned eyes, I
became aware that my position was not an enviable one,
particularly since I felt little disposed to set the law on
the track of the real culprit. For this man who now lay
dead at my feet was doubtless one of the pair who had
attempted the life of the fireman of the *Jupiter*.

That my seafaring acquaintance had designed to kill
the Chinaman I did not believe, despite his stormy words:
the death had been an accident, and (perhaps my morality

was over-broad) I considered the assault to have been justified.

Now my ideas led me further yet. The dead Chinaman wore a rough blue coat, and gingerly, for I found the contact repulsive, I inserted my hand into the inside pocket. Immediately my fingers closed upon a familiar object—and I stood up, whistling slightly, and dangling in my left hand the missing pigtail!

Beyond doubt Justice had guided the seaman's blows. This was the man who had murdered my dark-eyed visitor!

I stood perfectly still, directing the little white ray of my flashlight upon the pigtail in my hand. I realized that my position, difficult before, now was become impossible; the possession of the pigtail compromised me hopelessly. What should I do?

"My God!" I said aloud, "what does it all mean?"

"It means," said a gruff voice, "that it was lucky I was following you and saw what happened!"

I whirled about, my heart leaping wildly. Detective-Sergeant Durham was standing watching me, a grim smile upon his face!

I laughed rather shakily.

"Lucky indeed!" I said. "Thank God you're here. This pigtail is a nightmare which threatens to drive me mad!"

The detective advanced and knelt beside the crumpled-up figure on the ground. He examined it briefly, and then stood up.

"The fact that he had the missing pigtail in his pocket," he said, "is proof enough to my mind that he did the murder."

"And to mine."

"There's another point," he added, "which throws a lot of light on the matter. You and Mr. Harley were out of town at the time of the Huang Chow case; but the Chief and I outlined it, you remember, one night in Mr. Harley's rooms?"

"I remember it perfectly; the giant spider in the coffin——"

"Yes; and a certain Ah Fu, confidential servant of the old man, who used to buy the birds the thing fed on. Well, Mr. Knox, Huang Chow was the biggest dealer in illicit stuff in all the East End—and this battered thing at our feet is—Ah Fu!"

"Huang Chow's servant?"

"Exactly."

I stared, uncomprehendingly, and:

"In what way does this throw light on the matter?" I asked.

Durham—a very intelligent young officer—smiled significantly.

"I begin to see light!" he declared. "The gentleman who made off just as I arrived on the scene probably had a private quarrel with the Chinaman and was otherwise not concerned in any way."

"I am disposed to agree with you," I said guardedly.

"Of course, you've no idea of his identity?"

"I'm afraid not."

"We may find him," mused the officer, glancing at me shrewdly, "by applying at the offices of the Planet Line, but I rather doubt it. Also I rather doubt if we'll look very far. He's saved us a lot of trouble, but"—peering about in the shadowy corners which abounded—"didn't I see *somebody else* lurking around here?"

"I'm almost certain there was someone else!" I cried. "In fact, I could all but swear to it."

"H'm!" said the detective. "He's not here now. Might I trouble you to walk along to Limehouse Police Station for the ambulance? I'd better stay here."

I agreed at once, and started off.

Thus a second time my plans were interrupted, for my expedition that night ultimately led me to Bow Street, whence, after certain formalities had been observed, I departed for my chambers, the mysterious pigtail in my pocket. Failing the presence of Durham, the pigtail must have been retained as evidence, but:

"We shall know where to find it if it's wanted, Mr.

Knox," said the Yard man, "and I can trust you to look after your own property."

The clock of St. Paul's was chiming the hour of two when I locked the door of my chambers and prepared to turn in. The clangour of the final strokes yet vibrated through the night's silence when someone set my own door bell loudly ringing.

With an exclamation of annoyance I shot back the bolts and threw open the door.

A Chinaman stood outside upon the mat!

IV

HOW IT ALL ENDED

"Me wishee see you," said the apparition, smiling blandly; "me comee in?"

"Come in, by all means," I said without enthusiasm, and, switching on the light in my study, I admitted the Chinaman and stood facing him with an expression upon my face which I doubt not was the reverse of agreeable.

My visitor, who wore a slop-shop suit, also wore a wide-brimmed bowler hat; now, the set bland smile still upon his yellow face, he removed the bowler and pointed significantly to his skull.

His pigtail had been severed some three inches from the root!

"You gotchee my pigtail," he explained; "me callee get it—thank you."

"Thank you," I said grimly. "But I must ask you to establish your claim rather more firmly."

"Yessir," agreed the Chinaman.

And thereupon in tolerable pidgin English he unfolded his tale. He proclaimed his name to be Hi Wing Ho, and his profession that of a sailor, or so I understood him. While ashore at Suez he had become embroiled with some drunken seamen: knives had been drawn, and in the scuffle by some strange accident his pigtail had been severed. He had escaped from the conflict, badly frightened, and had run a great distance before he realized his loss. Since Southern Chinamen of his particular Tong hold their pigtails in the highest regard, he had instituted inquiries as soon as possible, and had presently learned from a Chinese member of the crew of the S. S. *Jupiter* that the precious queue had fallen into the hands of a fireman on that vessel. He (Hi Wing Ho) had shipped on the first available steamer bound for England, having in the meanwhile communicated with his friend on the *Jupiter* respecting the recovery of the pigtail.

"What was the name of your friend on the *Jupiter?*"

"Him Li Ping—yessir!"—without the least hesitation or hurry.

I nodded. "Go on," I said.

He arrived at the London docks very shortly after the *Jupiter*. Indeed, the crew of the latter vessel had not yet been paid off when Hi Wing Ho presented himself at the dock gates. He admitted that, finding the fireman so obdurate, he and his friend Li Ping had resorted to violence, but he did not seem to recognize me as the person who had frustrated their designs. Thus far I found his story credible enough, excepting the accidental severing of the pigtail at Suez, but now it became wildly improbable, for he would have me believe that Li Ping, or Ah Fu, obtaining possession of the pigtail (in what manner Hi Wing Ho protested that he knew not) he sought to hold it to ransom, knowing how highly Hi Wing Ho valued it.

I glared sternly at the Chinaman, but his impassive countenance served him well. That he was lying to me I no longer doubted; for Ah Fu could not have hoped to secure such a price as would justify his committing murder; furthermore, the presence of the unfortunate Jewess in the case was not accounted for by the ingenious narrative of Hi Wing Ho. I was standing staring at him and wondering what course to adopt, when yet again my restless door-bell clamoured in the silence.

Hi Wing Ho started nervously, exhibiting the first symptoms of alarm which I had perceived in him. My

mind was made up in an instant. I took my revolver from
the drawer and covered him.

"Be good enough to open the door, Hi Wing Ho,"
I said coldly.

He shrank from me, pouring forth voluble protestations.
"Open the door!"

I clenched my left fist and advanced upon him. He
scuttled away with his odd Chinese gait and threw open
the door. Standing before me I saw my friend Detective Sergeant Durham, and with him a remarkable tall
and very large-boned man whose square-jawed face
was deeply tanned and whose aspect was dourly Scot-
tish.

When the piercing eyes of this stranger rested upon Hi
Wing Ho an expression which I shall never forget entered
into them; an expression coldly murderous. As for the
Chinaman, he literally crumpled up.

"You rat!" roared the stranger.

Taking one long stride he stooped upon the Chinaman,
seized him by the back of the neck as a terrier might
seize him by the back of the neck as a terrier might
seize a rat, and lifted him to his feet.

"The mystery of the pigtail, Mr. Knox," said the detective, "is solved at last."

"Have ye got it?" demanded the Scotsman, turning to
me, but without releasing his hold upon the neck of Hi
Wing Ho.

I took the pigtail from my pocket and dangled it before
his eyes.

"Suppose you come into my study," I said, "and explain matters."

We entered the room which had been the scene of so
many singular happenings. The detective and I seated
ourselves, but the Scotsman, holding the Chinaman by
the neck as though he had been some inanimate bundle,
stood just within the doorway, one of the most gigantic
specimens of manhood I had ever set eyes upon.

"You do the talking, sir," he directed the detective; "ye
have all the facts."

While Durham talked, then, we all listened—excepting

the Chinaman, who was past taking an intelligent interest in anything, and who, to judge from his starting eyes, was being slowly strangled.

"The gentleman," said Durham—"Mr. Nicholson—arrived two days ago from the East. He is a buyer for a big firm of diamond merchants, and some weeks ago a valuable diamond was stolen from him——"

"By *this!*" interrupted the Scotsman, shaking the wretched Hi Wing Ho terrier fashion.

"By Hi Wing Ho," explained the detective, "whom you see before you. The theft was a very ingenious one, and the man succeeded in getting away with his haul. He tried to dispose of the diamond to a certain Isaac Cohenberg, a Singapore moneylender; but Isaac Cohenberg was the bigger crook of the two. Hi Wing Ho only escaped from the establishment of Cohenberg by dint of sandbagging the moneylender, and quitted the town by a boat which left the same night. On the voyage he was indiscreet enough to take the diamond from its hiding-place and surreptitiously to examine it. Another member of the Chinese crew, one Li Ping—otherwise Ah Fu, the accredited agent of old Huang Chow!—was secretly watching our friend, and, knowing that he possessed this valuable jewel, he also learned where he kept it hidden. At Suez Ah Fu attacked Hi Wing Ho and secured possession of the diamond. It was to secure possession of the diamond that Ah Fu had gone out East. I don't doubt it. He employed Hi Wing Ho—and Hi Wing Ho tried to double on him!

"We are indebted to you, Mr. Knox, for some of the data upon which we have reconstructed the foregoing and also for the next link in the narrative. A fireman ashore from the *Jupiter* intruded upon the scene at Suez and deprived Ah Fu of the fruits of his labours. Hi Wing Ho seems to have been badly damaged in the scuffle, but Ah Fu, the more wily of the two, evidently followed the fireman, and, deserting from his own ship, signed on with the *Jupiter*."

While this story was enlightening in some respects, it

was mystifying in others. I did not interrupt, however, for Durham immediately resumed:

"The drama was complicated by the presence of a fourth character—the daughter of Cohenberg. Realizing that a small fortune had slipped through his fingers, the old moneylender dispatched his daughter in pursuit of Hi Wing Ho, having learned upon which vessel the latter had sailed. He had no difficulty in obtaining this information, for he is in touch with all the crooks of the town. Had he known that the diamond had been stolen by an agent of Huang Chow, he would no doubt have hesitated. Huang Chow has an international reputation.

"However, his daughter—a girl of great personal beauty —relied upon her diplomatic gifts to regain possession of the stone, but, poor creature! she had not counted with Ah Fu, who was evidently watching your chambers (while Hi Wing Ho, it seems, was assiduously shadowing Ah Fu!). How she traced the diamond from point to point of its travels we do not know, and probably never shall know, but she was undeniably clever and unscrupulous. Poor girl! She came to a dreadful end. Mr. Nicholson, here, identified her at Bow Street to-night."

Now the whole amazing truth burst upon me.

"I understand!" I cried. "This"—and I snatched up the pigtail——

"That my pigtail," moaned Hi Wing Ho feebly.

Mr. Nicholson pitched him unceremoniously into a corner of the room, and taking the pigtail in his huge hand, clumsily unfastened it. Out from the thick part, some two inches below the point at which it had been cut from the Chinaman's head, a great diamond dropped upon the floor!

For perhaps twenty seconds there was perfect silence in my study. No one stooped to pick the diamond from the floor—the diamond which now had blood upon it. No one, so far as my sense informed me, stirred. But when, following those moments of stupefaction, we all looked up— Hi Wing Ho, like a phantom, had faded from the room!

H. DE VERE STACPOOLE

THE STORY OF O TOYO

I

"The faculty of taking notice is above all others most essential to the detective," said Mynheer Amayat, Chief of the Tovas detective agency of North Borneo. To illustrate his reasoning he told me this story of a girl who "took notice." She was not a detective but she did the work of one. I give the story in my own words.

It was spring in Nagasaki, and the wind from the Hwang Hai coming across Fukaeshima was blowing bowler hats away and playing with the abbreviated skirts of the mousmees.

Through the crying of hawks in the rose-gold of the sunset and the shouting of the newsboys could be heard from beyond the Bund the syren of the Empress of Japan putting out from Vancouver, sounds of the present strange enough here in the Streets of the Wrestlers, where the past still lingers in fragments—vestiges of the dream that was Old Japan.

In front of Nijinska's bar a blind man with the dust of all Hondo on his feet was playing a mournful tune on a flute, whilst on a flaw of the wind from the lane of Yami came the distant call of a wood seller, wailing and long-drawn-out — "Moyayamoya — moy — moyayamoya" answered from the shop of the insect seller across the street by the tiny dingling bell of some caged mushi.

But in the bar Nijinska, backed by his bottles, heard neither the song of the insect, nor the cry of the wood-seller, nor the appeal of the flute. Young Japan was good enough for him. Young Japan and old Europe in the form of its more doubtful ambassadors.

Nijinska's was, in fact, well known both to the police of Nagasaki and to the card men and chevaliers of the Pacific coasts.

It was here Crook Keene was arrested after his attempt on the Mitsubischi Bank, and it was here Lemberg shot himself in the back room, where an eternal fat Chinese croupier in a yellow-flowered jacket presides over an eternal game of roulette.

But happenings like those are rare even in a place like Nijinska's, where the chiefs of the kingdom of crookery find themselves well received on their travels, first, because when the Japanese police are going to arrest you they don't, as a rule, give you time to commit suicide, secondly because they prefer to pounce in the street after their quarry has left the tavern where he has been drinking, or the gambling room where he has been spending other people's money.

Adams and Peter Richepin, seated this evening drinking in the bar, knew all about the Japanese police and their ways.

They also knew all about the Chicago police, the New York police, and the London police; that was their beat. They never touched Paris or Berlin, for, after all, a man can't be everywhere, and besides the methods of Paris and Berlin detectives leave much to be desired from the point of view of the yegg-man.

They had been this time in Nagasaki for over a month, having travelled here all the way from Singapore on the trail of a dope-hound who was also half a millionaire —and just as they had gingered him up to play and with two clear days before them in which to skin him well and good, the purser had intervened with a quiet hint.

Adams and Richepin hated pursers; it was wicked of them, but they couldn't help it. A ship has two sets of eyes, external the captain's, internal, the purser's; pursers more than once had put thousands of good dollars out of the pockets of Adams and Richepin, and that was why they hated them.

They had spent a month in Nagasaki for fun and also for business purposes; they had mixed with a good many people, and passed with most as good coin, but they had done little business, though they had acquired a vast amount of information that might lead to business.

"All the same," said Adams, in reply to some remark of the other's, "it has been a rotten year for work—sunspots or something maybe."

He paused and looked up.

The swing door had opened to admit a man, a mediumsized, well-dressed man. He came in as if he knew the place, and, nodding to the barkeeper, ordered a cocktail, and then stood, walking-stick under arm, looking at the board where the sailing lists of the Toyo-Kisen-Kaisha and the Eastern and Australian steamship companies were exposed.

He wore a beard cut torpedo-fashion, and he might have been a drummer in silks or a pearl buyer, only he wasn't.

No, indeed, and Adams, before Richepin had time to turn his head had not only read the stranger's profession, but his name as clearly as though they had been written on his back.

"Jack," cried Adams, turning to Richepin, "there's Kent!"

"Gosh! so it is," cried the other, and at the same moment Kent turned on his heel for his cocktail, and, noticing the others clearly, now came forward.

"Hullo, Adams!"

Next minute they were all together round the same table. Adams, clean-shaved and iron-jawed, Richepin, hawknosed, narrow-browed, stamped with a hint of that Gallic ferocity which distinguishes some of the faces you will see on the wharves of Marseilles or the sea front at Bastia, and Kent, quiet and ordinary-looking and mild of voice, but far the most terrible of the three.

He had only arrived in Nagasaki the day before from

D. S.—VIII—11

a Canadian boat; he was staying at the Bay Hotel. He told all about himself and how times had been going since the three had met last in Chicago, and it would seem from his talk that luck had dealt with him as hardly as with the others.

But you never can tell; these men don't boast of the possession of money, one to the other; and, anyhow, and however luck may have dealt with him, he was well groomed, well clad and most evidently well fed.

Adams, whilst Richepin and the other talked, remained silent, his eyes fixed on the face of Kent. He looked puzzled, then his brows cleared and he slapped his thigh and laughed and turned to Richepin.

"Jack," said he, "don't you see the likeness?"

"Which—what d'you mean?" asked Jack.

"Tanner," replied Adams. "Ain't he the spit and image of Billy Kent?"

"Sure," said Richepin after a moment's pause. "I seen the likeness at once, but I didn't seem to connect it up in my mind. Billy, you haven't got a long lost twin brother by any chance—for if so, he's here in Nagasaki doing fine under the name of Tanner."

"Is that so?" said Kent, "well, I'm glad he's prospering, notwithstanding the fact I was born single—Tanner, what's his business?"

"Jap curios," replied Adams, "and pearls. He does the two businesses separate. Got a shop in the concession. Me and Jack's met in with him and been to his place, had drinks and a look round. He wanted to sell us an idol, and we might have bought it only there was nothing doing, he won't play cards—don't drink, shoves the whisky under your nose, but opens a tonic water for himself. We turned him down after examining all his possibilities, so to speak. It's this cursed teetotalism is playing the cat and racket with things. The world's turning drier than bone dust, seems to me, and it's only in the States one has a chance these days of makin' the two ends meet."

Richepin had pushed his empty glass aside and was

sitting with his elbows on the table and his head in his hands, thinking.

That intellect swift as a hawk and subtle as a snake was sweeping above and wriggling round a problem. He broke out:

"We've got to make something of that—here's Providence giving us a chance, but there don't seem a handle to it. Here's two gentlemen as like as peas, one with a wad of notes, so to speak, and the other in want of dollars——"

"You're talking through your hat," cut in Kent. "There's not two chaps ever so much alike you can't tell one from the other. S'pose me and this guy were spit and images of one another and I'm only taking your word—stick us together and there's no man wouldn't see the difference."

"Maybe not in 'Urope," replied Richepin, "but Asia's different. Now I'll tell you. There was a ship built for the Chinks in Frisco harbour, and a Chink crew came to take her over and a bright young American girl she went and married one of them, and he did the natural and bunked from her when sailing day came. She got aboard after him to claim him, and the captain he lined the whole crew up and told her to pick out her man—and she couldn't.

"They were all different, no doubt; a Chink could have picked out one from the other, but she couldn't.

"In a way, it's the same with the Japs. Of course, they can tell the difference between a lantern-jawed slab like Adams and a good-looking chap like me, but get two chaps reasonably alike, not to speak of twin images, and they'd be done. Now if we could fix up any sort of business deal between Tanner and a Jap—pearls, f'r instance—mind all those pearls he showed us, Adams, in that big safe in his private room?"

"Showed you them, did he?" asked Kent.

"Sure. Free as if they were lumps of sugar. What reason would he have not, seeing they're covered by insurance, and we were honest American gentlemen, Mr. Stater—

berger and Mr. Hoover, of Rhode Island—weren't we, Ad.?"

"Sure," said Adams, "and Mrs. Hoover was at Nagoya, but coming along with a carpet-sweeper to sweep up net-sukes and any jade ornaments she could get at a reason-able price—remember that rose jade stuff he took out of the safe, Jack, and gave us to handle?—never bothered—lord, that's the insurance companies—the trust-inspirin' insurance companies—here's luck to them."

"But get back," said Kent, "suppose it's all as you say, where's the plan or the making of one?"

"It's buzzing in my head, but I can't catch it," replied Richepin. "It looks to me like a Jap merchant he'd take parcel of pearls to—no—it looks to me as if Mr. Hoover, staying at his hotel, sent to Mr. Tanner for a parcel of pearls to look at, see, the Jap messenger would bring them and wait whilst Mr. Hoover was looking at them. Then in would come Mr. Tanner himself—he always dresses in grey tweed, so we'd have to get you a suit to match, Billy—and he'd speak to Mr. Hoover, and Hoover would say to the Jap messenger: 'Your master says you can go, he'll take back the pearls himself!'"

"All that's too damn complicated," cut in Kent, whose genius was as much greater than the genius of the two others as was his daring and wickedness, "besides, it's too risky for a fistful of pearls. I want the safe—meaning all it contains, pearls and jade and maybe, money as well."

"You can't break into that place," said Adams, "the Jap assistants sleep there. We found out that."

"Who's talking of breaking in?"

"Of course," said Richepin, filled with sudden light and admiration. "Bill, you're a great man. I kow-tow, I put your foot on my head; why, Ad., you sumph, can't you see, he'll walk in as Tanner——"

"I see," said Adams, "but we'd have to get Tanner away."

"Naturally."

Meanwhile, Kent sat brooding, disregardless of the others as though they were children.

Then he spoke:

"There might be business in it," said he, "but it would take a month to frame up. First, I'd have to see this guy without him seeing me to make sure of the likeness. I don't take no man's word for that. Second, the clothes— you say Tanner always is dressed in grey; that means you've always seen him in grey—he may change to blue or Lord knows what. That doesn't matter much, it would be in the evening; the only thing is, he mustn't be called away in grey and come back in black. Then the hat—the whole of that business would have to be worked out fine. Detail is everything."

"Come a burst of hot weather, everyone will be in white or tussore," said Adams.

"Better still," said Kent. "Well, all that would have to be prepared for. Then again, you two guys would have to be in it up to the neck; it's a three-man job—and after it was done you'd have to change your looks so's to cover traces and get away."

"No," said Adams, "you're out there, Kent. Our passports wouldn't allow for that; where we'd have to change our looks would be here in Nagasaki or wherever we were handling the job. F'r instance, suppose I went to some place to send this chap a 'phone message that would fetch him away, I'd have to turn myself into another man in the train or somewhere before I went to the hotel to do the 'phoning. Same here in Nagasaki, wherever we touch the business. We mustn't leave no face prints behind us, but that's easy. As f'r you, when the job's finished the sweep of a razor would turn you into someone else."

"When all your talk's done, if you'll let me put in a word," said Richepin, "I'd advise, if you want to take up this business, that we'd put the whole matter in Jink's hands."

"Nijinska?"

"Yep. When the devil had done making eels, it's my belief he had a bit of stuff over and made it into Jinks; he's in everything from cocaine to faked passports, and for 10 per cent. on the profits he'd do all the details of the business, including the 'phoning and fooling Tanner's servants, and what's more, he'd dispose of the goods, and where his hand is mixed in any business all's as safe and innocent as buying doughnuts with silver dollars."

"Well, there's something in that," said Kent.

The determining point in the business, the something that threatened Tanner, was the fact the Kent had not lied when declaring that he had had a run of bad luck.

This was so. He wanted money and wanted it badly, badly as the questing tiger wants meat.

II

Tanner's shop is next to the new National Bank building, which stands on the site of the tea-house of the Tortoise, a house of entertainment long gone before the sweeping broom of Western civilisation.

The shop was long and broad, communicating by a passage with the room where Tanner lived and slept. Stairs on the left of the passage led to a lumber-room and the servants' quarters.

The sleeping arrangements of Japan enable one to subtract almost entirely the bed element from a bed-sitting-room.

Tanner slept on a *futon* under a blue gauze mosquito-net. The whole thing could be rolled up and put away out of sight; and, for washing arrangements, there was the bathroom opening by a panel door on the right of the sitting-room when you entered.

He had meals at a café—that is to say, dinner and sometimes luncheon; for the rest he depended on his servants, who were also his shop assistants.

From the servants' quarters, when he clapped his hands and gave the order, would come cups of tea borne by O Toyo, the little girl shop assistant, parlourmaid and watchdog (she slept in the shop at night on a *futon* under a blue gauze mosquito-net, just like Tanner's), and sometimes, staying in to lunch, the same hands would bring him a tray of tiny dishes—tunny, seaweed soup, lily roots, rice, with the inevitable saki bottle, and all conjured up from who knows where and without smell of cooking.

Sayémon no doubt could have told. He was the eldest male shop assistant; he wore horn spectacles, could price a Hiroshige print or get the better of any dealer over an Owari vase. Yet, called down by Tanner one day in a hurry from the servants' quarters, he came with a frying-pan in his hand, so betraying himself.

Goto, the apprentice, messenger, duster of idols and general slave of all work, was the youngest, younger even than O Toyo, who was only fifteen.

III

O Toyo did not wear silk stockings, at least she did not show them; in the house she wore white socks (*tabi*) that peeped beneath the edge of her kimono; in the streets she wore clogs. She was very antiquated, despite her age, and on dark nights carried a coloured paper lantern on the end of a little stick.

O Toyo, in fact, was a fragment of Old Japan. When Old Japan tumbled down the trick staircase set for it by Western civilisation and smashed itself to pieces there were lots of pieces left like O Toyo scattered here and there in Yezo, in Hondo, in Kiushiu and these cities, including the great city of Nagasaki, but there were few pieces prettier or more delicate and dainty.

She was scented like a flower, with a scent of her own, like the taste of vanilla made olfactory and crossed with the reminiscence of verbena once smelt in a dream, her hair was glossy with camellia oil without being ropey and her face had expression.

Finally, like Sayémon and Goto, she was Tanner's very devoted servant, and like them a true assistant in his dealing with the one god truly worshipped by the whole world, Diakoku—the god of wealth.

Not that Tanner was a blind worshipper of the deity. He made money by selling things, and he was rather tight-fisted and a not too generous master to these three servants who looked so well after his interests—all the same he loved the things that he sold when they were worth loving.

A passion for a tripping mousmee in ivory, seven inches high and carrying an open ivory umbrella pictured with storks, had lost him a most valuable customer also consumed with love for the lady, yet with sense enough to refuse the prohibitive price asked by her owner, and there was a rose jade plaque the size of a dollar, old Chinese carved and most lovely, in that safe of his, a plaque that no customer had ever seen, because he could not bear to part with it.

It was different with the Miochin bronzes and the Thibetan ghost daggers and carved masks, netsukes and whatnot that formed the movable furniture of the shop, things made to be sold, and amidst which to-day Tanner stood stroking his brown beard looking at a newly-acquired joss and talking to Sayémon.

"Sayémon," said Tanner, "I am called away to-day to Shimanara on the matter of some pearls which a lady wishes to sell. I go by the evening train, so that I will not return before to-morrow. Meanwhile, I leave all in your charge. You can deal with any customers that come in my absence. You will, of course, sleep in my room as usual when I am away."

Sayémon bowed.

He was used to looking after the place, and he felt no fear of not being able to deal with any customers that might turn up and no fear of robbers—the bolts and bars were too strong, there was a telephone, and robbers had never yet come.

Tanner, having given his instructions, went to his room, and at the appointed time, leaving the shop with a small attaché case in his hand, he got into a rickshaw and departed for the railway station.

IV

After he had gone came in a tourist, a woman with a blue veil tied round her hat; she was accompanied by a guide, and, after looking about her and after quarter of an hour's haggling, she bought a netsuke, price five yen, and departed.

Sayémon was used to customers like this, and having rearranged the tray of netsukes and smoked a whiff or two of tobacco from a pipe with a tiny bowl, he composed himself to do some accounts in a long notebook with a lizard skin cover, whilst Goto, who had been put to polish some brasses, pursued his job, and O Toyo, seated on the matting like a tiny tailor, worked on some embroidery that required mending.

Not a word from the three, one to the other, whilst from the street outside came the sound of the passers-by and the crying of the evening newspapers.

The picture houses would be filling now for the first house, and the cheap restaurants putting out their menus. Sayémon, as if in recognition of the fact or as though the dusk had dictated the order, reached out a hand without lifting his eyes from his accounts and turned on the electric; a few minutes later and in came Tanner!

O Toyo, Goto and Sayémon lifted their heads and stared at their master so unexpectedly returned, but he scarcely seemed to see them, for he was not alone.

He had brought in with him a companion, an American in horn-rimmed spectacles, and they were talking—at least, the American was talking, and so furiously that Tanner seemed unable to get in a word.

There was evidently some important deal on, and it was likely that Tanner had broken off his journey and come back with this stranger, so thought O Toyo, Goto and Sayémon as the two men paused whilst the American pressed home some argument that had to do with the sentence: "Well, Mr. Tanner, a thousand dollars is neither here nor there if you'll agree to the other terms I've just been indicating."

Tanner, without replying, and evidently turning things over in his mind, nodded to the three assistants, as, with hand on the American's arm, he led him along past the figure of Diakoku, the God of Wealth, past the stand of swords and the long glass case of ivory masks to the door of the passage leading to his private room.

Here they entered and closed the door.

The American took off the pair of horn-rimmed spectacles, also a moustache, and became Adams.

"Well," said Adams, "that's that. They haven't suspected, for I watched their faces, and you did it beautiful. I will say it."

"Put it down to Jinks," said Kent. "If he hadn't found out the sort of attaché case this guy takes with him on his nights out, we'd have been done. Those chaps' eyes in the shop out there were like gimlets."

He put the attaché case on the table, sat down on a chair by the desk and turned his eyes on the safe. His specialty was safes. Contrasted with the modern American safes, this was a simple affair—a simple-minded old English safe that had come out to India maybe forty years ago, and then had been sold off to one of the dealers who supply the further East with office ironmongery.

All the same, it would take him nearly an hour to open it—maybe more.

There were cigarettes and matches on the desk. He lit a cigarette; he had not smoked it half through when he crossed himself. Suppose Tanner was a non-smoker and kept cigarettes only for customers? The idea was improbable; yet high-class burglary is a fine art that takes cognisance of the minutest detail.

Well, anyhow, the thing was done and the evidence in the form of fresh tobacco scent could not be removed, so he might as well go on.

He finished the cigarette, rose, stretched himself and immediately sat down again. What was that? A faint jingle.

He had left the door slightly open so that he would not have to reply to a knock. Yet a knock came, from the corner of a tray borne by Goto, a tray containing a whisky decanter, soda-siphon and glasses.

Goto came in. His master, seated at the desk writing, glanced round with a little irritable movement as though angry at being disturbed, and went on with his writing.

Goto, imperturbable as the Sphinx, placed the tray on the table, and then, going to a corner and drawing a curtain, took out a *futor*, which he placed on the floor, a lighter one for coverlet, a pillow and a mosquito-curtain with a bar arrangement, which he proceeded to set up. Then he withdrew, closing the door behind him.

Gosh! What was this? A native bed set out for him! Had Adams misfired and forgotten to tell them that he was going out at midnight? If he hadn't, why the bed?

Was it just stupidity on that Jap's part or did he think that his master would want to snatch a sleep before going out?

Who could tell? Anyhow, he could now lock the door, and he did so. Then he stood looking at the bed.

If Adams had forgotten, or suddenly got cold feet, he (Kent) was trapped. To knock the assistants up at twelve o'clock might be fatal, or to try to open the shop door, sure to be securely fastened. And, oh, just remembered fact! It was on the bill that the girl slept in the shop!

Yes, if Adams had forgotten all was up.

He wiped the palms of his hands and turned to the safe, then, getting his tools from the attaché case, he set to work.

Never had he found himself in a position like this before. He had worked against time and against chance, but never with uncertainty as to his tools. He had always gone sure of himself, because sure of his preparations and his assistants.

He remembered now that this sort of thing was not Adams's specialty. Confidence business, card business, the disposal of notes not manufactured by Uncle Sam, the evasion of Customs laws—you could not touch Adams there, but this——

Well, well, the rat in the trap must use its teeth, not

stop to think, and, taking off his coat and opening the
attaché case, he set to work on the safe.

The thing was surprisingly easy, a new lock must have
been put on by some Eastern hand innocent of the cunning of the West in these matters, and ten minutes suf-
ficed to do the business.

The door of the safe opened on its hinges and there,
sure enough, was the plunder. Tin cases which, on opening,
disclosed pearls between layers of cotton wool. Jade ornaments, and, seated amidst the jade stuff like the guardian
of the safe, a solid gold cat, a crown weighing maybe an
ounce embellished with eyes, one a ruby and one a sap-
phire.

V

Meanwhile Goto, having returned to the shop, helped in
tidying up for the night. This business finished, the three
trooped up to the servants' quarters and the two men
sat down on the floor whilst O Toyo, with the rapidity of
a conjurer, served them with plates and a variety of
little dishes taken from a safe, also with rice which had
been kept hot in a bowl which had thermos-flask qualities.

She folded up and sat on the floor with the others, but
she did not eat, she had a headache; she was, in fact,
white as paper, and Sazémon, who had no holding with
fal-lals, instead of sympathising with her reminded her
that she had not set about preparing Tanner's supper.

"For he maybe will not have eaten," said Sazémon. "At
all events, you had better go see."

O Toyo rose and took a tray and began putting things
on it. Tanner, if he did not dine out, generally took
something light about this hour, leaving the choice of
things entirely to O Toyo.

Turning round, she magically cooked two eggs, and,
having heaped the tray with other things, left the room
and descended the stairs vaguely lit by the light from the
passage; but she did not go towards Tanner's room, she
turned instead to the shop.

The shop was lit. An electric permanently burning showed the gods, the monsters and the knight in armour with great slashes of shadow and points of brilliant reflection from wiry or polished steel.

Here, bending down, she placed the tray in a space of shadow and knelt beside it, a little soft figure, the lamplight touching the blue silk of her kimono. Her shoulders trembled, she was weeping.

A minute passed, then, rising and leaving the tray where it was, she came to the passage and stood looking at the door of Tanner's room, as if undecided. Then, suddenly, and like a fired rocket, she rushed up the stairs, burst into the room where the others were still seated, slithered down on the floor on hands and knees and, projecting her head like a tortoise, turned their souls with terror as she whispered:

"It is not the master in the room below—he did not come in. It was one in his image." She spoke with such assurance that Goto opened his fingers wide with terror.

"Is it then a demon?" asked Goto.

"No, perhaps, I do not know—perhaps it is a robber (dorobo)."

"Did you speak with him?" asked Sazemon.

"No. I did not go into the room. The food I placed in the shop."

"Then how know you——?"

"I know."

"Now that is dreams and foolishness," said Sazemon. "It was the master, I saw him—he is there waiting for the stranger who is to come at twelve."

"It will soon be that now," said Goto.

They spoke in whispers.

"Come," said Sazemon. "I will go down and see."

He left the room and came down the stairs, the others following. They walked softly on tiptoe, and in the passage the brave Sazemon paused; he did not go to the door of Tanner's room, he turned to the shop.

"We will sit here for a while," whispered he, "and wait for the coming of the stranger, to make sure; if it is

indeed the master in his room he would be angry were
he disturbed."

They sat down in the shop.

"Let O Toyo take in the tray of food," whispered Goto.
"Then she can see for certain."

But Sazemon somehow did not care for this suggestion.
O Toyo had managed to infect him, despite his brave
words, with a superstitious dread.

Suppose a demon were in there in the form of his master?
(And in fact such was the case.) Suppose it should come
out? Well, anyhow, the situation would settle itself if the
stranger came back. *He* was real enough, for Sazémon had
spoken to him, and demons don't inquire about motor-cars.

Oh, it was all nonsense—a fancy of the girl's; all the
same, it was curious that the master had not rung for his
supper—he would surely want something to eat, unless he
had eaten in company with the stranger—or was not hungry.

There was a telephone in the corner of the shop, and
his mind strayed towards it. But were he to ring up the
police on a false alarm like this what would Tanner say?

He would say: "You damn fool, why didn't you come
in and speak to me?" and Sazemon could only answer:
"I was afraid." No, they would wait till the stranger came
back—anyhow, they were guarding the shop, and who-
ever was in the room could not get out.

VI

At three minutes to twelve Kent, attaché case stuffed
with loot and the café closed, was smoking his sixth
cigarette. The room was hazy. He had not touched the
whisky. Better perhaps for him if he had, for his nerves
had almost reached the breaking strain.

Adams wouldn't come. Twelve o'clock. Two minutes
past. The Brute, The Beast, The Fool—stay, what was
that? The ring of a bell. He picked up the attaché case
and came to the door and opened it.

Sound of bars giving from the shop. A voice—Adams's
loud, cheery voice. Salvation!

He came along down the passage to the shop whose door was open. Sazémon and Goto, seeing truly their master in the flesh, bowed before him, and in another moment he might have been in the street had not something almost tripped him up. It was O Toyo. She had flung herself before him and was clinging to his legs. She was shrieking, and her shrieks filled the street outside: "Dorobo—Dorobo—Dorobo!"

"Hell!" shouted Kent.

His nerves had smashed. He tore her away from his legs and dashed her behind him. Sazemon and Goto at the sight closed on him. Adams rushed in, and then— shouts, screams, stampings—gods and josses and bronzes and masks dashed hither and thither—and then a whistle, closed doors and the Japanese police in charge of the situation armed with flashlights and guns.

Now I wonder had Nijinska anything to do with the appearance of that police squad?

VII

"But, O Toyo," said Tanner in the hospital next day, where the girl was lying with a broken shoulder. "How did you know it was not me, since Sazemon and Goto were deceived?"

"Because," she replied, "always on your going upon or retiring from a journey I have noticed that you have touched the god Daiokoku for luck, and last night you did not touch him; also—I knew."

Tanner laughed.

"That is so, but why have you watched me so closely, O Toyo?"

Her eyes half rose, fell, and then rose fully to his face. She did not speak the words with her lips, but with her eyes.

"O Master—because I loved you."

That was how Daikoku gave wealth to Tanner, for, though these mixed marriages are not always successful, his was.

GILBERT FRANKAU

THE TRAGEDY AT ST. TROPEZ

I

"CHI LIN, SIR MARCUS," I read out from the only English "Who's Who" between Toulon and San Raphael. "Knight, Created 1922. Born 1868."

"*C'est lui*," said Kyra. "Tell us all it says."

They had burst in on me, my lovely little Roumanian friend and the head of our district Secret Service, while I was breakfasting. But though I could see that both were excited, neither had vouchsafed any reason for disturbing me at so early an hour.

"Sir Marcus," I went on, "has been twice married. The second marriage, to a Miss Selene Wu, took place three years ago. He is childless; and was educated in Shanghai —at a native university. His business is finance. He possesses about twenty English and Chinese decorations. His hobby is yachting. He gives two addresses—one in London and one in Singapore. And now tell me why you require information about this distinguished Oriental at seven-thirty a.m."

"We require it," said Kyra, who can never resist a touch of the melodramatic, "because the big yacht which you and I saw anchor off St. Tropez yesterday evening is Sir Marcus Chi Lin's *Sea Joy;* and because in it Sir Marcus is lying, or rather sitting, dead."

"And he has died," continued the Chef de la Sûreté, who is also a bit of a melodramatist, "in circumstances which are so peculiar that the gendarmerie at St. Tropez had no option but to telegraph for me."

"Are you going to tell me those circumstances?" I asked.

"We are going to do more than that," smiled Kyra. "We are going to implore your assistance. We need an interpreter, quickly, both to help us interrogate witnesses, and to translate"—she paused, while the Chief drew a paper from his pocket—"this."

"This," handed across my breakfast-tray, proved to be a half-completed letter, headed "S.Y. *Sea Joy*," with the previous evening's date. Addressed, by a queer coincidence, to the head of the firm who are my own London solicitors, and marked "Confidential," it read:—

"My dear Carthers: I am sorry to trouble you. But on going through the entries in my private pass-book, just received from the Bank of England, I find various cheques—noticeably one for three thousand pounds, debited on May the seventh—which I cannot recollect having drawn. The pass-book is enclosed. The cheques about which I am doubtful, all of which you will note have been paid to bearer, I have starred with a red cross. As it will be at least six months before I return to England, would you mind going personally to the Bank and inquiring if the clerk who paid over the money for these starred cheques can possibly recollect who——"

"Who got the money, of course," I explained as I finished my careful translation. "He was writing this when he died, I gather?"

"Yes," said Kyra. "Alone in the yacht's library. They found a half-empty tumbler beside him. We suspect that the tumbler contained poison. Fortunately, Doctor Lancart is holiday-making at St. Tropez. He is analysing for us. Now won't you please come and interpret for us, like a dear?"

II

I continue repeating, while I remain the chronicler of her adventures, that I am not sentimentally interested in Kyra Sokratesco. Still, she certainly looked her boyish

best, bare-legged, in short white skirt and thin jumper,
as I took the tiller of my new twenty-knot motor-boat,
and we shot out across the blue Mediterranean bay.

"Strange," I remember thinking, "that anyone so attractive should be living alone, in this out-of-the-way part
of the South of France. Stranger still, that she should
prefer the investigation of what is at best a sordid business, Crime, to the gaieties of Paris or Cannes, of Monte
Carlo or her own Bucharest."

For quite apart from the various little mysteries we
have investigated together, there is also—about Kyra
herself—a mystery. And perhaps a tiny hint of that mystery revealed itself to me when—pardon the pride in
my recently-acquired seamanship—I brought my brand-
new boat smartly to the lowered gang-plank of the eight-
hundred-ton *Sea Joy*, and the three of us went aboard.

There is a way of going aboard yachts—and that way
was obviously Kyra's. The captain, a grizzled man in the
fifties, with lips like a rat-trap, noticed it immediately.
I could see, by the very salute of him, that he was impressed.

"We bring a translator," said Kyra, in her quaint
English; and introduced me.

"I'm glad you've come, sir," said the captain. "Nobody
on board speaks French, except Sir Marcus's secretary;
and his isn't up to much."

The four of us, the skipper leading, retired to his
cabin. As we went, I noticed two of the local gendarmes,
obviously on guard.

"Tell your friends," said Captain Middleton, once we
four were seated, "that nothing's been disturbed. Nobody's been into the library. Mr. Vivian, Sir Marcus's
secretary, is just having breakfast. Lady Marcus will see
them if necessary. But, of course, she's a bit overcome."
Then, "So that there sha'n't be any misunderstanding,"
he repeated what he knew of Sir Marcus's death.

His story was of the simplest. The *Sea Joy* had left
Marseilles, where she had called only for food and letters,
about eleven the previous morning. The short trip had

been uneventful. At eight o'clock they had anchored off St. Tropez. At eight-thirty, dinner had been served to the three passengers. At ten, Sir Marcus had retired to his library. At ten-thirty, his own steward had taken him his usual "grog-tray." At half-past eleven, the same steward—entering to remove the grog-tray—had found him at his desk, dead.

"I advised the authorities at once," ended Captain Middleton. "It's the only thing to do in foreign ports, you see. But I don't know why they're making all this fuss about things. If it's what I think it is, just an ordinary case of heart-failure——"

"Leave him," interrupted Kyra in quick Roumanian, "under that impression. Tell him we want to see first the steward, then the secretary. We're expecting Doctor Lancart. Tell him the doctor is to be brought straight to this cabin as soon as he comes on board."

I transmitted these orders; and could not help being aware, as I did so, of the captain's cold grey eyes, watching first Kyra, then the detective. "He knows more than he'll tell," I decided; and the decision confirmed itself when the steward, straight-faced and very English, came in.

Him, too, the captain watched—anxiously, as though doubtful what he might reveal.

"I prepared Sir Marcus's tray as usual," the steward told us. "Sir Marcus always had the same things—his little whisky decanter, his little ice-bucket, half a bottle of Perrier straight out of the refrigerator, and one glass. I put the tray in its usual place—on the ledge under the port-hole."

"Under which port-hole?" The question came from the Chief. "There are two in the library."

"The starboard one, sir."

"Was it open?"

"Yes, sir. Both port-holes were open."

"He says port-holes." This was Kyra, again speaking Roumanian. "But they're really windows. They give straight on to the deck."

The steward, withdrawing, received the order, "Ask Sir Marcus's secretary to come up." But before the secretary put in an appearance, one of the gendarmes entered without knocking to say, "Il y à Monsieur le Docteur Lancart. He wishes to speak privately"—and the Chief of the Sûreté, followed by Kyra, went on deck.

Alone with me, Captain Middleton's attitude was purely conventional. "A painful business," he declared. "Very painful for everybody—especially Lady Marcus." But when Kyra and the Chief came back to us, I sensed perturbation in him. Nor did the shock seem entirely unanticipated when I translated: "You had better tell him the truth. Sir Marcus was poisoned. Doctor Lancart has no doubt about it. Though by what poison, we do not yet know."

"Poisoned!" was all he said. "But who could have poisoned him?"

"That," I retorted, just to see how he would take it, "is what my two friends are here to find out."

He took my retort well; though I could see it worried him. But when the secretary came in, I forgot all about the captain in sheer pleased surprise.

For Vivian, Sir Marcus's secretary, and I had been at school together; and in the Far East before the War. The War had altered him, as it alters all of us. His dark hair, though still curly, had gone grey at the temples. A grey moustache covered the mouth—which I remembered as full-lipped, and slightly ascetic. He seemed to have grown taller and thinner. But his voice, and his hand-clasp, were the same.

"Well!" he said. "What are you doing in this *galère*, Gilbert?" And when I told him, "I'm glad. It was my idea they should get hold of somebody English. My French isn't up to official cross-examination. Not by a yard."

Vivian, always the coolest of mortals, had very little to tell us. He had been Sir Marcus's secretary ever since his marriage. On the previous evening, after Sir Marcus had retired to his library, he had sat with Lady Marcus until she went to bed at about ten-thirty. He himself had been in bed by eleven. "Of course, when the skipper woke me up and told me what had happened, it was a bit of a shock."

But when, at the Chief's bidding, I told him, "Look here, old chap, you'd better know everything; these friends of mine are practically certain that Sir Marcus was poisoned," his coolness left him—and he could only stammer, "Poisoned. Poisoned. Good God!"

"This is too ghastly," he said when he had recovered himself. "Has Lady Marcus been told yet?"

"No." I spoke in English. "Nobody knows except yourself and the captain."

"And nobody shall know," chipped in Kyra—also speaking English; "until we have made search of the ship." Then, to me in French, she went on. "Ask him if he knows the whereabouts of Sir Marcus's bank-books; who has charge of the money on board; and where Sir Marcus usually kept his personal keys."

"Sir Marcus," answered Vivian, "always kept his personal keys on him. You will find them, I imagine, attached to his watch-chain. His bank-books he kept in the middle drawer of the bureau at which he died. The money on board, which was made up to the full two hundred pounds at Marseilles yesterday, is in the safe in the dining-salon. The safe is a letter-lock one, of which only Sir Marcus and myself knew the combination."

"Write down the combination, please," demanded the Chef de la Sûreté—and after Vivian had written it for him, the search began.

I did not take part in that search. Neither did Vivian. We sat alone, in the captain's cabin, for the best part of two hours. And it was only towards the end of those two hours that I became aware of Vivian's nervousness; that it semed to me that he, in the same way as Captain Middleton, knew more than he would tell. Every now and again, too, he seemed to be on the verge of some confidence; and once, when I said, "I hope to goodness they don't give me the job of breaking the truth to

Lady Marcus," the queerest look betrayed itself in his dark eyes.

"Yes," he said slowly, "that'll be a rotten job, who-ever has to do it." And after that a constraint fell be-tween us; so that I felt glad, almost inordinately so, to see Kyra at the door.

Kyra came through the door, which was curtained, alone. Her mood seemed almost nonchalant. She nodded pleasantly to Vivian, saying, "Excuse us, won't you?" as she drew me outside. But once outside, her mood, in-deed her whole face, changed.

"That man," she said quickly. "Is he a friend of yours? Have you known him long? Tell me all you know about him? Has he ever been in the East?"

"He was in the East three years, rubber-planting," I began. "He's a gentleman by birth—with a little money of his own, I imagine. A bit of a rolling-stone. But noth-ing against him. A very ordinary English Public School type."

"Married?" asked Kyra.

"No."

"*Pour les femmes?*" (The French phrase is untranslat-able.)

"I should say not."

"But no St. Anthony?"

"Perhaps. Perhaps not. It would depend on circum-stances. But what the blazes are you driving at, Kyra?"

"Hold thy tongue. *Tache da lingura!*" she whispered suddenly—and as she did so the curtain rustled over the doorway of the captain's cabin and a shadow fell between us on the deck.

The shadow was a woman's; and a whiff of exotic per-fume accompanied it; and a minute later, Vivian, emerg-ing from the cabin, had presented us to his employer's wife.

To write that Lady Marcus Chi Lin was beautiful, would be an understatement. She possessed that rare ex-quisiteness which is sometimes given to the half-caste; and her eyes were the almonds of the East. Age, she had

none, though I judged her nearing the thirties. Her
European yachting-costume was of the simplest; but
pearls worth many thousands glistened at the lotus-flower
of her throat.

"I came to find you, Charles," she said, having ac-
knowledged our presentation without a handshake. "My
amah (maid) tells me that there are policemen on board;
that they are searching all the cabins. Will you please
inform me, and at once, why?"

There was something regal about Lady Marcus; and
we must have stood before her, all three of us, for the
best part of fifteen seconds, silent, looking like courtiers—
that is to say, like fools. Then, swiftly, before either
Vivian or myself could stop her, Kyra said, in that broken
English of hers: "We search the ship, my lady, because
somebody have poisoned your husband—and we must
know who."

What Kyra expected, I discovered later. What I expected was a shriek, a fainting fit. What actually happened was a perfect exhibition of Oriental self-control.
Nothing about Lady Marcus displayed the slightest emo-
tion. Hands, lips, eyelids, cheek muscles—every feature,
in that supreme instant, might have been carved stone.

"You are sure of this," she said at last.

"Quite sure, my lady."

"Then find me the poisoner, and quickly, so that he too
may die."

III

On the Côtes des Maures, where murder is an everyday commonplace, thieving only another name for business, and the coins current of every man's conversation
the quarter truth, the half-truth, and the full downright
lie, one decency of civilization is nevertheless sacred—
and that, the midday meal.

We took ours—Kyra, the Chief, and I—at the villa, all
embowered with bougainvillæa, which Doctor Lancart, the
famous Parisian analyst, had taken for his holiday, and
suddenly converted to his work.

There were test-tubes, and an electric heater, on the
side-table of the one living-room; and every now and then
the little ferret-eyed scientist jumped up from his
bouillabaisse to see how the work went on.

"I lack everything," he kept on saying. "The fool
chemist here has none of the reagents." And every time
he said this, the Chief and Kyra looked at one another—
the semblance of a twinkle in their eyes. But whenever
they looked at me, their eyes were doubtful; and when,
our meal over and coffee on the table, the Chief produced
a tiny phial from his pocket saying: "Perhaps this will
help you, Doctor. We found it in the yacht's safe while
we were searching," I seemed to understand why.

For the phial had a tiny Chinese label on it: and Doctor Lancart, who had practised several years in Saigon,
recognized it instantly—and, apart from the dead man,
only Vivian ("He was in the East three years rubber-
planting," I heard myself say to Kyra) knew the combination of the safe.

Yet that Vivian should be even suspected of such a
murder seemed to me an outrage. For though our old
School had seen more than one of its alumni in broad
arrows, none so far has merited the poisoner's rope.

The doctor, with the contents of the phial to guide
him, took a bare half-hour more to reach certitude. "I
will perform the post-mortem this evening," he said. "But
there is no doubt in my mind as to the result of it. If
you can prove opportunity and motive, you need not
hesitate to arrest."

"And Opportunity," said the Chief, "was ample. The
steward set down the tray by an open window. Motive,
too, may be provable."

But because an English boat is English territory, it
seemed to me, as I followed Kyra into the sunshine, that
he would have to consult the Parquet (the office of the
Procureur de la République) before arresting; and, strong
in that half-knowledge, I detained the pair of them in the
doctor's porch.

"One moment, my friends," I said. "If you want more

help from me, if you want me to go back to the *Sea Joy*
with you, let us be explicit with one another. Tell me
precisely what else you found when you searched this
morning—and tell me, very precisely, what you suspect."

The Chief—whose appearance, I repeat, I have promised not to describe in these chronicles—hesitated, murmuring that the position was "a little delicate." Kyra,
however, retorting, "Delicate or not, *mon ami*, he knows
too much not to know the rest of it," told me the truth.

They had found the bank-book, with the red stars
against the doubtful entries, easily; the phial, which was
a tiny one, only by supreme luck—wedged, as it had been,
between the back and the binding of another book,
obviously kept by Vivian, and marked, "Ship's Cash."

"There was the faintest bulge in the back of the binding," said Kyra. "But only the faintest one. As for what
we suspect, that is—alas!—obvious. Whether you go on
helping us or not, depends—I should say—on your feeling for *him*."

IV

Whether or no I was ethically right in returning to
the *Sea Joy,* is open to discussion. That I could not prevent myself doing so, is positive fact. I know Kyra's
methods, you see; and I knew, or thought I knew, the
exact line she and the Chief would take in their further
examination of the man who, whatever there might be
against him, had still been my pal.

"Once a pal, always a pal," I remember thinking.
"Vivian couldn't possibly have done this thing. And at
least I can take care, when they are putting their questions, that they don't lay any trap."

But once we were back in Captain Middleton's cabin,
it was not, to my surprise, Vivian, but Lady Marcus
whom the Chief, after a low-voiced consultation with
Kyra, elected to see.

Lady Marcus entered with perfect self-possession, re-
questing only that Captain Middleton should leave us
before the questions began.

"He was my husband's servant," she explained after he had left us. "And, though he was a most faithful one, I would rather not speak before servants." An explanation which prejudiced me against her from the first.

Prejudice, however—during the hour we had her under examination—was the least of the feelings I experienced about Lady Marcus Chi Lin. That she had a rare beauty, I acknowledge. That she answered my questions freely, intelligently, and with a great semblance of honesty, I acknowledge also. But—to use a forthright vulgarism—she gave me the creeps. And most of all did she give me the creeps when, right at the end, I put the inevitable, "You mustn't be offended, Lady Marcus. But my friends are very anxious to know whether you and your husband have always been on the best of terms?"

"Always," she asseverated. "Marcus and I adored each other. No other man ever interested me in the slightest. I used to tell Marcus everything. Even when other men tried to flirt with me, even when Charles——"

She bit her lip on the "Charles"; and I fancied, from a look which passed between us, that she wished me to slur the point over. But Kyra's sharp ears had fastened on it—and in two more questions, the thing was out.

Charles Vivian had been in love with his employer's wife. At any rate, he had tried to flirt with her. She had told Sir Marcus about it. Sir Marcus had wanted to get rid of Vivian. "But I persuaded him not to. Charles was so useful, you see. And when he saw I had no intention of—of flirting back at him, he left off."

"Did Vivian know that you had told your husband, Lady Marcus?"

"I'm not certain. He may have."

"And how long ago did this happen?"

"Oh, just before we left England, in May."

Sir Marcus Chi Lin's widow, having made this statement, left us—Kyra and the Chief satisfied, me in gloom.

"A double motive," said Kyra. "Sex—as always. And money—if it was he who cashed the cheques." Then she asked me to fetch Captain Middleton, whom I found just outside the door.

"Ask the captain," she demanded, "to be very frank with us. Has he noticed, since leaving England, anything peculiar about the relations between Lady Marcus and her husband's secretary?"

"Isn't that rather a brutal question?" I protested.

"You need not put it brutally." Kyra's lovely eyes hardened. "But in the interests of justice, we must know."

So I put the question, or rather a series of questions, after my own fashion; and succeeded at last in extorting a very reluctant, "I should say, though of course there was nothing wrong about it, that Lady Marcus was very fond of Mr. Vivian. They used to be a lot together especially when Sir Marcus was working. I should say, though, that on the whole she liked him more than he liked her."

Middleton, despite a good deal of quiet pressure, refused to add anything to this statement. "I oughtn't to have said as much as I have done," he protested. "If it hadn't have been for you, I'd have held my tongue altogether. Because I don't trust foreigners. And that's a fact."

Meanwhile "the foreigners"—I could see—had been a little shaken. If one were to believe the captain, Lady Marcus had lied to us. And if Lady Marcus had lied to us——

"She's half Chinese," said Kyra—displaying yet more of that racial prejudice which is so unfortunate for the internationalist. "If your friend rebuffed her, out of loyalty to his employer; if she wanted to marry him——"

"If she wanted to marry him," cut in the Chief, "she would hardly try to have him guillotined as a preliminary. To me what is really important is that we find out who forged the cheques."

Then, again murmuring about "the delicacy of the position," he asked me if I had any objection to putting a few further questions to Vivian: to which I replied, "None at all. Provided the questions are fair ones—and

provided that you will do nothing more than keep him
under surveillance until we have had time to communicate
with my solicitor, Mr. Carthers, who will probably come
over personally when he knows what has occurred."

The Chief demurred—as I had expected him to. Kyra,
however, took my side, saying, "Our position, too, is a
little delicate. Whoever we arrest may claim the right
to be tried in England"; and I got my way. Also, knowing the irregularity, to English ideas, of Kyra's and the
Chief's methods, I insisted on being allowed to warn
Vivian of what he must expect.

He came in a little later; perturbed, but not unduly
so considering the circumstances; and I warned him that,
Doctor Lancart having confirmed the fact of the poisoning, everybody on the yacht was bound to be more or
less under suspicion until the matter had been cleared
up.

"Including myself?" he asked.

"I'm afraid so, old chap."

"Well, it's natural, I suppose. Though, of course, *you*
must know I didn't do it. With Sir Marcus dead, I'm
left with about a hundred-a-year and my wound-pension.
Tell your friends to keep that in their minds, won't you?
And now, fire ahead."

I translated—and put the Chief's first question. "You
kept the yacht's cash-book. The cash-book was in the safe
of which you gave us the combination. Are you quite
sure that nobody except yourself and Sir Marcus knew
that combination?"

"I'm very nearly positive. Sir Marcus had it changed
before we left London."

"Could Lady Marcus have known it?"

"No." Vivian answered instanter. "Certainly not."

"He told us before luncheon"—it was still the chief,
note-book on knee, speaking—"that Lady Marcus went to
bed at about ten-thirty; he himself at eleven. Ask him
if he can remember his movements during that half-
hour."

"I remained in the saloon," answered Vivian, "reading

—one of your books as it happened, old man. When I'd finished it I turned straight in."

Half-a-dozen questions, all more or less along the same lines, followed. Then, abruptly, Kyra took a hand.

"*Je pense,*" she said, speaking French very slowly, and looking towards Vivian as she did so, "that you had better tell your friend everything, in your own manner. What we have discovered, we have discovered. It is for him to explain it—if he can."

"Everything?" I asked.

"Yes. Everything. You made a condition that the examination should be a fair one. Could anything be fairer than to tell this gentleman about the letter, about the pass-book, about the little phial we found, and"—Kyra, still looking at Vivian, spoke more slowly than ever— "about Lady Marcus's statement that he flirted with her, and Captain Middleton's statement that it was she, rather, who flirted with him?"

A silence followed; and during that silence I saw Vivian change colour; saw one little greasy bead of perspiration break out on his cheek.

"Could anything be fairer?" repeated Kyra.

"I—I suppose not," I admitted—and for a good ten minutes, feeling as uncomfortable as I have ever felt in my existence, I spoke with Vivian as only one man of the same race can speak to another, when there is need.

He heard me out unflinching; but I was aware, as I explained about the cheques and the poison-phial, of stark amazement in him; and when I came to his relations with Lady Marcus, of fear. After I had finished, he was like a man stricken with aphasia. His lips moved—but for many seconds he could not speak.

"What—what the hell's a fellow to do?" he said at last. "You say you're going to write to Carthers. You needn't. I cashed that bearer cheque for three thousand on May the seventh. The others, too. I always cashed his cheques for him. But they were all right. Sir Marcus signed them, and he had the money for them. As for the poison, I swear to God I never even knew he had been poisoned,

till you told me this morning. And there's nothing between me and Lady Marcus. Nothing, I tell you. Nothing
on earth!"

And Vivian, his grey eyebrows twitching, added: "For
God's sake believe me, old chap. Because—because any
fool could see that those two don't."

V

I think, looking back a whole year on what was at best
a sorry business, that I—even though I obeyed the Chief's
order and kept away from the *Sea Joy*—always did believe in Vivian's innocence. But that evening, as Kyra
and the Chief and I sat on my terrace watching the lights
of St. Tropez glimmer across two miles of silent water,
my belief in him may have been a little shaken. And two
evenings later, when I sat in the same place with Carthers,
arrived post-haste from London, it was more shaken
still.

"I can't agree with you," said Carthers. "The sex-
motive, though obscure, seems ample. He admits he cashed
the cheques. Whether they were forged or not, is im-
material. He could easily have induced Sir Marcus to
sign them. And nobody had a better opportunity of
dropping this poison, which is apparently odourless, into
the glass."

"Circumstantial evidence," I protested.

"More than that. The discovery of the phial——"

"Proves nothing. He could far more easily have dropped
it overboard."

"But he didn't. He was afraid of its being washed
ashore. And to-morrow, whether for trial in France or
for extradition, he'll be arrested."

Whereupon Carthers, tired with his twenty-four-hour
journey, went up to bed.

I went up to bed, too. But there was no sleep in me.
I just sat at my window—staring, staring, staring at the
riding-light of the *Sea Joy*. And as I stared, my brain

worked, and my blood shrank back into a heart sick with apprehension—till on a sudden, I saw the other light.

The other light was dead under the *Sea Joy's* riding light, almost at water-level. It winked—and kept on winking. Till presently, I began to read.

"G.F." read the light. "G.F. S.O.S. G.F." And when I had got my own torch, it signalled: "S.W.I.M.M.I.N.G. C.O.M.E. S.H.O.R.E."

My Morse, after ten years' disuse, was rusty. But I remembered the O.K.; and sent it; and five minutes later I stole—stole is the only word for it—out of my house.

It is no distance, if you take the path over the golf-course, from my house to the Beauvallon foreshore. But the moon was still up—so I went by the pine-woods; telling myself that there could be no hurry, because Vivian's swim from St. Tropez would take him, even if he made it, at least an hour.

I remember how, as I reached the foreshore, I was afraid he might not make it. I remember wondering whether I should get my boat out, and being afraid again —lest the boat should betray us to some watcher. In fact, I was in a pretty panic by the time the last rays of moon-light showed me the shadow of Vivian's swimming head.

He shivered as he came out of the warm water; and the breath whistled through his teeth.

"Good of you," he whispered. "I thought you'd be coming on board again. I tried to write you. I tried to come over this afternoon. But those gendarmes wouldn't let me. Haven't got a spot of brandy, have you? I—I'll need it before we talk."

There is always drink, and a change of clothing, in my boathouse. I led Vivian there; found him flannels and a sweater; and set drink before him—in the dark.

"Carthers must be here," he began. "I overheard some talk about the *avocat anglais*. Does *he* think I'm guilty?"

"He——" I hesitated.

"All right." The teeth had ceased their chattering. "You needn't make any bones about it. I'm as good a judge of evidence as the next fellow; and Selene——"

"Selene!"

"Lady Marcus. Hell holds no fury, old chap! You know the rest of the quotation. But thank your stars you don't know what it means to a fellow, when he can only hold a thousand-a-year job by playing Joseph to a half-caste . . ."

He told me exactly what holding such a job meant; but because that part is real life, and not fiction, I have cut it out.

"One couldn't tell that to a jury, could one?" he ended. "At the best, they'd only think she and I were accomplices. And besides, there's no earthly proof. The letter was too well forged, you see. And poor old Marcus'll never let on now, how she wheedled the combination out of him. Or what he did with the three thousand, either. And, and, oh damn it, Gilbert, what's the use of pretending? I loved her—even if I wouldn't behave like a blackguard to poor old Marcus. I love her still even if she is trying to have me guillotined. And that's why—that's why *you've* got to help me. Because nobody else can."

My wife, usually the most tractable of women, found it almost impossible to forgive me the loss of our brand-new twenty-knotter. Carthers, to whom, from the very moment the theft was discovered, she never ceased appealing, "Would any man in his senses leave a motor-boat which cost a thousand pounds lying about loose with enough petrol in her tanks to cross the Mediterranean?" contented himself with a malicious, "No doubt, Mrs. Frankau, your husband's loss will be made good by his insurance company." The two gendarmes on board the *Sea Joy* lost their chances of promotion. The Chief de la Sûreté, after one of the most fruitless inquiries in police history, departed for Toulon. And Kyra—whose friendship, though always platonic, is always precious to me—sulked like a spoiled princess.

"Never again, my friend," said Kyra, sulking, the night after the *Sea Joy* had sailed for England, in my library. "Me you cannot fool. How it was done, I know not. But you had a hand in it. And he was guilty. He merited the death-penalty. His flight alone proves it. Though she, too, that sly one, is not altogether blameless. In all crime where there is a sex-motive——"

"Sex-motive," I interrupted. "Or race-motive." And because any Boswell may be proud of out-distancing his Doctor Johnson, I could not help feeling a little superior as I took a thin book printed on vellum from my pocket, and read the first paragraph of that thousand-year-old story which begins: "In the great walled city of Soochow lived Wong Whei Yui, the rich old merchant; and his lovely young wife, Peach Blossom, and Wen Chen Ming, the servant of Wong Whei Yui, who was also his friend."

"What on earth?" began Kyra.

But I silenced her, and read on.

"Now the young wife of Wong Whei Yui," I read, "fell amorous of Wen Chen Ming, who would have none of her. But Wong Whei Yui, not knowing this, imagined that Wen Chen Ming had betrayed him. And because, in that age which the scribes of Far Cathay call golden, no man might kill with his own hand, however great the wrong suffered; and because moreover it seemed to Wong Whei Yui that life without the love of Peach Blossom were better ended, he ended his life—doing so in such a way, for he was a man of great cunning, that suspicion for his death should fall upon his friend. And after Wong Whei Yui's death, Peach Blossom, about whom the story is told, being still angry with Wen Chen Ming, who had rebuffed her, forgot that it is written, 'Who does not help the innocent is himself guilty.' And she——"

I did not, however, succeed in finishing that thousand-year-old story; because Kyra snatched the book from me; and when she had re-read those opening paragraphs, picking her way very slowly through the quaint English, her face lost something of its loveliness—going, indeed, almost grey before my eyes.

"Did—did _he_ know this?" she stammered.

"Wen Chen Ming thought Peach Blossom guilty," I answered.

"And you?"

"The book only came yesterday."

"Then why?"

"Why what, Kyra?"

"Why did you—why was your motor-boat——"

"Sheer carelessness, Kyra."

"You—you needn't lie to me. He was your friend——"

"Sheer carelessness, I repeat, Kyra."

"No. No. No. It wasn't. It was——"

And before I could quite realize what had happened, Kyra had seized both my hands and was kissing them, sobbing as she did so: "Providence, Gilbert. Providence! God forgive me. It was suicide. And I—I'd have had an innocent man guillotined for it, just—just to keep myself from being bored."

Which last, though a trifle disingenuous on Kyra's part, is no bad reason for becoming a detective—or for reading about one, if it comes to that.

EVELYN JOHNSON
AND
GRETTA PALMER

THE CRAWLEY ROBBERY

AT three in the afternoon the snow that had been falling steadily for several hours appeared to be stopping. Tommy Gallagher swung his cab into the main street of town and headed toward the Leighton National Bank with a reasonable expectation of picking up one final fare before finishing the day's work.

As he neared the banking institution an unimpressive little man carrying a newspaper and a small package emerged from the doorway, and hailed the approaching taxi with a wave of the newspaper. Beside him was a slight woman of indeterminate age and coloring. They gave an address a good two miles away, on the very outskirts of town, and in precisely the opposite direction from Tommy's own ultimate destination. Tommy spat expressively. "Rotten roads, long drive, come back light, and a dime tip. I know 'em!" Tommy considered seriously the advantages of joining the police force like his brother Patrick. Pat got free drinks, anyhow.

Behind him the couple for whom he felt such a lively scorn were in a far more cheerful frame of mind. During the halt necessitated by the passing of a railroad train even the harassed driver was forced to smile as his lady passenger undertook to describe to her spouse the elaborate garment which she planned to wear to a party that evening:

". . . with a bouffant skirt of honey-colored taffeta,

(From "Murder," by Evelyn Johnson and Gretta Palmer. Copyright, 1928, by Covici, Friede, Inc., New York.)

Henry, and a bodice of natural colored lace. That's to set off grandmother's emeralds."

"All right, Mary," said her husband indulgently. "Here, you better take them now and put them in your bag. Don't want to forget them in the taxi, Mrs. Crawley. Here, take 'em and be careful of 'em."

"I certainly will, and remind me to phone the drugstore before I go upstairs, Henry. I have to have those curlers by the time I've had a bath." Just then the gates lifted, and they went on.

The car ultimately drew up before a neat suburban villa such as one would have expected. The snow had ceased, and a thoughtful negro was languidly sweeping the last of it from the ten-foot brick walk that led to the front door. As he had anticipated, Tommy Gallagher's tip was in strict accordance with the budget system by which the Crawleys had regulated their lives for the past decade.

Tommy stopped to light a cigarette and glance over the house. Then he started back to town and headed for his brother's apartment. Patrick would be there with that quart of Rye that he received every week as honorarium from the bootlegger on the beat.

Mrs. Crawley's preparations before the dinner they were attending that night were somewhat more elaborate than one might expect from her unassuming appearance. Her charms were of the mousy order not calculated to set off emeralds to advantage, and the honey-colored taffeta seemed to reduce her to the single tone of an albino carrot. None the less she commenced to dress a good two hours before the time that they planned to leave, and at six-thirty, when the telephone rang, she was by no means ready.

Mr. Crawley, who was downstairs at the time, answered the call, and heard a man's voice ask for Mrs. Crawley. He called upstairs to her, and presently she appeared in a mouse-colored dressing-gown, and came down fervently hoping that no unexpected contingency had arisen which might interfere with the plans of the evening.

By the time that she reached the telephone, however,

the gentleman had either been disconnected or had grown tired of waiting, for she received no response. She replaced the receiver and planned to wait a few moments before returning upstairs on the chance that it would ring again. As she stood a moment undetermined, there was a low knocking at the front door.

Mrs. Crawley stepped into the library as her husband answered it. She heard soft voices for a moment, and soon he appeared, several shades paler than her *poudre blanche* had rendered his wife.

"It's a policeman, Mary," he gasped. "He just saw a man climb up a ladder and go in a window upstairs."

"The emeralds!" she exclaimed. "On the dresser!"

They reëntered the hall together and stood, rapt in horror, while the intrepid Irishman tried to reassure them in hoarse whispers. They remained huddled at the foot of the stairs while he mounted cautiously with drawn revolver. They heard him move about, and utter a hoarse command.

After a few breathless minutes their champion reappeared and descended the stairs in great haste. Brushing past them, he exclaimed, "He got down the ladder! I'll get him!" and, tearing open the door, rushed off into the night.

After their terror had somewhat abated and a brief search had shown the emeralds to be missing, Mrs. Crawley gave herself over to the fit of hysterics that she considered her due, and her husband, assuming the rôle of audacious male, ventured forth to see what could be seen from outdoors.

He found the ladder which had been lying along the side of the house to be propped up against it in such a manner as to give access to the window of his wife's room. Likewise he found footprints in the snow leading to where the ladder had been and to the base of it as it stood, and leading away from it again toward the road.

Mr. Crawley was surprised to notice, however, that the footprints leading away from the base of the ladder, which had evidently been made after the burglar had been

disturbed, had been made by a man who was walking and
not running. A burglar who is disturbed at work will
most certainly run, Mr. Crawley knew, and he was frankly
puzzled.

Mr. Crawley called the police station.

A large sergeant whose countenance had achieved an
unbelievably high degree of polish and color, came and
took their testimony. Of course Mrs. Crawley had the
emeralds when she got home. Didn't she put them on the
dresser? Yes; she hadn't been out of the room after she
took them out of her hand-bag. They were not insured.
There was no one in the house except George, the "butler," and they'd had him ten years. She had been downstairs probably three minutes when the other officer came.
She didn't remember what he looked like except that he
had a big black mustache.

Mr. Crawley did not make the best witness imaginable,
as the officer began his examination by suggesting that
Mr. Crawley was probably an inveterate gambler and
drunkard who had taken his wife's emeralds to procure
the means to satisfy his vices. Mr. C. waxed indignant.
He brought to the attention of the law's noble representa-
tive that he had been right at his wife's side all the time
she had been on the ground floor. She had answered the
telephone in the library where he was reading, had started
upstairs, and had stepped back into the library when the
door bell rang. He had let the policeman in, and in the
excitement, she had forgotten her natural modesty and
had stood with him at the foot of the stairs while the
policeman had rushed up only to find the burglar gone.
He was most likely tracking down the culprit while the
sergeant stood around asking idiotic questions of honest
householders. No, he had not noticed his number. There
was no other entrance to the house except the back door.
The sergeant could see for himself that there were no
tracks at all from the back door. He didn't see why it
was necessary to make insinuations about George who
was certainly far more trustworthy than policemen. They
had no garage, so when Mr. Crawley had borrowed Mr.

Jeliffe's ladder to fix some weather-stripping, he had left it by the house. No, he did not think that was a foolish thing to do. Any one was likely to leave a ladder around for a little while.

George was hardly more illuminating. He certainly did not go around catching his death propping ladders up against windows in the dead of winter. Anyhow, his Sarah wouldn't like them old green stones. The sergeant could see for himself that George's feet were built on more distinctive and massive lines than the footprints on the lawn. The sergeant was disgruntled. Then he had a bright idea. He had the operator trace the call that Mrs. Crawley had answered. He came back smiling at Mr. Crawley in disagreeable triumph. "I guess you won't see them jools again," he observed. "That phone call was from the cigar store at the corner here."

What became of the emeralds?

THE SOLUTION

Tommy Gallagher was in luck when he picked up his unpromising fares, and he did not miss the reference to the emeralds. He also heard Mrs. Crawley intimate that the only telephone was downstairs, which suggested a plan by which he might decoy her from the neighborhood of the jewels. After pocketing his tip, Tommy hurried back to seek Patrick and the loan of his uniform. He returned to the Crawley home dressed like an officer of the law, and was delighted to see a ladder leaning against the house. This he placed against the window as a realistic touch, walking across the lawn to the street. His footsteps on this occasion were not, of course, those of a man running away from capture. According to plan, Tommy then crossed the street to a drug store and telephoned the Crawley home, asking for Mrs. Crawley. When he was sure she had been called, he crossed the street, rang the bell, told the startled Mr. Crawley his tale of the second-story man, and hurried upstairs alone. He had ample time to secure the emeralds and carry them out of the house past the unprotesting owners.

EVELYN JOHNSON
AND
GRETTA PALMER

FINGER PRINTS CAN'T LIE

THE morning of the day we declared war on Germany, I was aroused at one o'clock by a phone call.

"This is Mrs. Booth," said a voice. "I've heard of you and you're badly needed. Will you come over?"

I went to the address she had given, and found a nice little semi-detached villa.

"Mrs. Booth?" I asked.

"Yes," said the pleasant-faced middle-aged woman who answered the door. "But the trouble is next door. I was awakened by screams about half an hour ago coming from the Marcus's. I knew that the Doctor had gone to Germany on his lecture trip this afternoon, so I thought I had better go over. Mrs. Marcus has been quite sick; that is why the Doctor couldn't take her with him, although he is so devoted to her, and they had been planning to make this trip together for months. I got my clothes on and ran over, and found the door closed but not locked. I went in and called the maid, Mary, and no one answered, although it was not her regular night out, and Mrs. Marcus was still in bed. I ran upstairs and found Mrs. Marcus writhing on the bed in horrible agony. She was dead a minute after I got there, and never said a word. The maid came in as she died. I called Dr. Mills and he said it looked like strychnine poisoning, so I phoned you. He is over there now."

We went over to the other house. The woman was lying

in a bed in a nicely furnished room on the second floor. Dr. Mills was bending over her, but as I came in he observed that there was no use. He pointed to a bottle of capsules on the bedside table.

"I thought I had better not touch that bottle," he said. "There are finger marks on it, and I'll guarantee it contains strychnine."

The autopsy confirmed the doctor's diagnosis. A fatal amount of strychnine was found in her stomach. Dr. Marcus's closet of poisons had been broken open and the strychnine tampered with. There were good finger prints there too. I got some excellent photographic enlargements. Nothing else in the laboratory had apparently been touched. The Doctor had had very varied tastes, evidently, as I found photographic and engraving materials as well as the most elaborate chemical and medical equipment. There were finger prints all over. I got some good ones of the Doctor's, but to make certain, I developed prints from instruments no one but he had had access to. Besides, there were no other finger prints in the laboratory except the ones I took to be his and a few I afterwards found to be Mary's. I then questioned Mary, the maid. Her story was that the Doctor had told her that she could go out that evening, as Mrs. Marcus was much better, and had given her tickets to a play. The only train she could get from London to the suburb they lived in was one that go there at twelve-two. It was a short walk from the station, and when she got to the house she heard horrible screams. She had gone up and found her mistress dying, with both Mrs. Booth and Dr. Mills there. They often left the door unlocked.

I took her finger prints, and went home. I developed all my finger prints and looked at the bottle of capsules curiously. In what I ascertained to be Dr. Marcus's handwriting, it said, "One at Bed-time." Each of the ten or fifteen capsules contained enough strychnine to kill a horse.

My finger prints were ready, so I compared them. The prints on the capsule bottle and on the poison closet were identical, and both tallied with Mary's. The Doctor's were utterly different.

I went back to the house where the tragedy had taken place, but the only important thing I found was an envelope in the waste basket in Mrs. Marcus's room, containing capsules of a harmless sedative. Mary was finally acquitted, however, as no motive was ever adduced and an English jury does not like to convict a woman on circumstantial evidence.

Several other interesting facts had come out. Dr. Marcus had been a German spy of no small importance, so it is not odd that his "lecture tour" took place just when it did, as he had in all likelihood known that war would be declared.

One day after the trial, I paid a visit to Mary. I felt somehow that there had been a mistake, and I wanted to make further investigations. My efforts at the time of the trial had been greatly hampered by the fact that her lawyer was convinced that she was guilty, and had resented what he called my misplaced zeal in trying to vindicate her. He had refused to let me see her and had convinced her that I was working against her.

With a great deal of difficulty, I managed to persuade her that I was really friendly, and begged her to allow me to question her. She finally agreed. I asked her to tell me everything she had observed in the house the day of the murder. She told me that the Doctor had wakened up at seven-thirty as he always did, and she had given him breakfast downstairs and taken a tray up to Mrs. Marcus. The Doctor had shut himself up in his laboratory from nine to twelve, and Mrs. Marcus had worked at a tapestry. The Doctor's mother had come for lunch. It seems that she detested her daughter-in-law, feeling that her constant illness was mere malingering. They had had a stormy interview until the Doctor had intervened. The old lady had spent the time while he was getting ready to leave for Germany down in the living room, while Mary helped the Doctor with his packing.

"Was the mother alone downstairs?" I asked.

"Oh, yes," said Mary.

"Was the laboratory unlocked?"

"Yes, I noticed the door was open when I went down to get a duster."

"Go on," I said.

"Then the Doctor asked his mother if she wouldn't come up and make up with his wife, as he did not want to go away and leave them estranged. He seemed terribly excited and insistent about it. He was awfully fond of his mother."

"Were the capsules there then?"

"Yes, he had just given them to her and told her to be sure and take one if she couldn't sleep, as she needed plenty of sleep. Then his mother came in and kissed his wife rather unwillingly and the Doctor and I went to tie up his luggage, and pretty soon the Doctor went down to close up his laboratory. I came down to the kitchen just before he left and found him by the stove. He was putting something in the fire. There was a terrible fire going, and I told him it was too hot. So afterwards I lowered the fire in the range, and when I took out the ashes I found it must have been some rubber gloves that he had been burning, as I found the wrist and stubs of the fingers of one although all the rest had been burnt up."

I was deep in thought. If it had been the mother-in-law, that would account for the fact that the other pills had been discovered. She had only had time to toss them in the waste basket before some one came in. But Mary's finger prints? And the rubber gloves?

There was nothing I could do at the time of my interview with Mary, but early in 1919 I determined that I would unearth Marcus and get to the bottom of the mystery. I won't stop to recount all the vicissitudes that I went through to locate him. Finally I thought I had the Doctor, anyway. The mother had died in 1917.

I took the train for Munich. On the train I studied a photograph of the Doctor that Mary had given me. It was a full-length portrait that I had ascertained from several neighbors to be a perfect likeness. He was a straight, well-built man, slender, with a fine sensitive face, a long pointed nose with sculptured nostrils and a thin-lipped mouth. The brow was high and smooth and straight. He had delicate hands with long, tapering fingers, and small feet. Mary had also given me a careful description of him. He had very fine, smooth skin, she said, and she was sure he was five-feet nine, because she had seen his passport. I would be certain to know him.

When I reached my destination, a nurse opened the door, and told me that Dr. Schwartz was out. Dr. Schwartz was the man I was sure was Marcus. She asked me to come into the waiting room and I gladly accepted the opportunity to have a look around. I was in luck, for the door to his office was open. I looked about the desk carefully, but everything there was thoroughly impersonal, except for a book which was lying open. It had markers in it and had been much thumbed. I looked at the title. *"Cushing,"* it said, *"The Pituitary Body."*

I rushed back to the waiting room, hearing footsteps, and a man came in.

He looked at me inquiringly.

"Dr. Schwartz?" I said.

"Yes," he replied.

It was not my man at all. This man was six feet tall with great rugged, craggy features. His eyes were sunk, and his brow furrowed; he had a thick heavy nose, and great pendulous lips. His skin was thick and wrinkled and pachydermatous. He had large nobby hands and huge feet. He was terribly stooped and dull-eyed.

But I wanted to be sure; so when I saw that as he talked to me about my purely imaginary ailment, he fingered his paper cutter, I took the liberty to put it in my pocket when his back was turned.

I took out the paper cutter when I got home, and developed the beautiful finger prints with which it was covered.

They were exactly like the prints Dr. Marcus had left all over his laboratory!

Who murdered Mrs. Marcus, and how do you account for the confusion in finger prints?

THE SOLUTION

Dr. Marcus murdered his wife to prevent her from giving away his state secrets. He broke into his own poison-cabinet before his departure for Europe and placed the strychnine in a bottle from which he wiped his own finger prints. He had photographed the finger prints of Mary, had engraved them and transferred them in the positive onto a pair of rubber gloves. Wearing these gloves, he handled the bottle, leaving traces that correspond to Mary's own hand. His instructions to his wife about the medicine insured that she would not take the poison until after he was well on his way to Europe. During the four years that elapsed before the detective reached him, he entirely changed his appearance by inducing to a marked degree a disease called acromegaly, which can be brought on by eating enormous quantities of pituitary extract. Such changes as a gain of several inches in height and unrecognizably heavier features are a result of this disease.

Self-Development

A Handbook for the Ambitious

By H. ADDINGTON BRUCE

Author of "Nerve Control and How to Gain It," "The Riddle of Personality," etc.

A wonderfully clear-cut analysis, in plain, conversational English, of certain mental actions and reactions, every page radiating encouragement and helpfulness for ambitious men and women. It explains how to develop will power, memory, poise, and personality; elaborates on the simple methods all must adopt—and which are easy to adopt—to achieve marked success in social and business life. It points out the insidious pitfalls that must be avoided—and which are easy to avoid after the author points them out.

All that Mr. Bruce advises will appeal to every reader with ambition—young or old. And every one who takes his advice will be better able to win friends, fame, and fortune and to get all the good out of life that life has to offer. Founded on the soundest principles of psychology as established by the latest research, and written in a style which all may easily understand, the author has produced in "Self-Development," a remarkable volume of practical, sensible self-help.

" 'Self-Development' contains more good advice, more information that can be turned to practical account, than almost any other book that could be mentioned."—Rochester (N. Y.) *Democrat and Chronicle.*

12mo. Cloth. 342 pages. $1.50, net; $1.62, post-paid.

FUNK & WAGNALLS COMPANY, Publishers
NEW YORK AND LONDON